"If I'd rejected
certain I woul

"Garin became your sword then," Annja said.

"That's one way of looking at it, I guess. He came along at just the right moment, much like the sword did with you. I guess that's one of the great mysteries of life, how things seem to happen at just the right moment."

"No coincidences," Annja said. "That's too easy an explanation. And I've seen enough to not believe in coincidence anymore."

"It does seem to be the crutch for the unimaginative." Sheila smiled. "Garin told me you were something else."

Annja smirked. "That's only because he's been trying to seduce me for years."

"There aren't many who can resist him," Sheila said.

"I never claimed it was easy," Annja replied with a laugh.

"You're honest," Sheila said. "I appreciate that."

"So the question now seems to be how do we deal with the shark terrorizing this boat and who would dive?"

"You're going to have to deal with it, Annja. You're going to have to kill the shark so we can get to the treasure."

Titles in this series:

ROGUE Angel™

Alex Archer

PHANTOM PROSPECT

A GOLD EAGLE BOOK FROM

W★RLDWIDE®

TORONTO • NEW YORK • LONDON
AMSTERDAM • PARIS • SYDNEY • HAMBURG
STOCKHOLM • ATHENS • TOKYO • MILAN
MADRID • WARSAW • BUDAPEST • AUCKLAND

Recycling programs
for this product may
not exist in your area.

First edition November 2010

ISBN-13: 978-0-373-62146-0

PHANTOM PROSPECT

Special thanks and acknowledgment to
Jon Merz for his contribution to this work.

Printed in U.S.A.

The
LEGEND

...THE ENGLISH COMMANDER TOOK
JOAN'S SWORD AND RAISED IT HIGH.

The broadsword, plain and unadorned,
gleamed in the firelight. He put the tip against
the ground and his foot at the center of the blade.
The broadsword shattered, fragments falling
into the mud. The crowd surged forward,
peasant and soldier, and snatched the shards
from the trampled mud. The commander tossed
the hilt deep into the crowd.
Smoke almost obscured Joan, but she continued
praying till the end, until finally the flames climbed
her body and she sagged against the restraints.

Joan of Arc died that fateful day in France,
but her legend and sword are reborn....

1

The waters off Montauk, New York, surged, frothing white as waves crashed into one another, spraying mist through the air. Annja Creed stood on the stern of a boat she thought seemed far too small for the job at hand. She watched as a sleek dark shadow glided just beneath the waves, its torpedo body reflecting the four hundred million years of evolution that had landed it atop the food chain of the ocean.

Cole Williams scooped another ladle of chum into the water. Annja swallowed and tried to ignore the sickly stench of pureed herring and tuna chunks mixed with an assortment of other matter designed to lure great white sharks to the boat.

"You sure you need to put so much of that into the water?" Annja asked.

Cole glanced at her and grinned, his cropped brown hair lightened by the sun beaming down. "You're not nervous, are you? Not the bold adventurer Annja Creed," he said.

Annja pointed at the water. "There's already one down there."

Cole nodded. "I'd like to see if we can get a few in the area. This study is all about how great whites interact with one another. Conventional science likes to paint them as solitary creatures but new research is proving they have a hierarchy when they encounter one another."

"So, it's not enough to have one proven killer in the water. You want as many as possible."

"Yep." Cole threw another scoop overboard. "You want to help me do this?"

Annja held up her hands. "I'm good here, thanks." The journey out from Montauk had been anything but calm. Despite the sunshine, the ocean seemed angry today and the little boat that Cole had converted from a deep-sea fishing charter to his own personal research vessel bobbed relentlessly in the violent swells. Annja's stomach wasn't in a forgiving mood.

Cole pointed at the triangular fin slicing through the water. To Annja, it almost reminded her of a sword.

Her sword.

"Look at that one."

Cole's voice did little to soothe Annja's nerves. In keeping with Cole's twisted sense of humor, he'd insisted they watch the movie *Jaws* the previous night while they shared a bottle of wine. Recalling the giant great white devouring a bunch of people on film didn't do much for Annja's nerves just then.

She glanced at the steel shark cage strapped down on the deck. "Does that thing actually work?"

Cole smiled. "There's nothing to worry about. I've done this loads of times and never had a problem."

"I find the choice of location unsettling given what we watched last night," she said.

Cole's laughter at least made her smile. Then he shook his head. "They actually filmed that on Martha's Vineyard, but I get your point." He pointed at another shark that had silently cruised into the area. "Thing about this place is the Long Island

Sound opens up into really deep water. The great whites out here are big. And that means we get a look at some healthy fish."

"They got that way by being hungry," Annja said. "I don't want to end up on the business end of those teeth." Cole had also insisted on showing her his shark tooth collection and Annja had marveled at how the great white's teeth looked exactly like steak knives, serrated along the edges and designed for cutting through the thick fat of their favorite meal, seals.

Looking at Cole in his wet suit, Annja could understand why great whites mistook divers for seals. They looked similar, especially underwater.

Cole finished tossing the chum over the side of the boat and hailed the deckhand. "Time to get the cage in the water."

They worked together. Annja unhooked the fastening cables and slowly they winched the cage over the side of the boat until the top of it sat at the waterline. The sea had calmed and the boat seemed to steady itself. Annja gave a silent prayer of thanks and felt her stomach stop lolling about.

Cole glanced at Annja. "Tom's going to heave a few tuna chunks out on lines and he'll drag them toward the cage."

"You want the sharks coming at the cage?"

"Yep."

Annja shook her head. "And this will help your research somehow?"

"We'll be able to see how the sharks separate themselves and who seems to be the ruling class. What researchers have observed is the deference certain sharks will have for another. But why they do that is something we don't know. Yet," he explained.

"Have fun," she said.

Cole smiled. "Time for you to get changed, Annja."

"Excuse me?"

"There's an extra wet suit in the cabin. I've got tanks all set for you. And there's room for one more in the cage."

Annja looked out at the sea. The dark shapes slid past the boat and surfaced, showing rows of jagged teeth as they sampled the chum line. Annja's stomach heaved again. "I'm not sure about this."

"I know how you feel. The first time I dived with great whites, I puked over the side of the boat."

"And then what?"

"I got the hell in the cage and did my job." He heaved the air tanks onto his back and checked his regulator. "You won't regret it, Annja. I promise."

Annja sighed and wandered back to the cabin. Cole had left the wet suit hanging on a door hook. She fingered the material and wondered what the sharks would see when she entered the water.

Dinner, most likely.

She took a deep breath. This was what she'd come out here for, she thought. When Cole had called and asked for her help, she'd had nothing pressing to do. And she'd always had a thing for sharks, even if they did scare the crap out of her.

This was her chance to try to put some of those fears to rest.

She took some calming breaths and stripped down, quickly climbing into the wet suit. The material clung to her skin and she noticed how much warmer she was inside of it. That was a good thing. The water temperature was fairly warm at this time of year, but it could still cause hypothermia if she was in it for too long.

She padded back out onto the deck and saw Cole sliding his mask over his face. He smiled when he saw her. "Glad you decided to come along."

"If I get eaten, I'm coming back to haunt you."

"I don't doubt it."

Annja pointed at the cage. "You sure those bars are strong enough to ward off any attacks."

Cole nodded. "Relax, Annja. Cages these days are much stronger than they used to be. You've got nothing to worry about. Besides, I'll be right there with you. Anything goes wrong, just follow my lead."

"That's comforting."

Tom helped her get the air tanks on and she tightened her waist belt, and then checked her regulator. She took a couple of breaths and tried to consciously slow her pounding heart. Adrenaline pumped through her veins and she knew that her nerves would take over unless she stilled them.

"Give me a second," she said.

Tom stepped away. While Annja busied herself with relaxing, Tom heaved a tuna carcass out into the water.

The surf exploded as a shark surged up from below and took the bait firmly in its mouth, ripping from side to side as chunks of flesh tore off in its mouth. Annja watched the grim spectacle and felt a strong desire to grow wings and fly home.

"Thanks for the help, Tom," she muttered.

He glanced back at her. "You okay?"

"Fine. Just fine."

"Let's go, Annja," Cole called. Annja watched him slide over the side of the boat and into the cage. She saw the splash and moved to make sure he'd made it into the cage.

Cole stuck his hand out and waved her on.

Annja took another deep breath and slid the regulator into her mouth. Tom handed her a mask and she settled it on over her hair. She tightened the straps and then nodded.

Tom helped her move to the side of the boat. The water seemed to be alive with sharks. Annja looked at Tom. He smiled. "There are only four of them down there."

Only four, she thought. Great.

She braced herself. The opening of the cage was directly in

front of her, but for some reason, it looked a lot farther away. One misstep would plunge Annja into the ocean, unprotected against the massive predators gliding through its depths.

Annja wanted to run. She wanted to puke like Cole had. But she steeled herself, took a breath and then stepped toward the cage opening, falling in through the open part with a splash.

White water bubbled up around her as she adjusted to the sudden change in her environment. She felt the reassurance of Cole's body next to hers. She took a few breaths and settled herself down.

The water felt warmer than she expected. And she was almost calm when a giant mouth suddenly loomed open in front of her. Annja blinked, saw rows of jagged teeth and fell back against the bars of the cage.

The great white in front of her bit the bars separating them and then slid off into the deep.

Cole patted her on the shoulder and gave her the hand signal to make sure she was okay. Annja nodded and gave him the thumbs-up. She blew out a long line of bubbles and again tried to calm herself.

On the floor of the cage, her balance felt sure enough. But the ocean floor was at least thirty feet below them.

She heard a splash and turned to see that Tom had tossed another bait hook over the side of the boat. Annja saw it tracking through the water toward the top of the cage.

Like a missile being shot out of a submarine far below the surface, Annja saw a flashing streak arc right past the cage as a huge shark shot up from below them, lancing into the tuna chunk. Incredibly, Annja thought she could hear the rending tears of the mighty jaws clamping and sawing through the fresh meat.

She forgot her terror and was instead awed by the mastery of evolution sailing through the waters before her. The sharks slid through the depths with complete ease. Their bodies had long evolved into almost perfectly aerodynamic shapes that met minimal resistance as they swam.

As they bit into the bait hooks, Annja could see the protective membranes slide up over their eyes, shielding them from any danger that might lurk as they attacked. She noticed the incredible flexion as the viselike mandibles sank into the flesh, exerting almost two tons of pressure per square inch.

But even as the sharks fed seemingly without regard, Annja could discern something else about them. She knew they were incredibly intelligent. She could see there was a rhyme to their reason. Annja realized that they seemed to almost feel with their teeth, making sure that what they attacked was suitable food for them.

She marveled at how they operated. And she knew why great white shark attacks were usually so deadly. It wasn't necessarily that the sharks sought out human beings to eat, but that they had no real way of probing something without committing to it fully. Their bites would naturally cause grievous wounds in anything, humans included. Blood loss and tissue damage would often cause death, even when the shark realized that the human victim wasn't the seal it was supposed to be and broke off the attack.

There was a great deal of misunderstanding about the creatures, Annja thought. She spent the next half hour entranced as Tom brought the big fish in close to the cage. She looked into their eyes; she tried to fathom their souls.

When Cole finally tapped her on the shoulder and motioned for her to get back on to the boat, Annja was almost upset. Maybe Cole wasn't crazy, after all. Maybe he just loved studying these fish so much that they took over his life.

Annja made her way back to the boat and spit out her mouthpiece. Tom beamed at her. "How'd you make out?"

"They're incredible!"

He nodded. "Cole's done some great research. Might even win himself some awards."

"I was terrified before, but now…"

Tom nodded. "I know. You get to the point where you see them as something more."

"I used to think Cole was crazy," Annja said.

Tom frowned. "Oh, he's definitely crazy," he said.

"What do you mean?"

"Didn't he tell you?"

"Tell me what?"

Tom pointed off the boat's port side. "See?"

Annja looked and felt dizzy.

Cole was out of the cage, in the open water with the sharks.

2

"He'll be killed!" Annja shrieked.

But Tom held up his hand and shook his head. "I know it certainly looks like that, but wait and see."

Annja could hardly breathe. She watched as Cole, who must have left his oxygen tank in the cage, swam with just a mask and snorkel within feet of the cruising predators. And while the ocean still held streaks of red and bits of tuna, curiously the great whites seemed to be almost nonchalant about Cole's presence.

After ten minutes of free swimming, Cole climbed over the side of the boat, his flippers touching the deck while a huge smile blossomed across his face. "That was an adrenaline rush."

Annja watched him lean back, the smile growing wider by the second. "You really didn't have to do that," she said.

He shrugged. "Free diving with them is an important part of the research for me. Along with their hierarchy, I also need to know how they behave when there's a human in the water with more than one of them."

"Yes, but you had no speargun, no backup. If they had turned on you at any moment—"

As if underscoring that fact, one of the big fish suddenly slammed into the side of the boat, splashing the water with its tail. Cole caught a shower of spray and wiped his face. "I think that was Martha," he said.

"You *named* them?"

"You get to know the distinctive shapes of their dorsal fins," Cole said. "And for me, it helps to establish that bond so I don't view them as mindless killing machines. Surely you noticed that, too?"

Annja grinned. "It was exhilarating, but I wouldn't ever recommend doing what you just did to anyone."

"Neither would I. But I have to control my own life. My destiny is always in *my* hands, not in the hands of someone else. That's what I love about my life so much. I make my own decisions. I know you understand that."

I used to, Annja thought. She watched one of the sharks break away from the boat suddenly and disappear into the depths.

Cole noticed, too. "They're bored now that there's nothing in the water."

"No more food?"

Cole sighed. "Sometimes I think it's not just about the food with them. I think they realize that we're curious and want to know more about them. They're active in the research as much as I am."

"I don't know," Annja said. "I think that sounds sort of insane, but then again, I didn't just swim naked with them like you did."

Cole laughed. "Annja, if you swim naked with anything, you'll get eaten right away."

"Flattery will get you killed, Cole."

He winked at her. "Well, maybe."

They set about winching the cage back on board the boat and secured it to the deck. Cole patted it. "I told you that nothing would happen while you were inside. Didn't you have a blast?"

"I hate to admit it, but I did. They were fascinating to watch. I could see how they tried to mouth the tuna first before chomping into it."

Cole nodded. "Exactly—they're smart. Not a lot of people give them credit for that. Oh, sure, scientists and researchers do, but the general public is still a long way from realizing how intelligent these fish are."

"Can you blame them?"

"No, not when they've been exposed to so much fallacy. But if people knew how close they swim in proximity to these fish without ever being attacked, I think that would go far toward raising people's consciousness."

"You won't change opinions overnight."

"No, I suppose not. But we can expose people through research. Look at what we accomplished today, for instance. I got you to change your mind about them, didn't I?"

"Somewhat. I'm still terrified," Annja said.

Cole patted her arm. "No worries. We'll have you free swimming with them soon enough."

Annja shook her head. "There is no way in hell I will ever do that, pal. Put that one out of your mind right now."

Cole laughed. "Okay, okay. Can't blame a guy for trying."

"Weren't you scared?"

"Absolutely. But this is the fourth time I've done it. The first was really terrifying. But when you get out there and touch them—"

"Touch them!"

"I give them a pat every now and again. I can grab their dorsal fins for a ride once in a while, as well."

"Good God."

"Once you do that," Cole said, "it just becomes this marvelous experience. I can't explain it without you doing it."

Annja nodded. "Yeah, well, that will have to be one experience I don't go through."

Tom called down from the wheelhouse. "We set to go?"

Cole nodded. "Fire 'er up."

The engines on the boat kicked into gear and the water behind churned into a frothy white of sea and spray. Wind blew through Annja's hair, drying it as she held on while the research vessel skipped over the waves back toward shore.

Cole busied himself jotting down notes on his observations. Annja went inside the cabin and changed back into her clothes. When she reemerged, Cole was still making notes. He glanced up at her.

"How about dinner tonight? I know a little Italian place with a fantastic wine selection and a veal cutlet to die for."

Annja nodded. "I'm starving, actually."

Cole finished his notes. "Great, I'll go make the call."

Annja followed him into the wheelhouse. Tom stood behind the wheel. He looked a lot younger than his twenty-four years. Fresh out of college with a degree in marine biology, Cole had scooped him up as his assistant and they'd been fast friends ever since. He smiled at Annja as she came in. "Feeling a bit more human again?"

"I need a shower to do that," Annja said. "This salt water is probably not doing wonders for my hair."

"Looks fine to me."

Cole elbowed him. "Mind your manners, boy."

Tom chuckled. "Why would I let the old guy have all the fun?"

"Old guy? I'll have you know I don't turn forty for another

year yet." Cole grabbed the ship phone and dialed into Montauk. He spoke for a moment and then hung up. "All set. Reservations for seven o'clock. That should give you enough time to grab a shower and change into something that will make me drool."

Annja punched him in the stomach. "Watch it, pal. I might get the impression all of this was done just to woo me, instead of in the name of science and the betterment of humankind."

Cole held up his hands. "Oh, hey, it's definitely for the betterment of humankind. I'm just starting out with me first."

Tom shook his head. "You know he's incorrigible, right?"

"Apparently," Annja said. She walked back into the main cabin and slid into the booth. Cole came in a second later and sat down across from her.

"I'm really glad you came out here, Annja."

"Me, too."

Cole leaned back. "The great whites we have access to here are among the largest in the world. They feed in the deep waters and it always astounds me how big they are."

"What's the biggest one ever caught?"

"You'd have to go back," Cole said. "There have been claims of thirty to forty feet about a hundred years back. Nowadays, it's rare you see one over twenty feet in length."

"That's still three times bigger than a full-grown man. Plenty of room to fit in the belly, huh?"

"That's nothing compared to the long-lost ancestor of great whites, the megalodon. Now that was something to behold."

"Why's that?"

"It was at least forty feet long when it cruised the prehistoric seas. Its teeth were as big as your hand with the same deadly serrations as great whites. Terrifying in its destructive power."

"Glad they're not around anymore."

Cole frowned. "I wouldn't be too sure about that."

Annja smirked. "C'mon. They died out ages ago. There's no way they could survive in today's oceans."

"Why not?"

Annja stopped. "Wouldn't someone have seen one by now?"

Cole shook his head. "Not necessarily. You know what's amazing about the oceans? Every year we find new species of fish or rediscover species we thought had long since died out. The depths that we are able to gain access to through advances in technology are enormous. We can't swim miles below the surface, but the robots we've built that have journeyed there have recorded a fascinating world."

"But giant sharks?"

Cole leaned forward. "Take the giant squid. For years, people swore it couldn't exist. We had corpses wash up on shores or sometimes get caught in fishing nets, but never found a live specimen. And then that Japanese team got the first video footage of it swimming in the silent depths. And we know that sperm whales love to eat those things."

"And you think that somewhere out there a megalodon could be swimming around?"

"Why not? We don't know everything and, sometimes, even the most implausible ideas turn out to be true."

Annja shrugged. "I guess. I just can't see it. I mean, a meg swimming out there would need to feast on a lot to sustain it, wouldn't it? So, I guess my question would be, if it's not extinct, then what is it eating?"

"I don't know," Cole said. "Perhaps it dines on the sperm whales that dive after giant squid. Maybe it's taken to living down far below the ocean surface where it can remain unseen except in its native habitat. All I'm saying is, we can't discount its existence merely because we haven't see one."

Annja shivered. "The idea of something that large and dangerous doesn't exactly make me all warm inside."

Cole laughed. "If it makes you feel any better, I wouldn't try to free swim with it, either."

"Well, there's a brilliant decision."

Cole smiled. Annja glanced around. "Are we close to the harbor? Sounds like Tom's throttled down."

Cole slid out of the booth and looked outside. "Yep. We're coming in through the outer channel now."

Annja followed and she and Cole joined Tom in the wheel-house. She could see the other boats lined up at the wharves. A few fishing charters meandered their way back into dock.

Tom pointed. "Hey, isn't that Sandy?"

Cole peered through the window and nodded. "What's she doing at the dock? She ought to have knocked off by now."

"Who's Sandy?" Annja asked.

"She works with us, handling calls in the office," Cole said. "She never goes out on the boats, though. She's terrified of the water. Her brother drowned when she was just six years old and she never goes near the water."

"That's horrible," Annja said. "And she's waiting down at the docks? That seems a bit odd."

"Sure does," Cole said. "Something must be up."

He and Annja went out on deck so they could secure the boat as they docked. Tom eased the engines down even further as they approached their mooring. He reversed, and then as the side of the boat touched the dock, Cole leaped on to the platform and Annja tossed him the lines. Cole tied the knots and Tom cut the engines.

Annja stepped off the boat and looked up at Sandy. She had a short blond haircut that fell just by her ears. But what made Annja stare was the expression on her face. She looked intensely worried.

Cole led the way up the gangplank and nodded at Sandy. "I didn't expect to see you here. Everything okay?"

Sandy shook her head. "No."

"What's the matter?"

"I just got a call from your brother. There's trouble up at the dive site."

"What kind of trouble?"

Sandy laid a hand on Cole's arm. "There's been a death, Cole."

3

Cole's face went ashen. "Not my brother—?"

Sandy shook her head. "No, but someone else on the dive went missing. This afternoon, they recovered a body. Well, part of it, anyway."

Annja frowned. "Part of it?"

Sandy looked her over. "There wasn't much left."

Cole shook his head. "Let's get back to the office and talk some more. I don't like discussing my business out in public."

Sandy led them back up the gangplank and toward the row of small wooden buildings scattered along the dock. At a pale blue row house, Annja saw the brass nameplate of Cole Williams Research and they entered. The narrow staircase up to the second floor seemed to be warped and it creaked underfoot as they climbed. But at the top Annja smelled coffee brewing and suddenly realized how much she wanted a cup.

Sandy pointed to the small coffeemaker. "Figured you all might be in the mood after being on the water."

Cole got himself and Annja each a cup and then sat down at an old table that must have served as a conference table by the look of it. He smiled at Annja. "It's not fancy here, but we make do."

Annja sipped the coffee and found it was a good roast. She smiled at Sandy. "This is delicious."

"Peruvian blend." Sandy glanced at Cole. "You didn't mention you had a visitor coming out."

Cole shrugged. "Annja's a good friend. Known her for years." He sipped his coffee. "And since I'm the boss, I don't think it's necessary that I keep you in the loop on everything that happens in my life."

Annja looked down into her coffee and wondered what sort of history Sandy and Cole had. Whatever might have once been, it certainly didn't appear to be intact any longer.

Sandy brushed off Cole's comment. "It would have been nice for me to know so I could make sure she's set up in town."

"Why don't you tell me about what's going on at the dive site?" Cole said. "Then I can figure out where to go from there."

"What dive site?" Annja asked.

"It's off the coast of Nova Scotia," Cole said. "My brother is up there heading the expedition to discover where the HMS *Fantome* went down back in 1814."

"*Fantome?*" Annja frowned. "You mean the ship that was supposedly carrying treasure looted from the White House during the War of 1812?"

"The same. My brother has been after it for years. Guess you could say that the love of the ocean runs deep in my family."

Annja sighed. "Great pun."

"Sorry." Cole shrugged. "But whereas I want to study the ocean and its wildlife, my brother is a bit more fixated on the economic aspects of it. He's been a treasure hunter for years."

"After all the time we've known each other," Annja said, "I never knew that."

Cole sipped his coffee. "Yeah, well, it's been a bone of contention between us for a while. Neither of us approves of the other's work. My brother thinks I'm a fruitcake for swimming with sharks and not making a buck off of my research. I think he's a money-grubber after fame and fortune."

"And never the two shall meet?"

Cole smiled. "Only during the holidays at my mother's house. She usually starts the visits by telling us that if we fight she'll smack us around."

"Smart woman," Annja said. "What's your brother's name?"

"Hunter," Cole said. "How tragically fitting, huh?"

"The problem is the death of one of his guys," Sandy said. "Hunter told me that they've spotted a big shark in the area."

Annja leaned back. "Sharks off Nova Scotia? Isn't that a little far north for any of the dangerous species?"

"Not at all," Cole said. "Great whites can regulate their internal body temperature and keep it higher than the surrounding water. They've adapted so they can hunt the seals that prefer to stay in the cooler waters. It's not uncommon to find great whites that far north." He took a breath. "Now, whether one is attacking divers at the dive site, that would be another matter entirely."

"Would it?"

He looked at Annja. "As you've seen, just because a great white is around doesn't automatically mean that someone's going to die. If that was the case, there'd be bodies everywhere."

Sandy laid her hands on the table. "It's pretty apparent from the evidence on the body that something large, with huge teeth, killed the diver."

"Huge teeth?"

"The bite radius was enormous. Hunter says the body was cut in two."

Cole frowned. "That would mean a great white of huge proportions. Something like that would be pretty unusual."

"Larger than a twenty-footer?" Annja asked.

"Sharks that large don't usually bother coming in close to shore. They're more deep-water fish. Hardly ever seen. That sort of thing. But if one is stalking the dive site, then that would be unusual behavior as well. It would mean it was a rogue shark. And unlike in the movies, that just doesn't happen all that often," Cole said.

Tom had been silent at the other end of the table, but he looked up and smiled. "Well, we could always offer to go and check things out. If Hunter's worried about his team and knows there's a shark in the area, that might be why he decided to call you."

Cole grinned. "Well, he needs to keep me in the loop anyway: I'm financing the operation."

Annja frowned. "I thought you said Hunter was always riding you because you don't make any money."

"He is," Cole said. "And he's right to some extent. I don't make much money. But I have money left over form a trust fund set up by my father."

"Didn't Hunter have one?"

"Absolutely. But he blew through it years ago financing his own dives. It was only after he went bankrupt that I staked him and he ended up striking a good find down in the Caribbean. Now, we work together with me fronting the money on his expeditions and reaping a decent return on my investment."

"Interesting."

"Well, it enables me to keep the research going," Cole said. "And that's the most important thing to me."

Sandy cleared her throat. "Thing is, with a shark in the area, the dive crew isn't exactly excited about getting back into the waters."

"Understandable," Annja said. "I wouldn't be crazy about it, either."

Cole looked pained. "It kills me to say it, but we've got to do something about it, then. Time is money on these things."

Sandy nodded. "That's why he called. He wanted you to know that there was some chaos up there."

"And?"

"He wants you to come up."

Cole took a long sip of his coffee and swallowed. "I don't know. I've got a lot to do around here."

"Like swim with more great whites?" Annja grinned at him.

"You know the plan, Annja."

"Yes, but this is something you should look into. If there is a shark hunting through the dive site, then maybe you can figure out why it's there and why it's attacked a diver already. That research could prove just as useful as what you're doing here."

"I've always tried to keep my business investments separate from my love of the ocean."

"Not always possible," Annja said.

Cole nodded. "I've been somewhat idealistic in that regard." He smirked. "Possibly naïve as well."

Sandy got up from the table. "I can make the flight arrangements if you'd like. Get you up there for first thing tomorrow."

Cole glanced at Tom. "Interested in coming along for the ride?"

Tom fixed him with a gaze. "Now, why would you even ask that question? Of course I am."

Cole smiled. "I don't like to assume things."

"Yeah, well assume all you want. I'm not going to miss the

chance to see what's going on up there." He shrugged. "Besides, it's a hunt for treasure. What guy didn't dream of doing that when he first heard about Treasure Island?"

Cole turned to Annja. "I know you've got plans to fly out soon, so I won't bother asking—"

Annja held up her hand. "The dive site actually sounds like something I'd enjoy. And like Tom said, it does involve the search for relics and treasure. That's something I'm always interested in, in case you didn't know."

Cole looked at Sandy. "Flight arrangements for three, if you please."

Sandy nodded and left the room. Cole watched her go for a moment and then, noticing the silence that hung in the room, turned back. "She's a good worker. Knows everything I need to keep up with."

Annja eyed him. "She didn't seem too thrilled with me being around here."

"Ah, that's just Sandy. She's had a thing for me ever since she started working here."

"That's awfully modest of you," Annja said with a laugh. She took a sip of her coffee and put her cup back down on the table. "Clearly, she thinks I'm a threat. Just make sure she doesn't throw me overboard to the shark."

"Sure thing." He looked at Tom. "I suppose we'd better get the charts out and study up on the site if we're going to be a de facto replacement crew."

Tom walked to the nearby metal file cabinets and yanked one of the drawers open. With a sheaf of charts and papers, he laid them out on the table and spread them around. Annja could make out pictures of the ship itself, lists of what its inventory was rumored to have been, and even notes form an old journal.

"Where's it supposed to have gone down?"

Cole sighed. "That was always the problem. The ship sank

near Prospect, but attempts to find it so far have proven futile. It was 1814, after all, so maybe the location was wrong. Back then there was no Coast Guard to help fix a position. It always amazes me to think of what people must have thought about when they cast off from dock. There was no guarantee that you'd ever make it home alive. Between storms, dangerous shoals, prowling marauders, you had a slim chance of completing a journey."

"And yet they did it," Annja said. "And they opened up the world to exploration."

Cole jabbed his finger at the east coast of Nova Scotia. "Hunter always thought the ship went down here. In about a hundred feet of water. But the currents are strong and there's no telling where the remains of the ship might have been dragged to since that time."

"Almost two hundred years have passed," said Tom. "That ship could be scattered halfway between Nova Scotia and Greenland."

Cole frowned. "Hunter has always based his hunts largely on his intuition. Until he learned to trust it, he never hit it big. The first time he went with his gut, he struck gold, literally. It's something he tries to abide by to this day. And he seemed pretty convinced he knew where he'd find the wreck."

"You believe him?" Annja asked.

"I'd better," Cole said. "I'm sinking two million dollars into the hunt for the *Fantome*. I expect to make that back and then some. The treasure on board would be worth tens of millions of dollars."

"If not more," said Tom. "Remember that a lot of it was taken right form the White House. There'd be gifts and such from all the powerful world leaders at the time in the wake of the Revolutionary War. That stuff today would be an incredible draw for collectors."

"Good point." Cole studied the maps. "I wonder where

Hunter is right now and whether he thinks that he knows where he'll find the largest stock of loot."

Annja studied a picture of the *Fantome*. "So this is the ship?"

"Loaded down with all that booty, she must have weighed tons," Cole said. "Imagine setting off bound for England and running into the storm they took the brunt of? No thanks."

"After weathering the strong ocean today en route to the sharks, I don't even want to think about that," Annja said. "I doubt I would have been a very good sailor."

"You get used to it," said Tom. "But even still, there's nothing like a strong storm at sea to turn anyone into a true believer in the power of Mother Nature."

Annja pored over the pictures and notes. "And to think, now there might be a prowling shark in their midst."

"Nothing like the promise of death in an already dangerous job," Cole said. "I'm sure Hunter is stalking around his boat furious at the sea for the delay this is causing."

"What about the body?" Annja asked. "Are they flying it home?"

"It was a local guy," Sandy said coming back into the room. "Luckily, they didn't have far to transport him. Although, with the ceremony being a closed casket, I'm not so sure those he left behind wouldn't just as soon see him buried at sea."

Annja looked up at her. Sandy's expression didn't betray a hint of emotion. But she locked eyes with Annja and then broke away long enough to look at Cole. "You're all set for departure tomorrow morning."

Then she glanced back at Annja. "Have a safe trip."

4

Annja, Cole, and Tom flew into Halifax International Airport the next morning. Annja hadn't slept much the night before, trying to use her laptop to dig up information on the infamous Megalodon that Cole raved about. What she found didn't cheer her up much. With teeth the better part of six inches long, Meg, as it was more affectionately know, could chomp through whales with ease. And humans were much softer than whales.

But most scientists agreed the species was long extinct.

Except for Cole.

A couple of authors had written some novels about a few remaining species swimming in the vast depths of the oceans, but otherwise, there'd been nothing to ever confirm or even hint at the suggestion there might be others still lurking in the waves.

She'd eventually fallen asleep with images of giant teeth running through her head.

Storm clouds blew in as they were making their final approach to the airport and the plane jumped a few times before its wheels finally gripped the tarmac. Annja gave a silent prayer of thanks for having her feet back on terra firma.

In the terminal, she saw a man standing by himself wearing a Dive the Marianas Trench T-shirt. She elbowed Cole. "That him?"

Cole smirked. "He always did have a twisted sense of humor."

"At least he doesn't free swim with great whites, huh?"

"Annja—"

The man came over and hugged Cole. Annja looked him up and down. He was a few inches taller than Cole and maybe a few pounds lighter. His lean build started with his close-cropped hair and chiseled face that bore a few interesting scars.

"Hey, bro."

Cole hugged him back. "When Sandy told me—"

Hunter nodded. "Yeah, I know, man. But I'm still here. Don't have any plans of shoving off any time soon, either." He turned and faced Annja. "Hi. I'm Hunter."

"Annja."

He shook her hand and Annja felt the rough sandpaper texture of it. Hunter was used to working hard. "Nice to meet you."

Hunter shook hands with Tom. "I see my brother's still got you working for him, huh?"

"At least until that other job offer comes through."

"Yeah, right." Hunter led them across the terminal. "We'll get your bags and then head down. I'll fill you in on the way. Less chance of being heard, if you catch my meaning."

Annja frowned. How come Hunter didn't want to talk about the attack now? She assumed the local media would have the story all over the wires now. A shark attack in Nova Scotia was a rare thing indeed.

At the baggage terminal, they got their gear and checked through the customs line quickly. The customs official gave

Annja's passport a whistle as he flipped through it. "You're quite the world traveler, Miss."

Annja smiled at him. "Sometimes, I don't even know what day it is."

Hunter guided them outside and Annja found the temperature pleasant with a warm breeze blowing in. In the parking lot, she spotted a van and Hunter pointed. "That's our ride. We shouldn't be on the road all that long."

"How far's Prospect from here?" Cole asked.

"About twenty three kilometers to the southwest. We'll just hop on the 333 and be there in no time. If the traffic's decent."

Tom stowed the gear in back and then they all climbed aboard. Cole took shotgun and Annja and Tom slid into the back. Annja leaned forward as Hunter eased the van out of the parking space. "You mind me asking why you wanted to wait until we're outside before we started talking about the shark attack?'

Hunter shrugged. "No surprise. But we managed to keep the attack out of the local media."

"How the hell did you manage that?" Cole asked.

"I paid off the local police chief." He glanced at Cole. "By the way, bro, I'm going to need some more money."

"What a surprise."

"You paid off the local police chief? To do what?"

"To say that the death was an accident."

"But why?"

Hunter put his hands on the wheel and steered them on to the highway. "Look, the thing is, we know where the wreck is. If we all of a sudden start blabbering about shark attacks, then the place will start crawling with media and fishermen, and even rival treasure hunters. That's a lot of publicity that we don't need right now. If we can get in, do our thing and then get gone, we'll be so much the better."

"And if it turns out there really is a shark up here?"

Hunter grinned. "Oh, there's definitely a shark in the water. I have no doubt of that. Even saw the damned thing register on the sonar."

Cole looked at him. "How big?"

"Big. Like, real big. Over thirty feet."

Annja put a hand on Cole's shoulder. "Don't get your hopes up about a Meg. What if it's a basking shark?"

Hunter laughed. "I've seen basking sharks before. Plankton eaters like the whale shark. Let me tell you something: this was no plankton eater did that to my man. Chomped him into two pieces and then some."

"A great white of that size would be an enormous specimen," Cole said. "I'd need to document it."

"Document it all you want, bro," Hunter said. "Just keep everything under wraps until we're done here."

"And how long will that take?"

Hunter shrugged. "Could take us two weeks to excavate everything from the site. Maybe longer if the currents have strewn it all over the place."

"You found the main wreck site?"

Hunter nodded. "Hull's intact. Parts of the ship aren't there, but the main hold is. I think we've got a big one here, bro."

"Why's that?"

Hunter shrugged. "A lot of people over the years claimed that the *Fantome* wasn't carrying loot from the White House simply because it wasn't involved in the raid on Washington. Some thought it might just be carrying goods from parts of Maine that the British controlled to Nova Scotia. But if that was the case, then why was it in convoy? A simple customs run wouldn't dictate such elaborate security."

"You never bought into that theory?" Annja asked.

"Nope. The *Fantome* was originally a French privateer that the British took possession of in 1810 and commissioned directly into the British Navy as a brig sloop with eighteen guns on her. She had a good kick in terms of firepower and she had a hold that could handle a large quantity of booty." He shook his head. "Nah, she was hauling some serious stuff when she went down."

"And it's off Prospect as the records claim?"

Hunter nodded. "That was the benefit of survivors from the wreck. They were able to confirm where they went down. Of course, that was over two hundred years ago, and the shifting tide can change things a lot underwater."

"Not exactly easy to explore when there's a shark cruising nearby," Annja said. "Why don't you tell us about what happened?"

Hunter nodded. "Yeah, sure. We were out just the other day. Good day for salvage work. Sunny, not strong surf. We made it out to the next grid on our search string and one of my guys, by the name of Jock, went down to lead the way for the rest of the team."

"He always go first?" Cole asked.

"Yeah, kinda like that. He's from the UK, former Special Forces guy. They lead that way, you know. Likes to be in the water and all that stuff."

"So, he went down…"

Hunter shrugged. "The rest of us were a little slow getting into wet suits. I was nursing an awful headache that I woke up with and the team was a bit slow. All of a sudden, the captain calls me on to the bridge and jabs a finger at the sonar. I thought it was a submarine at first, you know? This big thing just moving along."

"You think about radioing down to Jock?" Cole asked.

"Would have if he'd gone down with a radio unit. But Jock didn't like them. Said they didn't allow him the freedom he liked underwater. He used to rely on hand signals only."

"And he was down there all alone," Annja said.

"We saw the shape moving—Jock didn't show up on the sonar—and then it was gone. Someone screamed off the stern and when we went out, we saw an upwelling of blood break the surface of the water. We knew something was wrong so we went down."

Annja leaned back. "You went down there knowing that the shark might still be around?"

"My man was down there," Hunter said. "It's my responsibility to get him back, even at risk."

"What'd you find?"

"Two pieces of body. Shredded wet suit with these long tears. His air tanks were crushed. It was a horrible sight. His head was gone, too."

Annja frowned. "You sure it's him? The body, I mean."

Hunter stared at her. "Why would you even ask that question? Of course we're sure. Jock was the only one down there, then this big thing cruises by and then Jock's remains are found. Seems like an easy equation to me."

Annja held up her hand. "Just asking."

"Well, it was a bad question," Hunter said. "Jock was a good man and I don't like the memory of him being questioned."

"But you'll lie in order to protect the salvage operation you've got going on here," Annja said. "I get it."

Hunter frowned and glanced at Cole. "Just who is this chick, bro?"

"This 'chick,' as you call her happens to be a pretty damned good archaeologist. You'd do well to remember that she's not only pretty smart, but also a pretty tough woman."

"Pretty tough?" Annja smirked. If only you had the first clue about that one.

Cole turned around. "I don't want your ego getting out of check."

"Thanks for the concern." She looked at Hunter. "Look, I don't want to get off on the wrong foot here, so let's just agree that this is a real tragedy and that we will do everything we can to help you make sure it doesn't happen again."

Hunter paused and then nodded. "Yeah, okay."

Cole pointed at the sign for Prospect. "Not much farther now, is it?"

"Five minutes or so to get down to the harbor and catch the dingy out to the boat. That shouldn't take that long."

Annja looked at the small town as they drove through. It didn't look like there was a lot of traffic in the area. Small homes bordered streets and she could make out eateries and neighborhood taverns. It was a cozy town.

"There haven't been other shark attacks here, have they?"

Hunter laughed. "You kidding? The Canadian Atlantic is considered to be one of the safest places to swim. I mean, the water temperatures are fairly cold year round, so that's a major factor. Less people in the water, means less chance of interaction with sharks."

"Yeah, but great whites swim these waters, too," Cole said. "They can tolerate the cooler temps."

"Last great white seen around these parts was five years ago," Hunter said. "I checked."

"Maybe they're migrating north," Cole said. "How's the seal population?"

"Don't know," Hunter said. "They would like that, though, wouldn't they? And Jock always did like his gray wet suit."

Cole shrugged. "It could have been a case of mistaken identity, I suppose." His voice trailed off.

"But you don't think so," Annja said.

Cole shook his head. "I don't know. It just doesn't feel like it. I could be completely wrong, of course. I've been wrong before. But a shark that big as what showed up on sonar, well, I don't know."

"A rogue shark hunting these waters would be unbelievable

unusual," Hunter said. "Like I said, it's not like there's a lot of people up here to sustain it."

Cole nodded. "I know. I know." He sighed. "Well, I suppose we'll see when we get out there, won't we?"

Annja felt the bump in the road as Hunter directed the van down on to the town dock. Small fishing charter boats bobbed in subtle tidal surge. The waters looked a deeper blue than the blue green of warmer climates.

Annja cast her glance farther out beyond the harbor. The sea stretched before them: mighty, massive, and unknown.

Just like the thing that killed Jock.

5

They boarded a smaller dinghy and sped out toward the main salvage ship, which from a distance looked nothing like it was equipped for any type of recovery operation. Annja pointed at it as they approached. "That doesn't much look like a salvage ship, Hunter."

"That's the point." Hunter smiled. "We've learned some hard lessons since we got started a number of years ago. The number one lesson is to not let your competition know what you're up to."

"There's a lot?"

"Of rival treasure hunters? Oh yeah." Surf spray washed over them all and Hunter wiped his face. "It's mostly minor league stuff. No one's taking out contracts on another company or anything. But if people know what you're planning to do, they can get a head start on jumping the claim ahead of you."

Annja could see some activity on the deck. "Can't you just claim the site as belonging to you?"

"Not really. You have to jump through loopholes with the

nation whose territorial waters you're in. Then there's the question of who might own the contents, and all that stuff. If enough time has passed, it's not really an issue, but there are plenty of ways to get hung up in paperwork."

"Which is why we have lawyers," Cole said.

Hunter nodded. "Amen to the lawyers. At least this time."

Annja grinned. "What's that supposed to mean?"

"It means his ex-wife ran him through the cleaners," Cole said. "And she was merciless."

Hunter shook his head. "I won't ever make that kind of mistake again. Mark my words."

Hunter eased the throttle down on the dinghy motor and the little boat bobbed on the waves, closing the final distance down between them and the salvage ship. Annja noted that it was about a hundred feet long and had more of the appearance of a luxury yacht than anything else.

A ladder came over the side and Cole motioned for Annja to lead the way. She found the grips and went right up, finally stepping aboard the ship. Cole came up behind her, followed by Tom, and then at last Hunter stepped aboard.

"We would have come up from the stern, but I think we might have some work going on right now so I wanted to leave it clear. If people are in the water and that shark comes back, I want them able to exit quickly."

Annja nodded. "Fair plan."

Hunter spread his arms. "Allow me to welcome you to The Seeker. As grand a ship as there ever was what sailed the seas."

"Got a parrot to go along with that accent?" Cole asked. "You never could resist the urge to showboat."

Hunter stepped back. "I am slain by your tainted barbs, dear brother."

"I'll bet."

Hunter winked at Annja. "Right, well, let's get you settled

down below and then see if we can make some sense out of this whole situation."

They entered the cabin and Hunter led them down a flight of steep stairs to the sleeping quarters. He turned as he walked. "We're a little short of space, but I managed to find some room. I hope the accommodations are acceptable."

He opened a wooden door and Annja saw that the cabin was more luxurious than she'd expected. A double bed stood near the porthole and a small bureau would hold her gear, the little she'd brought with her. There was a small television as well. She glanced at Hunter. "Very comfortable."

Cole rolled his eyes. "This is probably the only worthwhile investment he's ever made."

Hunter sighed. "Are we going to get into this all over again? I'd rather focus on the actual reason you're here, rather than how to make me feel like crap for some of my past decisions."

"All right, all right." Cole held up his hands. "Show me where I'm staying and then we'll get to work."

Hunter looked uncomfortable. "Uh…"

"What?"

Hunter leaned against the doorjamb. "Well, it's just that, when I called and you mentioned you were bringing Annja along…I just sort of assumed that it was because you two were…you know…"

"Together?" Annja asked.

"Yeah."

Cole sighed. "I don't get my own room?"

"I don't have any to spare. Your pal Tom is being stuffed into an old storage closet that we managed to fit a mattress into, but even that's a stretch. And not in a good way."

Cole took a deep breath and looked at Annja. "I apologize for this. If you want to leave, I don't blame you in the slightest."

Annja smirked. "Do I look like some little innocent miss you've got to save from the perils of man? I've been in awkward situations before. I'll manage with this one." She looked at Hunter. "Don't worry about it. It's fine."

"You sure?"

"Yeah. Let's not lose sight of why we're here. If I can help out somehow, then that's all that matters."

Cole shrugged. "Suit yourself."

He started forward, but Annja lobbed her bag onto the bed first. "I sleep on that side. You get the porthole."

Cole looked at the bed and then back at Annja. "I don't do well on the porthole side."

"Why not?"

"I don't know. I just never have."

Hunter chuckled. "That's true. One of the first boats our dad bought, Cole there slept funny and woke up heaving halfway through the night. He blew chunks all over dad's teakwood finish. Hoo boy, the old man was furious about that one."

"Thanks for bringing that up," Cole said.

"Anytime."

Annja sighed. "All right, take the door side. But if any trouble comes through that door, I'll expect you to be up and defending the room. If you can't do that, I'll take over. Just hold them off long enough for me to wake up."

Hunter and Cole looked at her.

"What?" Annja asked.

"That sort of thing happen to you before?" Hunter asked.

"You'd be surprised," Annja said. "A lot of things have come through my bedroom doors over the years and not all of them have been good. Or even remotely pleasant."

Hunter glanced at Cole. "That's some roommate you scored for yourself there, bro. Best of luck making it through the night."

Cole nodded slowly. "I might need it from the sound of things."

Annja clapped her hands. "No use dwelling on it. Just that my work has exposed me to a lot of potential risks is all."

"And here I thought you were just a mild-mannered scientist with an outdoor streak," Cole said.

Annja grinned. "And I used to think you had some common sense rattling around in that skull of yours."

Hunter frowned. "Oh, no, don't you tell me he's swimming with great whites again."

"He is."

"Jeez." Hunter shook his head. "Dude, how many times have I told you that's not a good idea?"

"It's fine," Cole said. "I've done it a few times now and there's nothing to worry about."

"Famous last words."

"Annja was there on my most recent swim," Cole said.

Hunter glanced at her. "You were? You let him go and do it?"

"Hey, I had no clue anything of the sort was going on. We were in the cage, he motioned for me to get back on to the boat so I did. Next thing I know Jacques Cousteau there is off trying to catch a ride on a giant dorsal fin."

Hunter looked at Cole. "You're trying to ride them now?"

"It was a thought."

"Yeah, a bad one. How in the world can you think that grabbing a dorsal fin on a shark is a good idea? One wrong move and you'll end up down their gullet as a noontime snack."

Cole shook his head. "Not going to happen, Hunter. I've researched this. There's no danger provided I keep my wits about me."

"Did you chum the waters this time?"

"I need a way to attract the fish."

Annja looked at Hunter. "Sounds like you've been witness to his swimming with sharks before."

"Yeah, I saw him do it. Damn near scared me to death. He

didn't tell me he was going to do it until he was actually in the water with them without a cage. I'd had no time to prepare or be ready in case he needed help."

"If I needed help," Cole said. "There would have been nothing you could have done. It would be too late."

"Yeah, well, forgive a brother for wanting to help out in case of emergency. It's not like I love you or anything."

Cole smiled. "You're a pal, really. And I know your heart is in the right place, but it's not necessary to get all worked up over this."

"Not necessary?" Hunter sighed. "Look, dude, I've already lost one man to some type of giant shark swimming around in waters where it's extremely rare. I don't want to have to bury my own flesh and blood because of some foolish act."

"You think it's foolish?"

"I think we might both have some unaddressed issues that makes us do reckless things," Hunter said.

"You with money," Cole said.

"And you with your life," Hunter replied. "Tough knowing which is worse, huh?"

"At least you two aren't beating the crap out of each other like some other brothers I know," Annja said. "The fact is, it's risky stuff swimming with apex predators. I think we all know that. And hopefully, Cole will keep his focus when he does and we won't need to figure out how to put all the chewed-up bits of him into a trash bag for the funeral."

Cole laughed. "Colorful."

"I like her," Hunter said. "She's not afraid to give it back to you, huh?"

"Or anyone else," Cole said. "You'd do well to remember that."

"I will." He looked around the cabin. "All right, you guys want to rest? Catch a nap or something? I can arrange for lunch in about an hour if you want. Just let me know."

"I'm ready to go, actually," Cole said. "Let's get to it."

Annja took a breath. She could have used a nap. Plane travel sometimes made her weary. But since Cole had jumped the gun, she wouldn't miss the chance to get started.

"I'm good," she said.

They exited the cabin and Hunter led them back topside. "I'll introduce you to the rest of the crew."

"How are they handling the death?" Annja asked.

"As well as can be expected," Hunter said. "Given that Jock was a bit tough to get along with due to his work ethic and the fact he used to clean them all out with his poker face, there's a lot more sympathy than I might have reasonably expected."

"Anyone quit the project?" Cole asked.

"Nope. The promise of fortune is too great to scare anyone away just yet."

"And competitors?"

Hunter shook his head. "So far, so good. We've kept the search pretty well buttoned up and haven't seen another ship in days."

Cole nodded. "Good."

Bright sunlight greeted them as they emerged from below-decks. Annja looked up into the clear blue sky and smiled. Being on the ocean was always invigorating.

"Hunter!"

They turned as a young girl came rushing up to them. Hunter frowned. "What's up, Holly?"

"Got a blip on the screen again."

"Blip?"

"That thing—the shark? The captain thinks it's back again."

6

Hunter led them up to the wheelhouse where Annja was surprised to find a young woman studying the bridge console. She looked up as Hunter entered and jabbed a finger at the scope.

"Can't be sure. At least, not yet," the captain said.

Annja couldn't see past Hunter's shoulder. "How come?" she asked.

The captain glanced at Annja. "Who's she?"

Hunter pointed at Annja. "That's Annja Creed. Annja, meet Jax, our captain."

Captain Jax nodded. "Hey."

"You said you couldn't tell if it was the shark. How come?" Annja asked again.

"Too far out right now. I'll know more if it comes closer."

"Will it?"

Jax shrugged. "Who knows? It might just be cruising around looking for lunch. As long as none of us are in the water, I don't care. Let it eat something other than humans and I think we'll all be better off."

Cole pushed his way onto the bridge. "If the actual shark expert could maybe manage to get a look at the scope, that would probably be helpful for all involved."

Hunter stepped back. "Sorry, bro."

Cole studied the instrument. Annja moved forward and she could make out the slow line circling around the scope. As it passed the lower left section, it grazed what appeared to be a very substantial shape in the water. Cole frowned and leaned back. "You weren't kidding."

"About what?" Hunter asked.

"It's big."

Annja looked at Cole. "You think it's a shark?"

Cole shrugged. "Kinda tough to tell from here."

She looked out of the wheelhouse at the back of the boat in the direction she thought the shark would be cruising based on what she'd seen on the scope. To imagine that something that large was swimming the waters was extremely discomforting. Like so many others, Annja had considered colder waters to be relatively free of dangerous sharks.

So much for that, she thought.

Cole stepped away from the scope and stared out the back window with Annja. "There's not a lot I can do from here."

Annja looked at him. "I don't like the way that sounds."

He smiled. "But you know it's the truth."

"It seems to be what you do, crazy one."

Cole shrugged. "My life, my calling." He glanced back at Hunter, who was now talking with Captain Jax. "I don't think he'll be crazy about the idea, however."

"Of course he won't be. He's your brother. He doesn't want to see you in harm's way."

Cole eyed her. "Will you help me?"

"With what?"

"I'll need another set of eyes down there with me."

Annja watched the ocean and noticed that it seemed to have

gone almost glassy still. "You want me to get in the water with you?"

"That would be the idea, yeah."

"Um, did you bring a cage?"

Cole smiled. "No. But then again, this will give you a chance to get into the water and see that these sharks aren't necessarily the bad guys we make them out to be in movies."

Annja frowned. "Cole, this shark, if it's the same one, has already killed one person in recent days."

"We don't know for sure if this is the same shark."

Annja leaned against the wall of the wheelhouse. "Why do I feel like I'm living in a bad remake of *Jaws*?"

Cole grinned. "Because you're fighting the stereotypes that have plagued the sharks since that damnable movie came out. Everyone sees them as nothing but mindless predators, just killing machines. But they're not. They are extremely intelligent."

"I don't know if I'd go that far."

"You saw them swim with me in the open water. And they didn't attack." He smiled. "And don't forget that I'd chummed that water pretty heavily."

Annja sighed. "Yeah, but that was with sharks that hadn't attacked anyone. Maybe this one has developed a taste for human flesh. I'm not excited about the thought of meeting that fish."

Cole shook his head. "Human flesh isn't what feeds these incredible fish, Annja. We're not a staple of their diets. What probably happened here was a case of mistaken identity. The victim was caught in the wrong place at the wrong time, is all. Could happen to anyone, but unfortunately, he just got caught."

"That's not much consolation if you're trying to sell me on this idea." Annja felt her stomach turn over. This wasn't a good idea. And she didn't need the hard-won instincts she'd gained from countless battles and struggles to tell her that. Anyone who'd ever seen a shark special on the Discovery Channel would tell her this was a *bad* idea.

Hunter came over. "The blip's gone."

"It's gone where?" Annja tried to hide the relief in her voice.

"I don't know," Hunter said. "But the blip is gone. It might have moved out of range. Maybe it's still there." He stopped and stared at Cole. "What's going on here?"

"Nothing."

Hunter frowned. "Bullshit. I know that look."

Cole shook his head. "There's no look, Hunter. You're imagining things."

Hunter looked at Annja. "Is that true?"

Annja held up her hands. "Leave me out of the sibling confrontations. My stomach hurts."

Hunter turned back to Cole and jabbed a finger at him. "I know you too well, bro. I know what you're thinking about doing. The answer's no."

"What?"

Hunter pointed outside. "You want in. I turn my back on you and you'll probably dive right in without any tanks on."

Cole smiled. "Maybe."

"Water's awful cold, dude. At least take a wet suit."

Cole's eyes lit up. "You're serious?"

Hunter slapped him on the shoulder. "Are you nuts? You're not going anywhere near the water until we get some extra precautions up here."

"Like what?"

Hunter shrugged. "Like, for one thing, a shark cage. I notice you didn't haul one along with you."

Annja smiled. "The carry-on baggage fee at the airport was a little steep so we had to ditch it."

Hunter smirked. "And that wouldn't have stopped the crazy one here from jumping right in, would it?"

Annja chewed her lip. Hunter nodded. "Yeah, I knew it. He was trying to talk you into going in there with him, wasn't he?"

Annja backed away. "I should leave you guys alone to work this out. Maybe I'll just head downstairs and get some rest."

Hunter shook his head and stared at Cole. "Are you really insane? You were trying to get her to go in there with you? What was she—bait? That's a new low for you, Cole. Seriously, man. You've lost your freaking mind."

Cole sighed. "We come from two different perspectives on this, Hunter."

"Yeah, you want to put your head in the mouth of every lion you come across while I know that lions aren't made to have human heads in them. Which one of us is right, huh?"

Hunter stalked out of the wheelhouse. Annja watched him stomp down to the back of the boat. Cole took a breath and sighed. "I'm sorry you had to hear all that, Annja."

"Forget it. You guys aren't the first siblings I've known who didn't have the perfect relationship. At least it's apparent that you guys love each other."

"I guess."

Annja put a hand on his shoulder. "Think of it this way. If he didn't care, he would have encouraged you to jump right in."

"Yeah."

Annja shoved him out of the wheelhouse. "Go. Talk to him and try to get some common ground back. You've both got objectives here. Maybe you can make some sense out of them."

"Thanks."

Annja watched him go. Behind her, she heard a flicking sound. She turned and saw Captain Jax eyeing her while she cleaned her fingernails with a switchblade. "That was smooth," the captain said.

Annja looked at the long blond hair tied back in a ponytail with a length of hemp. Captain Jax was about Annja's age, but the crow's-feet around her eyes belied a lot more years on the ocean than the rest of her appearance suggested.

"How long have you been a captain?" Annja asked.

"Why? You have issues with my skippering so far?"

Annja shook her head. "No. It's just that most of the captains I've ever known have been men. Kinda strange to see a woman in charge. Nice change of pace. That's all."

Captain Jax finished cleaning one hand and adroitly flipped the knife around to work the other hand. "Yeah, well, it hasn't been an easy slog for me to climb the ladder. I did time on tramp steamers and shitty freighters, working the south Atlantic between Africa and South America."

"What happened?"

"I got tired of turning a blind eye to the crap I used to witness."

"Like?"

Captain Jax stop cleaning her nails. "You ever seen eight-year-old kids forced to shovel coal into ship boilers for ten hours a day?"

"No."

"You ever seen teenage girls being sold into sexual slavery?"

Annja frowned. "Heard of it."

Captain Jax smirked. "Different when it's right in front of your face, lemme tell you."

"So you stopped working that route?"

"I came north after the skipper of the ship and I had a disagreement about a particular shipment of kids into the Brazilian brothels."

"What happened?"

Captain Jax shrugged. "I cut his throat while he slept. And I shoved his bloated carcass overboard where the sharks tore him to bits."

Annja almost smiled at the candor with which Captain Jax spoke. "You don't seem particularly upset."

"I'm not upset at all." Captain Jax pointed the knife at her. "You, however, don't seem the least bit fazed by what I just said."

Annja shrugged. "Let's just say it sounds like we've both left a few bodies in our wakes."

"Is that so?"

"Yes. It is."

Captain Jax eyed her for a moment without moving. Annja returned the stare. A heavy silence cloaked the wheelhouse and, in the distance, Annja could hear the breeze coming off the ocean. But nothing moved in the space between her and the captain.

Finally, Jax seemed satisfied. "Just so long as you understand that this is my boat. I have the authority here."

"I thought this was Hunter's boat," Annja said.

"I'm the captain."

"No one's trying to steal the job from you."

Jax nodded. "Good."

Annja started to leave. She took a step before she heard Captain Jax's voice. "Annja."

She turned. She saw the whiz of movement through the air. Annja shifted as the blade flew past her and sank into the wood paneling next to her head. The switchblade was deeply embedded.

Annja glanced back at Captain Jax. "You finished now?"

Jax smiled. "Good reflexes."

"They're better than you know." Annja pulled the knife out of the wood and checked the edge. It was razor sharp. She turned the blade over and then in the next instant sent it flying right back at Jax. Jax recovered quickly and dodged the blade as it shot into the clock next to her head.

"Not bad," she said.

Annja smirked. "Just remember—you aren't the only warrior on this boat. Not anymore."

7

Outside the wheelhouse, Annja ran into Hunter. He looked her over. "Everything okay back there?"

Annja smiled. "Just a couple of dogs having a pissing contest. Nothing to get excited about."

"If it's happening on my boat, I want to know about it," Hunter said. "I've already lost one crew member and I don't want any more going missing. If Jax is giving you shit, you need to tell me. She's pretty territorial."

Annja shook her head. "Don't expect me to come running to you like some lost sheep. I don't operate that way. If Jax has a problem with me, then we'll work it out between us. One way or another."

"As long as there's not another body to worry about," Hunter said.

Annja frowned. "What do you mean?"

Hunter held up his hands. "I know something of what Jax came from. She's got a history all her own. You, I don't know about. Only what Cole told me. And that wasn't very much. Except that he's very fond of you."

A stiff breeze blew across the bow of the ship. "We're really not a couple, if that's what you're hinting at."

Hunter shrugged. "None of my business if you were. But he still had no right to ask you to do what he did."

"I don't take it personally. It seems to be in Cole's nature to run toward danger." Annja looked at the swirling surf. "It seems to be mine, too."

"Yeah? What's that mean? You go looking for trouble?" Hunter wore an amused expression on his face.

Annja sighed. "Trouble usually has a way of finding me on its own without any help from me. As a result, I get into a lot of bad places. Crazy stuff, sometimes."

"Like a boat looking for sunken treasure being stalked by a giant man-eating shark?"

"That's actually a new one," Annja said. "But it takes all kinds." She looked toward the stern. "You and Cole talk yet?"

"No."

"You should. The boat's too small for any bad blood to ferment. It'll end up costing us all in terms of our safety."

Hunter sighed. "It's always been like this."

"Why?"

"Natural competition? I don't know. Sometimes it's just the way brothers have to be."

"That's ridiculous," Annja said. "Families don't come with instructions that read 'must always be at odds with one another.'"

Hunter leaned against the railing. "Fact is, I need him and he knows it. I blew my inheritance on treasure hunting. It's only been with Cole's help I've actually made something of myself. That tends to grate on my ego a fair amount."

"I imagine it would."

Hunter sighed. "I'll find him. We'll get this squared away."

Annja patted his arm. "Glad to hear it. Now, if you don't mind, I'm going to have a quick nap. Wake me if the shark comes back."

"You'll know," Hunter said. "The whole boat will be in a panic."

"Does that concern you?"

"Of course it does. I've got a major hunt going on here. The last thing I need is people freaking out over a fish."

"Even one that eats them?"

"They need to keep their heads in the game. Forget about the shark. It was probably a freak occurrence. Probably long gone by now."

"Didn't seem so a few minutes ago when it showed up on the scope."

"We don't know if that was the shark. Could have been something else. Maybe a whale."

Annja raised an eyebrow. "We would have seen a spout when it breached the surface of the water."

Hunter started to say something and then thought better of it. Instead, he pointed at the stern. "I'm going to go find Cole now."

"See you later."

Annja let him pass and watched him work his way down the steps to the deck. He and Cole might be brothers but there were a lot of differences between them.

Annja took a deep breath of salt air and felt herself yawn. A nap would do her some good. She made her way down to the crew compartments. The corridor led her back to her room and she pushed the door in, falling into the bed with a muffled sigh. The pillow cradled her head and, within a few seconds, she felt herself falling into a deep sleep.

As she slept, her body seemed to relax, her muscles almost

melting into the bed. Annja realized that she was truly exhausted and needed the nap badly.

Until something made her start and come awake.

A noise.

She kept her eyes closed. Her stomach knotted up and she risked cracking an eyelid. She could just make out a shadowy form rummaging through her bag. The daylight had faded outside the porthole and the coming evening made it difficult to see exactly who it might be.

Annja frowned. She hated thieves. There was one way to solve the mystery and she steeled herself to suddenly surprise the invader.

Adrenaline flooded her system. Annja checked to make sure her sword hung where she could pull it out if need be. It was ready, hanging in the dim mist that waited between her awake and dream worlds.

Annja steeled herself and then, with a shout, she came fully awake and launched herself off the bed.

She felt something crash into her from behind. A bright explosion of stars caromed around her head as tears flew from her eyes. Blackness rushed to greet her and Annja sank back onto the bed, consciousness already a vague memory somewhere far off in the recesses of her mind.

"Annja?"

Annja opened her eyes. The bright light made her wince. "Ouch."

"Kill the light."

Darkness returned and Annja blinked her eyes open again. "What the hell happened?"

"You tell us."

She recognized Cole's voice. "I was napping. I heard something. Someone was in my room. I was going to surprise them and, when I did, something or someone else clocked me from behind. That's the last thing I remember."

Hunter growled. "This isn't good. A shark attack and someone attacking a guest on my ship. All within two days." He paused and looked at Cole. "We can't afford this kind of distraction."

"I know it."

Annja put a hand to her head. "Any chance I can get some water?"

"Yeah, yeah, sure." Cole handed her a glass of something cold. "Take it slow, though. That's a nasty bump you've got on your head."

Annja ran her hand over the growing bulge on the back of her skull. "Concussion?"

"Can't really tell. Maybe a mild one."

"Add it to the scorecard," Annja said. "I've had more than a few in my time. Every time I do, it only reminds me how much they suck."

"Are you nauseous?" Cole peered into her eyes. "You might be sick."

"You get any closer and I will definitely."

Cole leaned back. "You can't be that badly injured. Your sarcasm has remained intact."

Hunter chuckled. "You always did have a way with the ladies, bro."

Annja took a sip of water. The cold liquid hit the back of her throat and she winced. Her stomach rolled once or twice but she fought it back and swallowed the water. When she was done, she handed the glass back to Cole.

"Who did this?" she asked. "Was it Jax?"

Hunter shook his head. "Couldn't have been. She was in the wheelhouse, remember? It wouldn't be like her to come down here and take you out."

Annja nodded slowly. "Fair point. I don't think she'd mind just going straight on at me if she felt the need."

"That's more her style," Hunter said. "I've seen her hold her own in a bar fight outside of Norfolk, Virginia. That chick can rumble with the best of them."

Cole sat down in the small chair. "So, who else is on the ship that would want to see Annja get hurt?"

Hunter sighed. "I don't know. I mean, are we assuming that Annja was the actual target?"

"I seem to have been," Annja said. "As my skull will testify."

Hunter smirked. "Not what I meant. Obviously, you got injured. But were you the primary target? Maybe they were after something that you have and you just got in the way. I don't think it would be too hard to see that, if they wanted you dead, they could have easily killed you without much effort."

Annja frowned. Hunter had a point. She would have been incapacitated and an easy mark if they'd really meant to harm her. So what did they want? What did they think she had that could prove useful to them?

She shook her head. "I have no idea what they could have possibly been looking for."

"Only because we don't know who they are," Cole said. "Maybe they think you have something. Did you bring anything with you?"

"Like what?"

"I don't know."

Annja gestured for the glass and Cole handed it back to her. She took a longer sip this time. "Listen, you guys are the ones running this operation. Apparently, I haven't made some people very comfortable. Maybe the best thing would be for me to leave."

Cole shook his head. "Unacceptable. I invited you to come along with me. I need you here."

"You don't actually need me," Annja said. "Fish aren't really my specialty. I'm more into digging in sandboxes, in case you hadn't noticed."

"I appreciate that," Cole said. "But your perspective is what's required. Someone who thinks outside of the box."

Hunter nodded. "Cole's right. We don't know what it is that we're dealing with. Could be a shark, could be something else. But the presence of people meaning you harm on this ship is an indicator that something bigger might be going on here. That means trouble any way you look at it."

"Which means," Cole said, "that we all must make sure we have one another's backs."

"And not get on one another's nerves," Hunter said.

Annja smiled at them. "Nice to see you guys have made up."

"We never stay mad at each other for long," Hunter said. "Must be a brotherly thing."

"Whatever," Annja said. "Just so long as neither of you is plotting the untimely demise of the other, I think we'll be okay."

Annja finished the water. "So, where do we go from here? I've still got a killer headache. And there's a fan of mine on board the ship apparently."

"You rest," Cole said. "Leave this other stuff to me and Hunter for right now. We'll start checking things out, seeing where folks were earlier."

"You don't know when this happened, do you?" Hunter asked.

"Only that it must have been late afternoon or early evening. I couldn't make out too much. The lighting was dim."

"A good hit you took there," Cole said. "You've probably been out for a few hours, then."

"You feel okay now?" Hunter asked. "One of us can stay with you if you need us to."

Annja shook her head. "I'll be fine. And besides, I think you guys have some more important work to do than babysit me."

Cole stood. "We'll be back later to look in on you. In the meantime, lock the door behind us and don't let anyone in. We've got to check on Tom, anyway."

"Why? What's wrong with him?"

"Seems like lunch didn't sit well with him. He's been vomiting and on the toilet ever since. Might be a touch of food poisoning. Anyway, he's down for the count right now. But I want to make sure he's all right or see if we need to evacuate him back to the mainland."

Annja tried to stand and the room spun. "Whoa."

Cole caught her. "You okay?"

Annja took a breath. "Yeah. I'll be okay."

Hunter and Cole left the room. Annja slid the bolt in place and then collapsed back into bed. Her head throbbed.

Despite what Cole and Hunter had said, Annja couldn't help feeling like someone on the boat wanted her gone.

But why?

8

When Annja awoke, darkness shrouded the cabin. Mercifully, her head had ceased throbbing and her stomach seemed to be relatively stable. Her throat was dry, however, and she wanted to get some fresh air. Cole was sound asleep beside her.

She made her way to the door without fainting and opened it slowly. She was unsure what to expect on the other side. The boat was quiet and lolled gently, anchored as it was.

Dim red lights illuminated the hallway leading out to the stairs. Annja padded down the walkway until she came to the steps and started up them. She could already feel the wind washing over the boat and her skin. Goose bumps broke out along her hairline and she shivered slightly as she crept higher.

Her stomach didn't hurt and Annja felt somewhat secure as she crept along the walkway toward the wheelhouse. The salt air refreshed her. Waves lapped at the sides of the ship and she felt some of the spray wash up on her skin.

Annja felt good. She kept her hands along the railing,

however, just in case she felt faint, aware that she was still recovering from the concussion she'd received earlier.

A weak yellow light came from the wheelhouse. Annja moved toward it. Maybe she could have a word with Jax about what happened earlier. Annja didn't like bad blood if she could avoid it. But if she couldn't, then she'd just have to deal with it another time.

She took a deep breath and swung the door to the wheelhouse open. But Jax wasn't there.

Hunter was.

"Hey, you."

"Hey." Annja glanced around. "No Jax?"

Hunter smiled. "Even the captain needs sleep sometimes. I gave her the night off so she could crash. She's been pulling hard since the attack."

"She close with the victim?"

Hunter shrugged. "Don't really know. Jax has a way about her. She can get guys if she wants 'em. Or she can turn 'em off like a light switch. I'm not sure how she felt about Jock. Or how he felt about her, for that matter. Not that that would have been an obstacle per se. Jock had a thing for anything with breasts."

"Nice."

"Sorry."

Annja shrugged. "Forget it. I know how guys think. You're honest and I appreciate that."

"How are you feeling?"

"Better." Annja glanced around the wheelhouse. "I thought I'd come topside for a little air."

"Always clears my head, too," Hunter said. "You want a drink?"

"What have you got?"

Hunter handed her a flask. "A little whiskey. It's aged. Got a taste of peat in it, if you like that sort of thing."

Annja took a sniff and then a sip. The smooth whiskey flowed down her throat and she took a deep breath. "Wow."

Hunter took the flask back from her. "Don't tell Cole. He'll kill me if he finds out how much this stuff runs me. But why waste money on crap if you have a chance to get the good stuff, right?"

"I guess." Annja felt the whiskey hit her hard. "That's some potent stuff."

"Keep you steady, it will," Hunter said. "And I've used it to do just that on some stormy nights at sea."

"You had many?"

Hunter nodded and took a deep drag on the flask. "Once or twice. We were off the coast of Florida when a gale blew up and knocked us sideways. We were cresting fifty-foot waves, crawling up one side and diving down the other. They were like mountains, you know. Fifty feet doesn't sound like much until you actually get out in the thick of it in a twenty-foot boat."

"You were in a twenty-footer?"

Hunter grinned. "First and last time, mind you. I came back and resolved never to sail anything less than a hundred foot."

"Those waves must have been terrifying."

"They were. I had to keep the ship on course because any mistake meant we'd have been swamped and gone before anyone knew we were there. A storm like that, they don't roll up all that often."

Hunter switched the radio on and Annja heard smooth music roll out of the speakers. He adjusted the volume, then took another sip and offered the flask back to Annja.

Annja shook her head. "I should stop. The booze and my concussion probably won't get along that well."

Hunter took the flask back. "Good point. Hang out, though. I can use the company."

Annja leaned back against the wall and watched him. He had the same type of chiseled face that Cole had. But Hunter had strong limbs that seemed longer than Cole's. Cole's upper torso was more compact while Hunter's reminded her of a languid jungle cat stretched out on a rock in the sun.

"How'd you get into treasure hunting?" she asked.

Hunter shook his head. "Not exactly the type of thing you go to school for, is it?"

"Nope."

Bars of music filtered out of the speakers, while Hunter closed his eyes in appreciation of it. After a moment he looked at Annja. "I could say it's all because of a girl."

Annja smiled. "Oh is it?"

"Yep. I fell in love with a girl in college and flipped out of my mind over her. Spent the summer chasing her all over the Caribbean. We jumped from island to island on my dime, just having a blast. Sleeping on the beaches, making love, drinking our brains into a permanent pickled state. Youth's a crazy thing, you know?"

"I guess."

Hunter eyed her. "Yeah, I don't suppose my experiences as a kid are universal or anything. I can see that."

"So go on."

Hunter shrugged. "I came across this boat anchored in the blue of the Caribbean one day. There were a couple of guys in the water. Real island dudes. The boat represented every dime they had in the world and they were out there diving off this patch of sand. We happened to sail up at just the right moment."

"Right moment?"

Hunter took another sip. "You believe in serendipity?"

"Depends, I guess."

"Well, these guys had come across a sunken Spanish galleon filled with chests of gold. I was there when one of the divers broke the surface of the water holding a single gold coin in his hand. I'll never forget how the sun caught that gleaming yellow coin and made it look as brilliant as the brightest star in the sky. It blew me away. I wanted that joy of discovery. And I wanted all those riches."

"So, that was it? You shelved the college life and threw your lot in with those guys?"

Hunter chuckled. "Those guys wanted nothing to do with me. Right after we came upon them, one of the guys still on the boat pulled a pistol and told us to sail away or they'd kill us. Treasure hunting's a dangerous gambit sometimes."

"Certainly seems to be." Annja shivered as a cold breeze blew through the wheelhouse. "So, how'd you get started?"

"I spent a lot of my own money—hell, all of it—on a boat and top-of-the-line equipment that I had little clue how to operate. I was a fool and a cocksure one at that. I thought that my money could make everything go right when all it did was foul it up even quicker than if I'd been broke."

"How so?"

"On my first dive I lost two people. Couldn't be helped. The wreck we dove on shifted and crushed them. There was no way to help them. You're not moving tons of rusted steel no matter how strong you think you are."

"Oh, my God."

"Yeah. And that venture cost me a lot more than I thought it would. I came back to the States and found myself facing a lawsuit from the families of the deceased. That pretty much wiped me out."

"But you kept going."

Hunter smiled. "You know what it's like to want something so bad that you can't even fathom it ever being wiped out of your soul?"

"Maybe."

"That's how it was. I just couldn't give it up. As much as I tried—and I did try. I went back to school and even did a year of law before I bugged out. I just couldn't get that image out of my head of the diver breaking the surface with the gold coin in hand. I'd wake up in a sweat and know that it could be me."

Annja shook her head. "You're obsessed."

Hunter grinned. "Some guys, they obsess over women. Some over work, some over other things. For me, it was the dive. The lure of the treasure wouldn't let me go. I was caught in the spell."

"So you went back."

Hunter nodded. "Yeah. I did a lot more research than I'd done before. I found some smaller wrecks, thinking that if I could get started on something more in line with my limited experiences, then maybe that would be the best way to go about it."

"Did it work out?"

"My second dive was better. It still wasn't great, but at least I was getting my feet under me. I had only a little bit of money but I managed to make back my investment by scavenging the bits I was able to bring up from the ship."

"What sort of ship?"

Hunter laughed. "It was an old landing ship that the Navy had scuttled years earlier. I found someone to buy the scrap metal off me. It wasn't much—most of the metal had rusted away—but I made back the investment. And it helped fuel my desire even more. While I was doing that salvage job, I was already planning my next outing."

Annja took the flask from him and helped herself to the whiskey. She could taste the peat now, and Hunter was right—it was very good whiskey indeed. "Don't keep me in suspense."

"I heard about a Dutch trading ship that vanished along the coast of Brazil. I went after it."

"Brazil? Did you have to wrangle permits?"

Hunter shrugged. "I was still making mistakes back then. And one of them was the idea that I felt I could operate outside the law. I hooked up with a local criminal type who insisted that the permits would be arranged with a simple bribe."

"Something tells me that wasn't the case."

"Yeah," Hunter said. "Who'd have thought it? I flew into Rio and found myself under arrest for piracy of all things."

"The guy double-crossed you."

"I was carrying ten thousand in cash," Hunter said. "All part of the bribe, of course. They busted me on that. I had to do six months in jail down there."

"Wow."

Hunter took a deep breath. "You know what jail's like in Brazil?"

"I haven't had the pleasure. No."

"It's hell," Hunter said. "The prisons are run by the gangs, and just trying to survive takes every ounce of courage and endurance you have. I was one of the lucky ones. They thought I was a fool and didn't bother with me. And by the time they realized that my family had money, Cole had figured out a way to get me out of there. Thank God."

"He never mentioned that," Annja said. "I'm kind of surprised he didn't."

"Yeah, well, I suppose that's one of the things he's not very proud of his brother doing, you know? No one likes to talk about the troubled child gone astray."

"You weren't astray," Annja said. "Just trying to find your way. It could have happened to anyone."

"But it happened to me," Hunter said. "I've been trying to live it down ever since."

"You've got Cole helping you now, though."

Hunter nodded. "And it's great that he is. His money has helped make this operation profitable. But I guess I've always regretted not being able to do it all myself."

"Isn't it better this way?"

"Maybe." Hunter switched off the radio. "But there will

always be a part of me that wonders if I could make it on my own. I would have gotten out of that jail eventually."

"The guy who double-crossed you would have had you killed before you were free."

Hunter looked at Annja. "You think?"

Annja tried to smile but it came out wrong. "I've met men like that before. They operate on strict rules and one of their rules is that you never let someone you victimized live. It just means they'll come back for you. No one wants to spend their life looking over their shoulder."

Hunter stared at Annja. "Maybe you're right."

Annja's response died when the sonar scope suddenly started beeping. On the scope, Annja could see the outline of a huge shape in the water.

9

"Is that it?"

Hunter leaned over the display. "I don't know."

"It looks like what was on there earlier." Annja watched as the line swept around the scope, and every time it reached the nine-o'clock position, it revealed the huge shape in brilliant orange.

"Doesn't seem to be moving all that fast," Hunter said. "I would have thought it would be."

Annja shuddered as another breeze swept in through the open window. "Maybe it's just cruising around."

Hunter nodded. "I suppose that could be it. Sharks like to hunt at night. Maybe it's down there tracking something."

"How do they see?"

Hunter shrugged. "Better ask Cole that one. I think I saw a television special last year that mentioned they could use tiny amounts of ambient light to spotlight things against the backdrop. This guy did some research down in South Africa and found the ambient glow of city lights on shore helped great whites hunt seals at night. Pretty wild."

"And you think that thing might be using our running lights as help in this case?"

"Like I said, you'd have to ask Cole. But I suppose it's a possibility. Sharks haven't evolved over millions and millions of years just to be thwarted by something as rudimentary as the darkness."

I wonder if they could handle my sword, Annja thought. She kept watching the sonar sweep around. The shape in the water seemed to have drifted more to their port side. "It looks like it's searching for something."

"Yeah."

"Should we go get Cole?"

Hunter checked his watch. "I don't know. I mean, it's after midnight and the guy probably needs his sleep."

"Yeah, but he might get upset if he finds out he missed this."

Hunter eyed her. "Or he might jump into the drink without a second thought."

Annja nodded. "I guess you're right."

Hunter smiled. "My brother doesn't let things like the dark stop him, either. And he probably should in this case. Maybe we'll just keep this sighting to ourselves, huh?"

Annja watched the scope. "Sure would like to know what it's doing."

"Probably looking for a midnight snack."

Annja had watched some shark specials on television, but she couldn't remember seeing anything that came close to this size. The creature was huge. And yet, there seemed something almost unnatural about it. Maybe it was the overall size of the shark or maybe it was because Annja hadn't seen any shows that did night research on sharks, but the whole event left her chilled.

Suddenly, she had an idea. "Do you have a flashlight?"

Hunter nodded. "Yeah. Why?"

"You mentioned that sharks would use ambient light to hunt. Maybe I'll give this thing some extra light and see if its behavior changes."

Hunter handed her the flashlight from the instrument panel. "How are you going to do that?"

Annja took the flashlight. "Keep an eye on the scope and tell me if anything changes."

"Annja—"

She grinned. "Relax, I'm not going in the water. I'm not nearly that suicidal."

"Okay."

Annja stepped outside the wheelhouse and found her way to the steps leading down to the main deck. She followed the port side toward the stern and then stood staring out at the inky sea.

Waves lapped against the side of the boat, but from her vantage point, she could see nothing to indicate that a huge shark was cruising nearby. She smirked. This was probably how it was all the time. Nature had crafted these incredible creatures and humans were, by and large, oblivious to when they were close by.

She switched on the flashlight and its bright beam cut through the swath of darkness, illuminating the waves nearby that foamed white as they slapped into one another.

Annja swept the beam across the surface of the water and waited. She hoped this would provoke some sort of reaction from the shark. If Annja could get it to surface, then maybe she could get a decent look at the thing.

Maybe.

She glanced up at the wheelhouse and could see part of Hunter's body still leaning over the scope. She whistled softly and he leaned out of the window.

"Yeah?"

"Anything yet?"

"Not a thing. It's still moving at the same pace and on the same course. Maybe it doesn't see the light."

Annja frowned. If a shark could use the ambient city lights miles away, then surely this shark could see a bright white beam on the surface of the water.

She looked out at the waves. She needed something else to help attract the shark. Something it wouldn't be able to ignore.

Annja checked to see if the crew had left anything nearby that she could use. But the stern of the boat was remarkably absent of clutter. The dive platform hovered a few inches below the surface of the water and, before she could think things through, she sat down and pulled her socks off.

Maybe I *am* crazy, she thought.

"Annja?"

Hunter's voice drifted down to her, but Annja ignored it as she stepped off the back of the boat and onto the dive platform. The water felt cold and she shuddered as her feet went into the water. She was standing in it up to her ankles.

She felt a wave of fear wash over her. Now she was actually in the ocean with this thing, even though she was technically still on the boat. If the shark rammed hard enough, she might lose her footing and that would be it.

Annja swallowed and used the flashlight beam again, aiming it just off the stern of the boat, closer to where she stood. With her other hand, Annja held the back railing for dear life. It would be her only link to the ship and she didn't want to lose it.

"Annja!"

She glanced back. Hunter had come out of the wheelhouse and stood halfway down the stairs leading to the stern. "What the hell are you doing?"

"I've got to see if I can get this thing interested in me or if it's doing something else."

"I can't help you if it attacks."

"Just keep watching the scope and let me know if it starts to change course. Give me as much warning as you can."

"Yeah, all right."

Hunter vanished back up the stairs, leaving Annja alone on the lolling platform. She felt cold and her legs wanted to carry her back up onto the boat proper. Psychologically, she knew that she would feel a lot safer with the deck between her and the ocean. Right now, all that separated her from the deep was a few inches of steel.

The flashlight beam cut into the darkness and then died only ten yards away from the boat. Annja could see the frothy white caps cresting in time to the sway of the boat. A stronger breeze blew and she shivered again. Her left hand ached from holding the railing so tightly, but there was no way she'd loosen her grip.

Annja's stomach cramped slightly and she realized that if the shark did indeed decide to check out the light, she had no way of summoning her sword if necessary. Both of her hands were fully occupied.

She couldn't very well risk using one of them to hold the sword. Plus, its appearance would mean an uncomfortable amount of questions from Hunter and who knew who else? How would she explain that she somehow possessed the sword that once belonged to Joan of Arc and that she could summon it at will?

No, the time for the sword would be later. If it got to that point. If this was just a shark acting like a shark, then Annja didn't see any real need to fight it. Jock's death notwithstanding, there was already enough shark slaughter happening elsewhere in the world and Annja didn't want to contribute to it any further.

She frowned. There should have been some reaction to the presence of the light by now. She glanced back at the wheelhouse, but her view from the stern of the boat was limited and she didn't know what Hunter was up to.

She heard him coming down the stairs a moment later. "Annja?"

"Yeah."

"You okay?"

"I'm wondering why this shark hasn't responded to my presence or to this flashlight beam."

"You thought it would?"

Annja frowned. "Hell, I don't know what I thought. It was more of an experiment than anything else."

"The scope isn't showing much. It's still there, but its movement is as slow as it was before. It's like it either doesn't know or doesn't care that you're there."

Annja frowned. "I could go for a swim."

"Don't you dare!" Hunter's voice grated across the darkness. Annja smiled at the reaction.

"Relax. I told you I wasn't suicidal. And even if I was, I wouldn't do it like that."

"All right. Don't make me haul you back aboard against your will."

"Like you could."

Hunter started to laugh, but then they both stopped.

Something splashed out beyond the range of the light.

Annja's heart started beating faster. "Did you hear that?"

"Yeah."

She could tell Hunter was coming closer to her. "Annja, why don't you get back on the boat now?"

"Hang on a second."

She could hear more splashing. It sounded like something was almost on top of the water. She swept the flashlight beam as far as she could but the inexorable darkness simply swallowed it up beyond ten yards.

"I can't see a damned thing."

"Neither can I. But I think you should get back on the boat," Hunter said.

"Get back to the wheelhouse and tell me what you see."

"I'm not leaving you alone out here."

"I'll be fine. Just do it, okay?"

"Annja."

"Hunter. Just do it. I need to know if this thing is coming at me or not."

"Fine."

She heard him stomp away and then turned back to look out at the ocean. More wind blew up and she felt her fear rising with it. The shark might be heading right for her and she wouldn't know it unless her flashlight beam cut across its shape in the dark.

"Annja!"

"What?"

"It's coming at you. But still slowly."

"How far?"

"Maybe fifty yards."

Annja frowned. She wouldn't see it yet. She just had to keep the beam on. She flashed the light across the waves.

And then the glow dimmed.

"Oh, crap."

The light beam vanished, plunging the area into total darkness. Annja sighed. In all of her adventures, there seemed a constant she could always count on—poorly charged batteries ruining something.

She heard another splash and suddenly felt a lot more exposed without the aid of the flashlight.

Time to get back on the boat.

Annja turned and stepped back onto the rear deck. As she did so, something large slapped down against the waves far out from the boat. Annja turned and tried to see, but she couldn't.

"It's gone."

She looked up at Hunter. "What did you say?"

"Gone. One moment it was headed right at you. The next, it vanished."

10

"Heard you had an interesting night," Cole said to Annja as she helped herself to scrambled eggs in the galley.

"Oh?"

Cole smirked. "Hunter mentioned that you guys tracked the shark on the sonar around midnight."

Annja shook her head. "I thought he and I agreed that telling you might not be the best thing to do."

"Why? Because he thought I would get the ol' wet suit on and go for a midnight swim?"

"Something like that." Annja bit into the eggs and chewed, appreciative of the peppers she'd added. "Hunter didn't want you going overboard without much to go on. We were just trying to get some sort of bead on the thing last night."

"Which is why you felt the need to taunt it with the flashlight?"

Annja looked at him. "Believe me, taunting was the last thing I wanted to do. But Hunter mentioned that there was research done with sharks using ambient light. I thought it might be kind of cool to see if that worked with this one."

Cole took a spoonful of oatmeal. "The sharks in that research were hunting seals. Do you know why?"

"No."

"Because the seals had adapted themselves to hunting at night in order to avoid the sharks that prowl the waters looking for them during the day. That part of South Africa, the rocks that jut out of the ocean are home to the seals. But they've got to swim into deeper water to get to the fish. The sharks know this and prowl just beyond in the deepwater channels."

"Okay."

"The seals were getting picked off constantly, so one colony decided to hunt at night. For a while, it seemed to work."

"Until the sharks noticed the change."

Cole smiled. "They went from eating well to hardly at all. And so they adapted, too. What was that line that Jeff Goldblum says in *Jurassic Park*? 'Life finds a way.' She really does."

"So, what's the problem with what I was doing last night?"

Cole grinned. "No seals around here. At least, none that I've seen so far."

"Which means what?"

"It means our shark might not have been hunting much of anything last night. It might simply have been cruising around."

Annja frowned. "The batteries in the flashlight died, anyway. I never saw a thing." She paused. "I heard some splashing, though."

"Splashing?"

"Yeah."

Cole frowned. "Interesting."

"How is it interesting?"

He took another spoonful of his oatmeal. Annja noticed that

he had a large amount of maple syrup on it. He swallowed and looked at her. "It just is, that's all."

"So what now? What's our next play?"

Cole kept eating. "I need to get out there."

"In the water?"

"That's generally where the sharks are, yeah."

Annja sighed. "It's not safe. Something tells me you shouldn't be in the water. No one should be."

Cole smiled. "Annja, in case you haven't noticed, this is a huge investment we're undertaking. And, for Hunter, it's something of a personal quest."

Annja nodded. "Yeah, he mentioned that to me last night before the shark showed up."

"I can't imagine what the poor guy's been feeling ever since Brazil. God knows I've tried to give him his space. But this dive is important to him. The *Fantome* wreck is a legend in treasure-hunting circles. A lot of people—most of them, in fact—tend to think it's a wild-goose chase. That there's nothing much of value on the ship itself."

"But not Hunter."

"No. And I don't believe it, either. I think she might just be the pot of gold at the end of the rainbow. And that would mean vindication. Hell, it would rejuvenate the guy and tell him that all his dreams weren't just some silly notion."

"Vindication's important."

"It's vital," Cole said. "When he came to me and had to ask for help, it must have broken his spirit. We'd always had a fair relationship, but you know—"

"It was him coming to you, hat in hand. I get it."

"No one wants to do that."

Annja finished her eggs. "Have you told Hunter you're going into the water today?"

"Not yet."

"What do you think his reaction will be?"

"He'll freak."

"Rightly so."

"And then I'll explain that, by not going into the water, we're putting this whole dive at risk. As soon as I do that, he'll encourage me to go for a swim."

Annja smiled. "It's really going to be that easy?"

Cole nodded. "Sure. It's the stuff that happens above the waves that I can control. Down there, though, it's a different story. Those fish are unpredictable and they're intelligent. Anything can happen."

"You ought to have a cage."

Cole nodded. "I will. It should arrive today."

"You're certain about that?"

"Hunter got a radio call from the shore. They'll be transporting it out in an hour or so. Once we get it on board, we'll assemble it and go over the side. I'll do some reconnaissance and check what's happening below us. See what the scene looks like. If it's all good, then we'll bring some divers down and keep the search on for the *Fantome*."

"And if it's not good? If the shark shows up?"

Cole smiled. "Well, then, obviously I'll be very happy indeed."

"And what if the shark happens to have an appetite for shark cages?"

Cole shook his head. "Not going to happen. And besides, this is the strongest shark cage designed. Even a giant megalodon would have a hard time dealing with it."

"You're still on that?"

"The meg? Sure. Why not?"

Annja took a sip of her orange juice. "Because we haven't seen anything to suggest this is some prehistoric shark yet, that's why."

"Hope springs eternal," Cole said with another grin. "I'm an optimist, anyway, so I'll just keep my wishes coming."

"You really want this thing to be a meg?"

"Can't you see how amazing that would be? A giant prehistoric shark swimming off the Nova Scotia coast would mean headlines around the world. The world's scientists would have to revisit the notion that the species died out. And if the meg has survived, then surely it might mean that other species have, as well."

Annja looked at him. "Something tells me that Hunter's not the only one on a quest for the Holy Grail here."

"Well…"

Annja nodded. "Just so long as you remember that people's lives are on the line."

"I know," Cole said. "I saw how badly Hunter got treated in those lawsuits. I've made certain, ever since I came on to help with the hunts, that we've always put safety first."

"So how will you handle Jock's death?"

Cole shrugged. "Doubt we'll have to do very much. Jock apparently had very little family back in the U.K. Left home at sixteen and joined the military. He's been on his own for so long, and on the move until he retired here. There's probably few people who would even miss him."

Annja frowned. "That's sad."

"Life happens," Cole said. "How many people do you keep close to you in the course of your travels?"

"Not many," Annja admitted.

"My point," Cole said. "Jock's not the only loner ever to go out without so much as a bang. I tend to think most of the world goes the same way. Only those with money or those who make a huge contribution to society in some fashion get recognized. You gotta buy your own coverage, even in death."

"Yeah?"

"That's what PR is for."

Annja laughed. "Interesting theory."

Cole smiled. "Hey, you think the guy who invented fire

got any buzz when he kicked off this mortal coil? I doubt it. A saber-toothed tiger or something probably ate him and that was that. People sitting around after didn't even think much of it as long as they could still keep warm."

"So Jock is like the guy who invented fire?"

Cole frowned. "Maybe that's a bad comparison."

"Maybe."

"Anyway, the cage will be here and I'll go for a swim." He eyed her. "You're welcome to join me."

"Why would I want to do that?"

Cole's eyes narrowed. "Because you almost did last night. Without the benefit of the cage, I might add."

"It was just an idea," Annja said. "And not my most lucid moment at that."

"But you had the urge, didn't you?"

Annja shook her head. "I was terrified." She leaned across the table. "Look, I've confronted scores of people before in combat. It happens with me a lot. I know how to stare death in the face provided that face is human. But a shark?" She leaned back. "That's not something I've ever had to deal with. Not sure I could."

Cole nodded. "I understand. But when you went into the cage off Montauk, you felt empowered, right?"

"I felt scared," Annja said. "But, yeah, it felt good confronting that particular demon."

"So come in with me and test your limits again." He looked at her intently. "Hunter thinks I'm scum for asking you to come along, but I know what you're going through."

"How's that?"

Cole smiled. "What—you think I just woke up one day and decided to go swimming with sharks?"

"I don't know, did you?"

"It wasn't like that at all. I was scared to death of them. I saw *Jaws* when I was a kid like everyone else. For several years

I wouldn't go anywhere near the ocean. If I couldn't see the bottom, I wanted no part of it. I stuck with pools and lakes, thinking they were safer."

"Well, they are."

Cole nodded. "Yeah, but at the same time, I used to marvel at the sharks themselves. There's something incredible about them."

"We discussed this."

Cole pushed his bowl away. "Can you imagine that nature gifted you with so many millions of years as to make you the perfect hunting machine? Your body is streamlined for flying through the water. You have the agility to twist and turn and maneuver like a jet in a dogfight. Your weapons are savage and beautiful at the same time. You're perfectly adapted for your environment and rule it without question."

Annja smiled. Maybe she did understand some of that.

Cole kept going. "That's what eventually won out over my fear. It took a long time, true. But the more I studied, the more intrigued I was. And when I went to the aquarium, it was always the sharks that swam in the huge tanks that drew my attention the most."

"And that was it?"

Cole shrugged. "Sometimes that's all it takes. I saw them for what they were, rather than what my fear wanted them to be."

"You can't deny the records of attacks on humans, though."

"Like any other animal," Cole said. "Sharks just get a bad rap. What humans need to remember is really very simple."

"And what's that?"

"That as soon as we step into the water, we're no longer the dominant species. We're in their world. And all the rules change."

"Are you going to be able to remember that later today when you go down there?"

Cole smiled. "If I don't, I'm dead."

11

By ten o'clock, Annja heard the telltale sound of an approaching motor. She went out on deck and saw a smaller boat powering up to the *Seeker*. Strapped down on the bow was a large cage, not entirely unlike what she had used back on Montauk when she and Cole had dived with the great whites.

Cole joined her on deck. "Ah, there it is now. Looks great, doesn't it?"

"I guess. You sure something like that will protect you from that giant cruising down there?"

"Only one way to find out," Cole said. "And that's to actually get it into the water."

"With the shark."

Cole looked at her. "Well, obviously."

The boat came alongside the *Seeker* and cut the throttle on its engines down to a low purr. A grizzled old salt dog came out of the wheelhouse. "Hey, there."

Cole waved. "I see you got the package."

"This for you, then?"

Cole nodded. "Yep. All for me." He glanced at Annja. "Possibly one other, if she's up for it."

The salt dog shook his head. "Wasting your time, mate. There haven't been any sharks in these waters for years and years. Nothing worth eating up here. The seals even avoid the area for some reason."

Annja stared at the scars running down the man's face into the turtleneck he wore. "Why is that?" she asked.

"Locals claim the waters are haunted."

"Haunted?"

"Lot of wrecks down below there. None that have ever really been found, mind you. Pretty much everyone that goes out looking for them winds up struck by tragedy."

"Like what?"

"Some of the ships go aground themselves. Others, well, a storm blows up and, when it's over, no ship."

"Great."

Cole shook his head. "And the locals think that the wrecks of the ships have something to do with that?"

"Everything to do with it, actually," the captain said. "They say the souls of those who died out here have never gone over to the other side and continue to haunt these waters. If their burial grounds get defiled, it's said they'll take their revenge."

Cole looked at Annja. "And here you thought this was just about the shark."

"Imagine that."

Cole waved the captain over. "If you can get the boat closer, I can unstrap the cage and transfer it over."

"You'll need some help, there, mate," the captain said. "It's a bit heavier than other cages."

"Is it?"

"No 12 mm on this one. They went a few more thick. Said something about needing it stronger than the usual ones. Know anything about that?"

Cole seemed to feel Annja staring at him but he only shook his head. "Can't say as I do."

"Liar," Annja said quietly.

Cole looked at her. "What?"

"You *are* scared."

Cole sighed. "Fine. I might be a little nervous. But I can't let it stop me from doing this. So I just took a few extra precautions, is all. Most of the cages in circulation these days have had some field-testing. They know they can withstand the bite pressures of the great whites cruising around."

Cole looked out at the ocean. "But something this big?" He shook his head. "I just thought I'd better be prepared for the worst-case scenario."

"Glad to hear it."

Annja turned and saw Hunter standing behind her. He smiled at his brother. "Seriously. It's nice to see you exerting some wisdom on this thing."

Cole held up his hand. "Don't try to stop me from going into the water today, okay? We both know I need to get down there and see for myself what we're dealing with."

"I'm not going to stop you. I am going to help you get the cage winched over here, though."

Annja watched Hunter and Cole swing the small winch at the back of the *Seeker* over toward the smaller boat. Cole jumped over to the boat and finished unsnapping the restraints before attaching the hook to the top of the cage. When he finished, he waved across at Hunter.

"That should do it."

Hunter cranked the small winch engine and Annja heard the hydraulics go into action. The winch shifted and swept over back toward the *Seeker*. The shark cage went aloft and then drifted out into the space between the two boats.

"Easy," Cole said. "Don't drop it now or I'll have a real problem."

"Just keep quiet," Hunter said. "I know what I'm doing."

Annja watched as the cage swung over toward the stern of the *Seeker* and then Hunter guided it to a small area on deck. The cage descended slowly and settled with hardly a sound.

Hunter crossed his arms. "Easy as pie."

Cole jumped back across to the *Seeker.* "Nice work."

Hunter shut the winch down. "I take it you're going to want to get right into the water?"

"That's the idea. Once I'm down there and make a positive identification on the shark—figure out what species it is—then we'll know how much work we have to do or if we need to somehow get rid of the shark."

"And if it turns out we do?" Hunter asked.

Cole frowned. "That's not something I'm looking forward to thinking about right now."

"But we might have to."

"We don't know that for sure yet."

"But if we do?"

Cole sighed. "If we have to kill the shark, we will, all right? Is that what you want to hear me say?"

"Honestly, yes." Hunter sighed. "Look, I know you want to keep the fish safe. I understand that. But you also have an investment here. You know that we can lose our money if this thing hangs around."

"Maybe it's a ghost shark," Annja said.

Cole looked at her. "Are you on drugs?"

Annja shrugged. "Just saying. Maybe it was killed here a long time ago and now returns to haunt these waters."

"That sounds like something some delusional psychopath would cook up in the basement of his grandmother's home in rural Illinois."

Annja took a breath. "Okay, then."

Hunter laughed. "It did sound kinda crazy. But keep working

on it and I'm sure one day soon you'll come up with something better."

"I didn't see you guys laughing when the salt dog over there suggested the area was haunted by sailors who went down here."

Cole shrugged. "That's because there are haunted bits of sea around the world."

Hunter nodded. "He's right. Been to plenty of them before."

Annja frowned. "Now you're just pulling my leg. There's no way that's true."

"Actually," Cole said, "there are plenty of accounts where you'd be hard-pressed to find another explanation to rationalize some of the things that have been documented."

"Ghosts of sailors?"

"Yup."

Annja looked at the shark cage. She could see it was large enough to accommodate more than one person. "You're really thinking about getting me down in that thing, aren't you?"

Cole smiled. "Well, it *is* big enough."

"I don't know if I have the stones to do it."

Hunter put up his hands. "I thought we were done talking about this. I thought we'd settled on the fact that Annja wouldn't go anywhere near the ocean unless it was something she wanted to do."

"Can't blame a guy for trying."

"I did yesterday," Hunter said.

Cole smiled. "All right, all right. I know when I'm beaten. But I will be getting wet."

Hunter shoved him. "Go. Get your wet suit on and then join us down by the stern."

Cole dashed off. Hunter watched him go. "He's like a big kid when he gets one of his new toys."

Annja heard the engine of the smaller boat rev and she turned. Hunter waved to the captain. "Thanks for your help."

The captain nodded. "Good luck to you, lads. Hope you don't see nothin' down there what you'd be needing that cage for." And then he laughed long and hard, the sound carrying across the open ocean as he guided his little boat away from the *Seeker*.

Annja glanced at Hunter. "Yeah, he's in good shape."

"You're being generous there."

"That I am."

Hunter led her down to the stern. Annja ran her hands over the galvanized steel bars of the cage. They certainly felt impressively strong. But would they be able to withstand the incredible pressures of a giant fish like what she'd seen swimming around down there? She didn't know. But she did think it was silly to test the cage with someone in it.

"Can't we do it another way? Maybe chum the water and coax the shark up to attack the cage, just so we can see if it can handle the bite?"

Hunter shook his head. "Cole will never go for it. He's the kind of guy who wants to get into the thick of things. If he's not right in it, then he's dying inside."

"Better that than dying in a cage that doesn't work."

"It should work," Hunter said. "Cole knows how to specify what needs to be done to make it strong enough. If anyone knows how to build these things, Cole does. He had a bad experience once where a cage did, in fact, fail him."

Annja gulped. "Are you kidding?"

"Nope. The bars had rusted and fell apart when a nosy great white came calling. Cole was lucky to get out of there with his life. That was the last time he ever trusted anyone but himself to make the call on the nature of cages."

"He studied their construction?"

"Yeah. Went and visited with Rodney Fox, the Australian

dude who first came up with the idea for them after he got attacked back in the sixties."

"Did it help?"

"Yeah, Cole returned with a better appreciation for the mechanics involved. It wasn't just about how to stave off the attacks. It was about teaching the sharks that there was a barrier they wouldn't get through. That added psychological bit helps protect the diver."

"I see."

Hunter looked at her. "None of this is doing much for your confidence, is it?"

"Nope."

"At least you're honest," Hunter said. "But here comes Captain Wet Suit as we speak."

Annja turned and saw Cole walking toward them. He was strapping on a weight belt and nodded at the dive locker near the cage. "How are the tanks?"

"Fully charged," Hunter said. "I made sure."

"Thanks."

Annja shook her head. "I don't know how you do it."

Cole shrugged. "No real difference between this and what you do. You confront scorpions and snakes and people who want to kill you, right?"

"Yeah."

"This is the same thing except it's a big fish trying to get up close and personal with me."

"I think I prefer my life," Annja said.

"Just keep an eye on me," Cole said. "That's all I ask."

Hunter helped him strap on the oxygen tanks and then checked the flow to Cole's regulator. Cole held up his thumb.

Hunter patted him on the back. "Just be careful, bro. Don't try to be a hero."

Cole smirked. "Like I could."

Hunter fired up the winch and then lifted the cage up and

over the side of the boat. Annja watched as the buoyant tanks kept it floating on the top of the water. Cole looked at it for a moment and then nodded.

"Time to go."

Hunter pointed at the wheelhouse. "I'll be keeping an eye on the scope. Take care of yourself."

Cole bit into his regulator, glanced at Annja and then stepped overboard, disappearing into the cold ocean water.

12

Annja watched the foam from the splash fade into a sea of bubbles from Cole's scuba gear. She could see him settling into the depths, looking all around him to make sure the immediate coast was clear.

She felt instantly worried for him. Maybe that old sea captain had freaked her out some. Annja hated that this adventure was unlike how she operated most of the time.

At any other dig site, she'd be up to her elbows in dirt and sand and mud, trying to uncover some long-forgotten treasure. And yet here she was, stuck on board a ship that was presumably being terrorized by a giant shark.

But there was promise here. If Hunter was right about the *Fantome* and its hold of booty, then that would surely make up for the distinct lack of dirt on this particular jaunt.

"He okay?"

Annja saw Hunter watching from the stairs. Annja pointed at Cole's head, which was visible just below the surface. "Seems fine. He's just making sure he's settled and then I imagine he'll be in better shape."

"Okay."

"Anything on the scope?"

"Jax says it's clear."

Annja frowned. "You trust her?"

Hunter nodded. "I know she's difficult, but she'll raise the alarm if there's one to sound. She knew Jock and doesn't want that to happen to anyone else on this trip. Neither do I, for that matter. If someone's not pulling their weight and compromises the safety of the boat and its crew, they're gone."

"Strict."

"I run a tight ship, even if appearances suggest otherwise."

Annja smiled. "I can see that."

Hunter pointed at the cage bobbing a few yards off the stern of the boat. "You let me know if he gets too far away. The only thing keeping him connected to the boat are those heavy ropes securing the cage to the back. If those get cut, then he's out there alone."

"Cut?"

Hunter turned around. "Just make sure they don't."

Annja moved back to the side of the boat and saw that Cole seemed to be checking in all directions. But she saw nothing from her perspective that would indicate that something was down there with him. Certainly nothing like the giant shark that had appeared on the scope.

Annja took a deep breath and leaned against the gunwale. Maybe this was all a mistake. Maybe it was a whale that had simply not breached the surface while they'd been tracking it. She knew that sperm whales could dive for up to forty minutes on one breath of oxygen. And they hadn't watched the screen all that long.

It was conceivable, she thought, that something else might be down there.

But what about Jock?

He'd clearly been torn apart by something, but was it a shark? Maybe it was a killer whale. Annja had heard they could be dangerous to humans.

She turned and looked at the cage again. Cole was hovering middepth and seemed fine—

Annja's instincts were already hauling her away from the side of the boat as the giant head breached the surface, showing a huge gaping maw of serrated teeth.

The head dropped back into the water with a splash.

Annja screamed.

Cole had turned toward the commotion and, even at distance, Annja could see his frantic movement as he registered the massive fish in the water. The dorsal fin broke the surface and stood fully three feet out of the waves.

"Hunter!" Annja shouted.

She heard him racing down the stairs. More crew members joined them on deck. Annja pointed. "Look at it!"

"Jesus Christ," Hunter said. "That's huge."

"Understatement," Annja said. "How big is your boat?"

"Just over a hundred feet."

"How big would you say that fish is?"

"Maybe forty feet long?"

Annja nodded. "It's heading for Cole."

She watched as the dorsal fin sliced through the water. She could see Cole shifting in the water to brace for the impact.

When it came, Annja thought the shark had lifted the cage almost completely out of the water. But it crashed back down into the surf. Cole's body seemed to bounce off one side of the cage.

"Haul him in!" Hunter started working on the ropes, undoing the knots that held the cage in place.

Annja and two other crew members helped him. Hunter was sweating furiously. "Jax!" he bellowed.

"Yo!"

"Get us closer to the cage! We've got to help Cole."

"Roger that."

Annja heard the engines kick into reverse and saw the churn of ocean water kicking up white as the *Seeker* reversed course. Hunter had his knots undone and started hauling the cage toward them.

"Where'd it go?"

Annja frowned. The dorsal fin had vanished. "I don't know. But we've got to get Cole back here. If he was knocked out by that ramming, he might drown."

They yanked on the ropes and slowly the cage started coming toward them. "That's it," Hunter said. "Reel him in."

Annja's stomach cramped and she leaned back, yanking the ropes hard.

There was a sudden spray of water as the shark's head broke the surface again and its teeth sliced through the ropes.

"Shit!" Hunter ran for a gaff and leaned out, trying to hook the edge of Cole's cage, which floated just out of range.

"I need more room!"

Annja yanked him back as the shark raced through the expanse where Hunter's body had been a second before. "Get down!"

They toppled back onto the deck. Hunter disentangled himself from Annja's grasp. "Jax! I need us back by that cage now!"

The engines kicked up faster and they were closing in on the cage. Hunter got the winch hook ready and handed it to Annja. "As soon as it comes in range, hook it and I'll get him out of there."

Annja nodded. "Got it."

She watched as the cage drifted closer. She could see the

dorsal fin still cutting through the surf farther away from the ship. The crew was watching in awe as they saw the fish circling.

Annja couldn't think about it. She heard Hunter cranking the winch to life. "Get ready, Annja!"

"It's coming back again!" she shouted.

Annja risked a look and saw the dorsal fin turning back toward the boat. It was on a direct path to intercept Cole's cage again.

"Hunter!"

"Almost there!"

She saw the cage coming closer. She just needed a little more space. She leaned out, aware that she'd just screamed at Hunter for doing the same thing.

But she couldn't risk Cole taking another hit like he'd sustained earlier. She didn't think the cage would handle it.

She could see Cole drifting in the water but he seemed unresponsive. He must have been knocked out against the bars when the shark hit the first time.

"Look!" someone said.

Annja saw the fin dipping below the surface. "It's going deep," she heard herself say. And she felt certain this attack would come from the bottom, lifting the cage clear as it hit.

The cage came closer slowly and then Annja realized that she was leaning way out toward it.

"Almost there…"

She snapped the hook into place and jerked herself back. "Now, Hunter! Now!"

She heard the hiss of the hydraulics pulling the cage free of the water. Cole slumped as the water receded and then lay down near the bottom of the cage, hoisted at an odd angle by the oxygen tanks.

Annja braced for the sudden reappearance of the shark breaching from far below, but it never came. The only thing breaking the smooth surface of the sea was the steady dripping from the steel cage.

Hunter winched the cage back onto the deck and then Annja waved over some of the crew. "We've got to get him out of there. Help me turn the cage on its side and then it'll be easier."

Together, they maneuvered the cage until it lay with the opening facing them. Annja scrambled inside and worked her way toward the other end where Cole's body was.

"Cole!"

She got no response and yanked his mask off and pulled the regulator out of his mouth. She wriggled him out of the oxygen tank straps, then he collapsed against her. Annja struggled to take his weight and, in the close confines of the cage, she found it tough to do so.

"Someone help me."

Hunter got there next. "Give him to me, Annja."

Annja backed out of the cage and watched as Hunter dragged Cole free and laid him out on the deck. Hunter tore off the wet suit and pressed his fingers to Cole's neck, searching for a pulse.

Relief flooded his face. "He's alive."

Annja sighed. "Thank God."

"The attack must have knocked him out," Hunter said. "He must have clamped down on the regulator knowing what would happen."

Cole's eyes fluttered open. "Annja?"

Annja nodded. "I'm here. Are you all right?"

He frowned. "Head hurts. That was some hit I took in the cage."

"That was some shark that hit you," Annja said. "Can you stand?"

"I think so." Cole got to his feet, helped by Annja and Hunter. He stood for a moment and swayed. Annja helped him steady himself. He smiled at her. "Thanks. Glad that you're here."

Hunter frowned. "I got you out of there, you know."

Cole smiled. "Yeah, but you're not nearly as attractive as Annja."

Hunter nodded. "Granted."

"If you two are finished…" Annja said. She stared at Cole. "So, you saw it."

"I think everyone did," Cole said. "It's massive. Definitely a member of the carcharodon carcharias family. But I can't tell if it's a meg or not. Going by size, it certainly could be."

"Could it just be a great white?" Hunter asked. "Maybe a really big one?"

"It might be, but the likelihood of it is remote. There's not much of an indigenous seal population around here. Certainly not enough to sustain a creature of that size. It must have been forty feet at least. Probably six tons worth of weight on that beast. It was incredible. The dorsal alone—"

"Maybe three feet," Annja said. "It was terrifying."

"Did you see it up close?"

Annja nodded. "It made its presence known to me pretty convincingly. Talk about smiling for the camera, holy crap."

Hunter took a breath. "All right, so what happens now? I mean, we've got a monster shark hanging around. How do we handle this? We've still got a business to run and something tells me that our being here won't dissuade this shark."

"It won't," Cole said. "This shark is here to stay."

"Then how do we handle it?"

"Carefully," Annja said. "I got a look at those teeth and they're saw blades, for crying out loud. We don't play this right, then we'll all be seeing the business end of them. And I don't have any inclination to do so. No, thanks."

"You weren't in the water with it," Cole said. "I may never sleep again. We're going to have to think about this long and hard because we can't just go back into the water without a plan. A good plan."

"Hunter!"

They all turned and saw Jax approaching. Hunter nodded. "Good work on that reversing there, Jax."

"We've got a bigger problem right now."

"What's that?"

"You'd better follow me to the engine room to see for yourself."

13

With Jax leading the way, Hunter and Annja threaded their way through the narrow corridors of the ship and down into the engine room. Cole stayed on deck to clear his head.

Annja could smell something burning and frowned. Fire on a ship is never a good thing. When Jax pulled open the engine room, clouds of dark smoke billowed out.

"What the hell?" Hunter said.

"Engine's got something in it. Maybe some water, maybe we ground the gears, I don't know." Jax frowned. "But this is bad."

Hunter waved some of the smoke away. "The *Seeker* has brand-new engines. This shouldn't be happening."

Annja peered around him and couldn't see much of anything because of the smoke. She coughed. "It can't be very good to stay in here. We'll suffocate if we do."

Hunter nodded. He looked at Jax. "Blow the smoke out and get Sammy down here to look at this. The engines are his game."

"All right."

Annja turned and found her way out, coughing as she went. Behind her, Hunter coughed a few times, as well. In the corridor outside, Annja stopped and bent low to take a deeper breath.

"Why are the engines doing that?"

Hunter shrugged. "Sammy will be able to tell us. For right now, let's worry about Cole. Even in a worst-case scenario, we'll be able to get help from the mainland. It's not like we're fifty miles offshore, you know?"

"Fortunately."

"But fire or anything burning worries me." Hunter frowned. "I'm just not sure what to make of it all."

They worked their way back on deck and Annja saw Cole staring out at the ocean. "You feeling better?"

He nodded. "I am now, thanks. And thanks for your help earlier. It must have been a little worrisome for you guys."

"A little, yeah."

Cole frowned. "I owe you an apology, Annja."

"Why's that?"

"Because I wanted you to come in the cage with me." He shook his head. "I've been around sharks a very long time. And I know the limits that are there before safety gets compromised. I thought for sure there wouldn't be a problem, and yet..." His voice trailed off.

"I think we can all agree this shark is something of an anomaly," Annja said.

Cole grinned. "Biggest one I've ever seen. I mean, whale sharks get huge, too, but not ones like this...well, I guess we'll call it a great white for right now until the jury comes back on the whole meg thing."

"Still clinging."

"Yup."

Annja sat down next to him. "You must have been terrified when you saw it coming for the cage."

Cole smirked. "I found myself very glad that I'd insisted on the custom job rather than the stock cage they wanted to ship me. That extra bit of steel helped cushion the attack."

"Such as it was."

"Indeed."

A breeze blew over them. Annja could see the surface of the ocean had gone still again—it looked like the polished glass of a mirror. She marveled at the different facets of an ocean—how it could go from a swirling maelstrom in one moment to pure calm.

And it never revealed the secrets that it kept concealed beneath the waves.

"What happens now?" she asked.

Cole shook his head. "I don't know. I'm still replaying everything in my head. Not that there's all that much, mind you. Getting knocked out cold on the first pass wasn't exactly my game plan for the day."

"What are you replaying exactly?"

Cole shrugged. "Something doesn't seem right. About the shark, I mean. Maybe I'm trying to drive the square peg of a great white's behavior into the round hole of what just happened, but something isn't making sense."

"Like what?"

Cole frowned. "Not sure yet." He glanced at her. "You ever have a gut instinct about something and you can't actually rationalize it or at least verbalize it? And yet, you know there's something, something that doesn't feel quite correct."

"More times than I can tell you about."

"Figured you would." Cole nodded. "I just have to let my subconscious process things for a while and work through it that way. But there's something there all right. It's weird."

Annja patted him on the shoulder. "You going to get changed out of that wet suit before lunch?"

"Guess I should." Cole stood. "I won't be so anxious to get

you in the water the next time we get a visit from that thing. I'm not sure I'm going to be anxious to see it again, myself."

Annja nodded. "Well, I guess we'll handle that when the time comes, huh?"

"Yeah."

Cole got up and walked toward the crew quarters. Annja watched him go and then turned back toward the ocean. She closed her eyes and felt herself expand outward, searching with her subconscious. What was it about this situation that had Cole upset aside from the obvious fact that something huge was swimming in these waters?

Something didn't feel right to her, either.

She'd had strange things happen to her before on her adventures. But she wondered what could be going on now that lurked out on the dive site. She knew it had Cole spooked and not just because he'd almost died.

There was more to it than that.

And Annja would have to find out what.

"THAT'S THE PROBLEM."

Hunter stared at the rusted three-inch-long screw and frowned. "Where'd you get that? A yard sale?"

Sammy, the boat's mechanic, wiped a layer of soot from his face. He stood about five feet tall and almost as wide, leading Annja to wonder how he could work in the close confines of the engine room. He huffed and pointed at the screw. "That's your culprit. Jammed up the gears on the engine transmission. That's why we started smoking. And if I hadn't found it in time, it probably would have wrecked the engines outright."

Hunter picked up the screw. "But what's it doing in our engines? Ours are brand-new. This thing looks ancient."

Sammy shrugged. "That'd be a bit beyond my department, boss. The fact that it was in the engines leads me to wonder who might have put it there."

Annja stared at him. "You think someone sabotaged the engines?"

"Screws like that don't appear out of nowhere. Someone had to put the damned thing in where I found it, which was tucked back nicely so a cursory examination would have missed it on the first few passes."

Hunter frowned. "A saboteur on the boat?"

Annja stared down at her chowder. In truth, she hadn't felt like seafood, but there wasn't a lot of alternative cuisine on the boat, so she tucked into it and found it delicious. The warmth of the soup made her feel a bit more relaxed than she had been when she'd come in from the deck.

But now, the idea that someone on board was actively looking to disrupt the treasure hunt made her worry. Especially when she thought back to her own encounter with the person or persons who attacked her.

Cole took the screw from Hunter and turned it over in his hand. "How well do you know your crew, bro?"

Hunter frowned. "I thought I knew them all well enough to trust them with the delicate aspects of this operation."

"It would seem that's not exactly the case. Someone might be playing for the other side."

Annja looked up. "What other side?"

Hunter smirked. "Cole gets a bit paranoid about this stuff."

"It's not paranoia. It's a genuine concern." He looked at Annja. "Any time you're talking about treasure, there's always the risk that someone else will hear about your hunt and then take steps to, shall we say, throw up challenges to your operation."

"So you think this is an active attempt to derail this treasure hunt?" Annja frowned. "That would mean the traitors are still among us."

Hunter glanced around at the few other diners in the galley

and frowned. "I don't like looking at any of my people like they're criminals."

Sammy cleared his throat. "Yeah, well, like I said earlier, that screw didn't find its way into the engines by itself. You've got a rat on board, Mr. Williams. God knows what they'll try next."

Cole watched as Sammy ambled away. "He's right."

Hunter nodded. "I know it, dammit. But the prospect of treating everyone like a suspect doesn't sit well with me. I've had my own run-ins with the law before. I know what it's like to face questioning. It's not something I take lightly."

"No one's accusing you of being a hard-ass," Cole said. "But for the sake of this trip, we've got to find out what's going on. Our investment's at risk and our lives could very well be in jeopardy. Combine this with the attack on Annja and we've got a real problem to tackle."

"And the shark?" Hunter asked.

Cole chuckled. "Well, fortunately for us, the last time I checked, sharks don't come on board the boats they stalk. I think he's innocent in the engine room sabotage and the attack on Annja."

"I meant, what about studying it?"

"I know what you meant, bro." Cole took a drink. "But I think that we have to put a stop to everything until we get to the bottom of this. We can't risk being distracted with anything else right now."

Hunter stared at his brother and then nodded. "You're right. We'll get this done and then finish the hunt."

"Good."

"Where do we start?" Annja asked.

Cole looked at Hunter. "You have personnel files on everyone on board?"

"Not exactly."

"Why not?"

"Things in this business are a bit looser than that. Hell, you think I'd have gotten Jax if she had to fill out some elaborate background check?"

Cole shrugged. "Not sure that would be a big deal, honestly."

"She's good, bro. She knows her stuff. And if wasn't for her putting the boat into reverse earlier, Annja would never have been able to snag your cage and get you out of the drink. You were on a dead run with that shark when we winched you out of the water."

Cole looked at Annja. "That true?"

"Yeah. Jax might be rough around the edges—"

"They're serrated."

"But she knows her stuff. It's obvious."

Cole took a breath. "Guess I wasn't sure how dangerous things got out there. Me being out of it and all."

"It was hairy."

Cole looked at Hunter. "All right, so what do you have?"

"Résumés and the like. Everyone gave me one of those."

"But you didn't check any of them out?"

Hunter nodded. "I called the reference numbers."

Cole sighed. "Easy enough to dummy those up. We don't have any leads to go on."

Annja finished her chowder and stood. "Well, there's always the direct approach."

"Which is what?"

Annja gestured around them. "Make an announcement and then start interviewing the people. One of them has to be guilty."

"And if it's more than one?"

Annja shrugged. "We could always cut them up and use them to attract our shark."

14

Hunter set them up his quarters, which really weren't that much better than the crew quarters Annja shared with Cole. But there was room enough for a small table and space for them to sit behind it. Annja nursed a cup of coffee while Hunter and Cole went through the résumés.

"How many?" Annja asked.

"Ten," Cole said. "Not including us or Tom."

Annja nodded. "Who are we starting with?"

Cole sighed. "Doesn't make sense to question Sammy or Jax right now. Both of them are doubtful on the suspicion meter, but we'll check them out later. I've got a friend I can radio back on the mainland who can look into their pasts if I want. I'd rather keep them where they are right now. Jax is manning the wheel?"

Hunter nodded. "She's not due to get relieved for a while. But everyone else is fairly suspect. Sammy's working on the engine to get it all fixed and make sure there wasn't any other damage."

"Good." Cole looked at the top résumé. "So that means we start with this guy…Dave Crosby." Cole looked at Hunter. "What's his position?"

"Dive master. He's good hands-on for the dig itself. He knows how to work the vacuum that we use to extract the sand without damaging anything under it."

"Let's get him in here."

Hunter picked up the intercom and paged Crosby to the captain's quarters. Five minutes passed and someone knocked on the door.

"Enter."

A man came in. Annja had seen him before. He was an average-looking guy with short sandy hair and blue eyes. But his chest looked like a barrel, no doubt from his diving experience.

Hunter smiled. "Just a few questions for you, Dave. Then you'll be on your way. All right?"

He nodded. "This about the engine room fire?"

"It wasn't a fire," Cole said. "Just a bit of smoke."

"Okay."

Annja eyed him. "You've been diving long?"

He looked at her. "Almost twenty years. Got my start in the Bahamas where my folks ran a dive shop. I left and joined the Navy."

"What'd you do there?"

"I started on a frigate and then put in my application for the SEALs."

"How'd that work out for you?"

Dave smirked. "You want my BUD/S class number?"

Annja smiled. "Sure."

"It's 263. Hell Week was in the middle of winter. We nearly froze undergoing surf torture."

Cole and Hunter looked at Annja, who was still staring at Dave. "Go on."

"You know about it?" Dave asked.

"I've met a few of your fellow comrades over the years. They told me something about what you guys go through to wear the Budweiser."

Dave smiled. "Less than four hours of sleep over the course of the entire week. You know what sleep deprivation can do to you?"

"It's not pretty," Annja said. "I take it you passed?"

"Everyone in my boat crew did. None of us would have quit if you'd put a gun to our heads. We just weren't wired that way."

"What happened after you graduated?"

"I saw action abroad. Not really sure I can talk about any of it."

Annja nodded. "When'd you graduate?"

"In 1996."

Annja counted back in her head and came up with a half dozen possible overseas assignments that Dave could have reasonably been expected to participate in. "When'd you get out?"

"After Afghanistan, 2002. Before they sent us into Iraq. I went back home and kicked around there awhile. People find out you were a SEAL they want to live vicariously through you. Tell you how they did something almost as tough as what you went through. But there's really nothing I've heard of that even comes close. Kinda sad, really."

Annja smiled at him. "Did you sabotage the boat?"

Dave chuckled. "If I wanted to sabotage this boat, it wouldn't be floating. I know at least three dozen ways to blow this thing in two and send her right to the bottom."

"I'll bet you do." Annja looked at Hunter and shook her head.

"All right, Dave, you're secure. Thanks for your time."

"No sweat. You find out who's doing this, I hope you'll let me have a crack at them. I don't like traitors."

He left. Hunter looked at Annja. "You sure about that?"

Annja shrugged. "Just didn't get that vibe from him. He seems very switched on, and the fact that he was a SEAL—"

"Unless he was lying," Cole said.

Annja shook her head. "Doubt it. Anyone who goes through Hell Week never forgets their class number. They'll rattle it off without a second's thought. I think he's legit and he'd certainly know how to blow this ship up if he wanted."

"All right," Cole said. "Let's keep it moving."

Hunter picked up the next résumé. "Yeah, okay, let's see what Sheila has to say. I was on the fence about her when I hired her."

"Why's that?" Annja asked.

"Said she specialized in antiques from the early nineteenth century. But something didn't seem right about her."

Cole looked at Annja. "You any good with that era?"

"Nope. I'm better with ancient civilizations, to be honest, and medieval stuff is my specialty. Don't know I could even fake it if I tried, but we'll see where the conversation goes."

Hunter paged Sheila to his quarters and she showed up a few minutes later, suddenly standing in the open doorway without any fanfare. "Yes?"

Hunter smiled at her. "Come on in."

Annja watched the way she moved. There was a litheness to her movements. Sheila fairly slid into the room like cream flowing out of a cup. There was no wasted movement. And Annja felt herself tensing slightly as she recognized someone who was very at ease in her own body.

"Just a few questions," Hunter said.

"About the fire."

Cole sighed. "Is that what everyone's saying? That it was a fire?"

"All that smoke," Sheila said. "Sure seemed like a fire to those of us not down there with you guys."

"Just a badly burned screw," Cole said. "Nothing more. Where were you earlier?"

"Why?"

"Because we want to know."

Sheila frowned. "You think I did it? You think I sabotaged the boat's engines? Why would I do that?"

"Why wouldn't you?" Annja asked.

Sheila turned and fixed her stare on Annja. "Sorry, who exactly are you again? And why would I answer to you?"

Annja smiled and got ready to respond when Cole cut her off. "Do you know who I am, Sheila?"

"Yeah, you're the nut who swims with sharks."

Cole frowned and looked at Hunter. "Thanks."

Hunter shook his head. "Your reputation precedes you, bro. I had nothing to do with that one."

Cole looked at Sheila. "It's my money that's backing this venture. You understand what that means?"

"You're the one in charge."

"Hunter's heading the crew but who stays and who goes is up to me. Now if I ask you a question, or Hunter asks you a question, you answer us. As for Annja, she's here as an expert. She's got a background in psychology and has worked for the FBI. So if she asks you a question, it would probably be in your best interests to answer it, as well. Got it?"

Sheila nodded and looked back at Annja. "Sorry."

Annja waved it off. "Forget it. Just tell me a little something about yourself. How'd you get interested in this stuff?"

Sheila grimaced. "I hate boats. I'm here for the chance to see some of the artifacts from the White House."

"You really think this is the place you're going to find them?"

Sheila nodded. "I know what the so-called experts think,

that the *Fantome* is a ghost chase and it doesn't really have anything on it, after all. But I don't believe them. I think this ship is carrying actual relics from the White House and I want to be here when they come up."

"How'd you find out about the operation here?" Cole asked.

"I answered a classified ad in the *Washington Post*." Sheila pointed at Hunter. "He put it there."

Hunter nodded. "The ad said that I was gathering a team of experts who specialized in early nineteenth century antiques. Nothing about the treasure hunt. Too risky to do that."

Sheila sighed. "Imagine my surprise when I get the gig and he tells me I'm going on a boat. I've been constantly seasick since I got here."

Annja cocked an eyebrow. "You sick yesterday?"

Sheila nodded. "Pretty much all day. I was in my cabin. You can inspect my toilet if you don't believe me."

"Why would I do that?" Annja asked. "You don't flush after you throw up?"

"Of course I do. But there might be some leftover on the bowl."

Annja stared at Sheila, who stared right back at her. "I think I'll take your word on that. No need for me to go poking my nose into your toilet."

Sheila nodded and then looked at Hunter. "Are we through here? I'm not feeling very well again and I'd like to go lie down."

"Sure. Take it easy."

Sheila left and closed the door behind her. Annja held up her hand before anyone could speak and waited a few seconds before getting out of her chair. She walked to the door and opened it a crack, checking the hallway outside.

Sheila was gone.

Annja came back inside and closed the door again. "Well, she gets my vote as a possible."

Cole frowned. "Really?"

Hunter shook his head. "I didn't see anything suspicious about her. Just struck me as someone who wasn't feeling very well and didn't want to have to bother with this line of questioning."

"She said she hates boats," Annja said.

"Yeah. So what?"

"Did you see the way she moved?"

Hunter frowned. "I wasn't really paying attention to that, to be honest."

"You should," Annja said. "For someone who hates boats as much as she claims, she certainly knows how to move. She's well used to being on boats. If she wasn't, she would have been a lot more unsteady on her feet. But she looked pretty damned graceful to me."

"So she was lying about it?" Cole frowned. "I guess she could be." He looked at Hunter. "How did she seem when you interviewed her for the position?"

Hunter shrugged. "She was the first person to phone. Kinda funny, actually. I got the call from her at eight o'clock in the morning on the day the ad ran. Talk about an eager beaver. And she was a bit put off when I decided to hire her and told her about the boat."

"Could have been an act," Annja said. "I'm telling you that she has been on boats for a long time. She wouldn't be able to move like that if she had such a fear of them. She's our primary, I think."

"I don't want to jump the gun on this, Annja," Cole said. "We need to be sure before we accuse her."

Annja nodded. "Fine. I understand. But let's keep her in our sights until we can rule other people out of the equation."

"How are we going to do that?" Hunter asked. "We can't sit outside her cabin on surveillance. We'd be kind of obvious."

"Leave that to me," Annja said. "You guys are okay here without me."

Cole looked up. "You're leaving?"

Annja nodded. "I've heard enough. I think Sheila is our target. But she might not be acting alone. That's where you guys come in. Try to ferret out her accomplice, if she's got one. I'm pretty sure there were two people in my cabin yesterday when I was attacked. That means there's still another traitor in our midst."

"And where are you going?" Hunter asked.

Annja smiled. "No place special. Just visiting a friend."

15

Annja walked down the corridor toward the crew quarters. She kept her footwork light, her hands out in front of her as she progressed. She felt confident that Sheila was the person who had attacked her. She just moved too smoothly to be anything remotely like a seasick bystander.

Annja crept closer to where Sheila's quarters were. A stillness swept over her like a soft mist.

She checked to make sure she could summon her sword, if necessary. It hovered in the gray mist. She considered drawing it, but part of her said no. Not yet. In the close confines of the corridor, she would have difficulty swinging it to ultimate effect. It would be better to wait until she knew exactly what she was dealing with.

Annja paused to allow more sounds to filter into her consciousness. She waited and listened.

She could hear the engines somewhere below still grinding away. Sammy must have been working hard to get them back online. Around her, she heard the dull sounds and pings that occurred on any boat.

But little else.

Maybe Sheila was already asleep.

Annja almost smirked. She didn't believe that. Sheila was probably perched somewhere behind the door to her quarters, waiting for Annja to knock.

Annja crept closer to the door and waited. Her instincts told her Sheila was definitely up to something.

Annja heard a shuffle on the other side of the door. She placed one hand on the doorknob and started to turn it.

The door was pulled open and Annja found herself dragged into the room.

She spun, already lashing out with a kick as she crashed across the bunk in the tiny cabin. Her foot caught Sheila across the bridge of her nose. Annja heard a crack and saw the rush of bright red blood cascade down the woman's face.

But Sheila didn't stop. She immediately rushed Annja, tackling her around her midsection as Annja started to move off the bed. Annja's wind rushed out as Sheila crashed into her and they tumbled back onto the mattress.

Sheila lunged, launching an elbow strike at Annja's head. Annja ducked under and drove her own elbow into Sheila's midsection. Sheila grunted and brought her hammer fist down on Annja's skull.

Bells rang in Annja's head. Taking a head shot a day after a concussion wasn't good and she fought off the fog that threatened to overtake her. She shoved back at Sheila and drove her off the mattress, across the room and into the wall.

Sheila's head snapped back against the wall and Annja heard her grunt again, but she didn't give up the fight. Sheila brought her knees up one after the other and it was all Annja could do to ward them off, until one got through her defense and sank into her midsection.

Annja retched, but drove down and locked the knee out before yanking back. Sheila lost her balance and fell.

Annja aimed a kick at her head and Sheila only just managed to bring her hands up in time to catch the brunt of it and deflect it away. She chopped down at Annja's exposed knee but there was no power in it.

Annja rushed her but then, at the last minute, saw the pistol coming up in Sheila's hand.

"Stop!"

Annja skidded to a halt and stared at Sheila. "So, you'll shoot me now? Is that it?"

With her free hand, Sheila wiped her sleeve across her nose and winced. "I think you broke it."

"I'd break your neck if I could," Annja said.

Sheila laughed. "I don't doubt it. I was warned that you'd be formidable. You're good, Annja Creed. I'll definitely give you that."

"Put the gun down and we'll continue," Annja said.

Sheila shook her head. "I don't think so. I'm worn out from that matchup and, frankly, I'm not really into unarmed combat when a gun can solve things a lot faster."

Annja didn't make a move, aware that the gun Sheila held didn't waver in the slightest. Whoever Sheila was, she was a trained killer. "Guns are always the last resort of the uncreative."

Sheila smirked. "Doing a bit of paraphrasing there?"

"Maybe."

Sheila gestured toward the bed. "Have a seat. You and I need to talk without Hunter and Cole being close by."

"You're going to shoot me," Annja said. "May as well get it over with now, don't you think."

"Sit down, Annja. I won't ask again."

Annja took a seat on the mattress, actually grateful for the chance to sit. The strike to her head had rung her bell and she wanted nothing more than to cradle her skull and wish the pain away.

But she wouldn't do that in front of Sheila. Plus, she needed to gather her strength before Sheila tried to shoot her.

Sheila watched her for a moment and then smiled. "You know, you and me, we're a lot alike."

"How do you figure that?"

Sheila shrugged. "Well, we're obviously both gifted fighters. I've fought a lot of people—as I know you have—and very few can hold their own against me. Not that I'm bragging or anything."

"Oh, of course not." Annja sighed. "That doesn't necessarily mean we're alike, Sheila."

"Means we're more alike than we are different," Sheila said. "Surely you can see that."

"What I see is a woman who has sabotaged this operation and nearly cost the crew their lives for some reason I don't yet fathom."

Sheila smiled. "I wonder if you always take such a literal approach to your problem solving."

"Meaning?"

"Are you only superficial? Do things look one way and you simply accept that as the fact or do you dig deeper? Do you see beyond the convenient and beyond the horizon to greet the grander vista."

Annja frowned. "You should probably save the psychobabble for someone who actually cares about it. I don't. I'm here for my friend. And he's in trouble so I do my part to help."

"Is he in trouble?"

Annja nodded. "He's got a traitor on board. That'd be you."

"Did I say I sabotaged the engine room?"

"Nope."

"So, why are you convinced it was me? I mean, if you don't mind me asking and all."

"I saw the way you moved."

Sheila started to say something and then stopped. Finally, she broke out into a grin. "Ah, yes, the seasick comment. It didn't jibe with the way I walked." She nodded. "I told you you were good."

"I don't need you telling me that. I'm well aware of my own talents. As much as I am my own weaknesses."

"Well, you're wrong on this one, Annja. Dead wrong, it would seem."

"About what—you?"

Sheila nodded. "I'm not what you think I am."

"You're not a traitor?"

"Nope."

Annja sighed. "Look, someone knocked me out yesterday. I suspect it was two people, actually, but whatever. And then today, we have the engine room mishap. Now, you're the only person I've met on board who seems capable of doing that stuff, so in my book, it's pretty apparent who the troublemaker is around here."

Sheila nodded. "Well, I did knock you out yesterday. But it was just me. No one else."

"And you'd tell me the truth, why exactly?"

"So we can build a little trust here."

"Why would I want to trust you? You've got a gun on me."

Sheila nodded. "That's true. I do." She smirked and lowered the gun. "Or rather, I did."

Annja frowned. "Why did you do that?"

"You feel better with that gone?"

"Who wouldn't?"

Sheila shrugged. "I can bring it back to bear on you in the

flick of an eye so don't give me cause to, okay? We need to have a serious conversation about what's going on here."

Annja leaned back. "So, what *is* going on around here?"

"First things first. Do you at least believe that I may not be the root cause of all the trouble here?"

"Maybe. I'm still getting over the knock to my poor skull."

"An unfortunate event, I assure you. You weren't supposed to be back at your cabin that quickly. I thought I had plenty of time to go through your gear."

"Why would you need to go through my equipment?"

"To make sure you were who you said you were."

Annja grinned. "Are there a lot of other women going around claiming to be me?"

"You'd be surprised."

"I would be." Annja looked at Sheila. The longer she did so, the more Sheila's guise of the antiques expert seemed to slip. Annja could read the steely resolve in her eyes. Whoever had trained her, they'd done one hell of a good job. But Annja knew of the organizations that were capable of training someone like Sheila to that level. And she didn't relish the involvement of any one of them.

"So, why exactly is the CIA involved in this operation?"

Sheila looked amused. "You think I'm CIA?"

Annja shrugged. "Well, forgive me for sounding like a fan girl, but you're obviously well trained. Your skills don't grow on trees. And you aren't going to find most young women with the kind of talent you have. I ran down the list of organizations that could churn out someone like you. It's a short one."

Sheila nodded. "True enough."

"So, you *are* CIA."

"I didn't say that."

Annja frowned. "I thought we were building up some trust here."

"We are."

"You're not being straight with me now."

"I'm not?"

"No."

Sheila sighed. "Annja, forget for a moment that everything has to be so literal with you. Imagine that I'm not CIA. In fact, put that completely out of your mind, because—put simply—I'm not."

Annja frowned. "If you're not CIA, then you're with some intelligence outfit. Maybe military?"

"Nope. You're barking up the wrong tree again, Annja. You can do better. I'm going to chalk this up to the whole sea air thing. Maybe that shark, too."

Annja shook her head and regretted it. "All right, I'm tired and that shot to my head has rattled me. Suppose you save me the time and effort and just tell me what the hell is going on here?"

"You want me to ruin all the fun for you?"

"Yes."

Sheila looked disappointed. "How about we do it this way—I'll ask you a question and see if that helps?"

Annja took a breath. "All right, fine. Whatever."

Sheila turned the pistol over in her hand and checked the slide. Then she looked at Annja. "Take the government out of the equation. Who could train someone like me...realistically?"

"Honestly?" Annja frowned. "I know two people who could. But it would take time. A lot of time. They'd need to make sure you turned out just right before they unleashed you upon the world."

"And who would these two people be?"

Annja frowned. "Suppose I don't feel like sharing their names with you?"

Sheila shrugged. "It doesn't matter. I think I've gotten your thought process back on track enough. At least enough that I'll finish the work for you."

She got up and walked toward the porthole. She turned and smiled at Annja. "Garin sends his best regards."

16

Annja stared. "How do you know that name?"

Sheila smiled. "You didn't think you were the only woman to have ever met him, did you? You don't strike me as that naive."

"Of course not," Annja snapped. "But neither did I think that a complete stranger would know anything about him, at least not here."

"As I said," Sheila replied, "this isn't what it looks like."

"It never is when Garin is involved," Annja said. "Why are you here, Sheila?"

"To help Garin recover something of interest. Something that shouldn't fall into the wrong hands."

Annja's head still throbbed. What she really needed, she decided, was a very long sleep. And perhaps when she woke up, this convoluted nightmare would be over. Or at least she'd have a decent cup of coffee waiting for her. "And whose hands would those be? Mine?"

Sheila shook her head. "Not at all. Garin's not trying to keep anything from you. Far from it. He'd like your help on this, if possible. But we weren't sure you'd even be involved, which is why I'm here."

"How did you even know that this job was tied to Hunter? From what he told me, he was able to keep all reference to this out of the advertisement."

Sheila smirked. "I don't need to tell you how utterly transparent most computer systems are these days. Even with their supposedly impenetrable firewalls, we can get into most of them without breaking a sweat."

"Is that so?"

"Actually, yes. All it took was a quick peek around to get Hunter's particulars and confirm that it was him launching this operation."

"Why the interest in Hunter?"

"Because he's the only one who's been convinced from the start that the *Fantome* was actually hauling captured booty back to Britain. Pretty much everyone else in the treasure-hunting community blows it off as a wild-goose chase. Hunter hasn't."

"And if he's determined to bring it up, then that represents a problem for you guys."

Sheila nodded. "Of course. Garin was never concerned about it before. As long as it stayed on the ocean floor, he was content to let it lie. But Hunter is not content to let that happen. So other steps had to be taken. I was told to insert and safeguard it."

"From me?"

Sheila shook her head. "This isn't about you, Annja." Her eyes narrowed. "Besides, from what I hear, you've already got your hands full with another relic. I don't think anyone's eager to see your workload compounded."

"You know?"

Sheila nodded. "Pretty much everything. Yep."

Annja frowned. "And Garin was comfortable with that?"

"That's beside the point," Sheila said. "The real danger here is that this relic falls into the hands of the other party."

"Who?"

"In time," Sheila said. "For right now, let's just say they are extremely dedicated to getting their hands on the relic first. We've already seen some of their attempts."

"Not the engine room fire?"

Sheila nodded. "Just a slight distraction. If they'd wanted it, we'd all be dead right now."

"Wonderful." Annja frowned. "What is this thing and why do they want it?"

"It belonged to the same woman as your sword."

"Joan of Arc?" Annja frowned. "What was it about her that prompted such attention?"

"Her single-minded devotion to God's service. When she was burned at the stake, the sword wasn't the only thing taken from her and believed to have been destroyed. When she was tied to the stake, they took the small crucifix from around her neck. Since they considered her a heretic, they said she wouldn't be needing it."

"So the crucifix is down there?"

Sheila nodded. "It was a gift from the French to Washington after his inauguration as the first president. The legend surrounding the necklace was whispered about in tight circles. Rumors of what it could do abounded but no one ever paid much attention to it. The necklace was to be kept safe and secured in the White House."

"What's it supposed to be able to do?"

Sheila looked at Annja. "Are you sure you want to hear this?"

"I'm here, aren't I?"

"It supposedly renders the wearer immortal."

Annja frowned. "Supposedly. You don't know for sure?"

"Can you tell me exactly what that sword of your does or where it goes or even every one of its powers?"

"I wouldn't even try to convince you of that," Annja said. "It seems to have plenty of hidden assets I can't understand."

"Exactly," Sheila said. "That's the problem with the crucifix. We don't really know how it works. It's not like we could experiment with it. But the threat of what it can potentially do is enough to spur our intervention."

Annja shook her head. "You want to keep this out of the hands of someone very powerful, I take it."

Sheila stretched. "Can you imagine what would happen if an evil party got their hands on this? If they could figure out how to tap into the hidden properties of the necklace? I think we can both agree that the world is filled with people who really should not be allowed to ingest any more oxygen than absolutely necessary."

"I've met my fair share of evil," Annja admitted.

"Now imagine if they were invulnerable, even to your sword. If they could continue sowing discord and terror among the population."

"They'd grow unchecked." Annja nodded. "I can see the threat. But how do we stop it?"

"By getting the crucifix first."

"That means going underwater," Annja said. "I don't think I need to bring up the danger that waits below the surface."

Sheila nodded. "The shark is a problem."

"A big one, near as I can tell," Annja said. "I'm used to dealing with humans. Giant flesh-eating fish are something else entirely."

"It's going to have to be dealt with," Sheila said. "We need that treasure brought up and the crucifix either safeguarded or destroyed."

"Destroyed? How would we do that?"

"Smelting it would render it useless. At least, that's what the legends tell us. We don't really know if it would work."

"Wonderful." Annja shook her head. "This is turning into quite a trip."

"If it makes you feel any better, I'm not exactly thrilled to be here, either," Sheila said.

Annja looked at her and realized how similar they seemed to be. Even the way Sheila carried herself reminded Annja of how she behaved on occasion. And Annja could see the resolve in Sheila's eyes.

"Garin's been training you for a long time?" she asked.

"Almost ten years."

"You don't look that old."

Sheila frowned. "I'm not, thank you very much. I'm your age. Garin recruited me when I was much younger."

"How'd he find you?"

Sheila shook her head. "I don't think that's germane to our conversation right now. We should probably just concentrate on the matters at hand."

"I'd like to know," Annja said. "After all, it feels like you have an unfair advantage over me in that you know all about my past."

Sheila sat there for a moment and said nothing. Finally, she sighed and nodded. "Fine. Let's just say that I was something of a wild child. I dropped out of high school and found my way to New York where I did some modeling. I didn't particularly care where my life led me. I met Garin at some high-class event. He took me home and seduced me. But when I expected him to just use me for his own enjoyment, he wanted something else."

"What was that?"

"To become an operative for him. He told me something about his life and how limited he was in being able to freely move around the world. He told me that if I agreed, he would train me to be able to handle any situation. And he would pay me very well."

Annja frowned. She wasn't getting paid and it seemed as though she was putting up with the same risks. That figured. "Go on," she grumbled.

"Garin spent five years teaching me all he knew about pretty much everything under the sun. He's been around an awfully long time. The fact that he was able to cram all that knowledge into my brain is something miraculous in and of itself."

"If you say so."

Sheila grinned. "I'm not egotistical, Annja. I long ago learned to be accepting of my own limitations. It's the only way to ever rise above them."

"So you know all about Garin?"

"I know about the ongoing struggle between the forces of good and evil. Of which Garin is a part. As are you."

Annja frowned. "I was drafted. Unlike you, I wasn't given much of a choice. I wish I had been."

"And if you had declined, you would most likely be dead by now."

"Thanks for the vote of confidence."

"It's not that I doubt your abilities, Annja. After all, I've had the chance to see them up close and personal. But have you ever thought about how our lives unfurl from the spool we're born with? Our actions and decisions always seem to lead us inevitably toward a crux. Your life led you to the point where you encountered the sword and it became a part of you."

"So?"

"So, if you had rejected it at that point, somehow—and I'm not saying you could have because I don't know enough about it—it seems like it would have been a rejection of not just the sword, but of your entire life. What would have been the point of living anymore?"

"Well, I wouldn't have become suicidal or anything."

"Perhaps not consciously. But your actions and thoughts would have subconsciously led you away from your destiny. And when someone rejects their destiny so completely, the universe seems to want to hit the reset button."

"You're saying I would have brought about my own death?"

"Most likely."

Annja fell silent for a moment. "What a rosy outlook on life that is," she said quietly.

Sheila smiled. "I only speak from my own experiences, Annja. I'm not casting judgment on you and yours."

"Are you sure?"

"Absolutely. Look at my life. I was headed for a cliff when I met Garin. If I'd rejected him at that point, I know for certain I would be dead now."

"Really?"

Sheila nodded. "The drugs, the sex, something. I don't know. Any one of them or a combination would have led me further and further astray until I overdosed or got some horrible disease. It was only a matter of time."

Annja sighed. "Garin became your sword, then."

Sheila shrugged. "That's one way of looking at it, I guess. He came along at a particular time, much like the sword did with you. I guess that's one of the great mysteries of life, how things seem to happen at just the right moment."

"No coincidences," Annja said. "That's too easy an explanation. And I've seen enough to not believe in coincidence anymore."

"Coincidence does seem to be the crutch for the unimaginative." Sheila smiled. "Garin told me you were something else."

"That's only because he's been trying to seduce me for years," Annja said.

"There aren't many who can resist him."

"I never claimed it was easy," Annja said with a laugh.

"You're honest," Sheila said. "I like that."

"So the question now seems to be how do we deal with the shark terrorizing this boat and all who would dive?"

Sheila looked at Annja. "Isn't it obvious?"

"Not yet."

"You're going to have to deal with it, Annja. You're going to have to kill the shark so we can get to the treasure."

17

"You're dreaming," Annja said. "There's no way in hell I'm going into the water with that shark. The thing's huge!"

Sheila shook her head. "We don't have a choice."

Annja frowned. "And what would you be doing right now if I wasn't here? You'd have to figure out something else, right?"

"Yes."

"Then figure it out. Leave me out of this. I'll be more than happy to help you recover the crucifix, but I'm not going into combat with some giant fish. No way."

Annja got up to leave, but Sheila put up her hand. "Remember what we were just talking about?"

"What?"

"Destiny and how it impacts us?"

"Fighting that shark is not my destiny. It's just a convenient way for you to get out of doing your job."

Sheila shook her head. "I wish it was that simple. But the fact that you're here is the same as it's always been. You are where you are for a reason. And for you to deny that is tempting the fates in the very worst way."

"I've been tempting fate a lot longer than you know," Annja said. "I just don't see how I can help."

"You can help because your sword is here on this boat, right now. And you know that the shark can't survive against it."

"The sword's not perfect," Annja said. "Neither is the wielder of it. You may have bought into the whole good versus evil thing, but I still struggle with it and my own place in this universe. Sometimes I don't even want this sword. Sometimes all I want is my old life back. Or at least the life I thought belonged to me."

"You're not the only one, Annja."

Annja sighed. "Suppose I agree to go through with it, how would we even do it? The shark is huge. I'll never last long enough to get close."

"We've got the cage that Cole had shipped in, right?"

"You think I can kill the shark from inside the cage?"

"Maybe."

"It'd be me sticking my sword out between the bars, poking at it and probably losing it in the process."

"You can't lose it," Sheila said. "You simply will it back to where it rests when you aren't using it."

"Garin told you about that?"

"As I said, Garin tries to explain a lot of things so I'm better prepared when I go out on operations. There was a chance you would be here, albeit a small one and one that we couldn't overtly manipulate to our advantage, but we hoped you'd show up."

"How so?"

"We know about your relationship with Cole. We knew about Hunter. And it was hoped there would be a convergence of situations."

"Cole and I don't really have a relationship. We're just friends."

"Call it whatever you want," Sheila said. "I'm not here to pass judgment on you or your lifestyle."

"Gee, thanks."

"But the fact remains we have to deal with that shark."

"We've got to deal with the traitor on board the boat, as well," Annja said. "Otherwise, the shark is going to be the least of our problems."

"Hunter and Cole should be able to figure out who the traitor is without our help. We've got bigger fish to fry, pardon the pun."

"How are they going to narrow it down?"

Sheila shrugged. "You left them to handle things while you came after me."

"Yeah, but I thought you were the traitor."

Sheila nodded. "And you told them to carry on because you felt certain there was someone else working on the ship, right?"

"How'd you know that?"

Sheila smiled. "Garin taught me very well. I've had this entire boat wired for sound for days now. I heard everything you said after I left. It's how I was able to be ready for your sudden appearance."

"Wonderful."

"The truth of the matter is: there is someone working on the boat to disrupt the operation. But it's not me. So in a way, you were absolutely correct when you told them there was another party on board."

"That makes me feel all warm and fuzzy inside."

"Well, the important thing is they'll be fine without our help. You and I need to figure out the shark. Once we get that taken care of, Hunter and Cole will have found the traitor and then we can get down to the business of securing the crucifix."

Annja sighed. "And just who are we keeping the crucifix away from? Because you never told me that."

Sheila looked at her. "Do you just pretend to not notice things as a way of ferreting out information?"

"Depends on who I'm talking to."

"I see."

"And you still haven't answered the question."

"I don't know if I can."

Annja frowned. "I thought you knew everything there was to know about these people."

"I do. To some extent, anyway. But it's not a lack of information I'm worried about."

"Then what is it?"

"It's about whether Garin wants you to know who they are."

Annja shook her head. "Why on earth wouldn't he want me to know about them?"

"I'm not sure. He didn't specifically tell me to share the information with you. 'Need to know' and all that."

Annja stood. "Let me make myself clear. If you expect me to go into the water and face down some huge shark that wants nothing more than to chew me into little bits and pieces, then I expect some quid pro quo here. You can get right on the horn to Garin and tell him I said that. If he wants my help, he'd better start sharing the goods on who is after this thing. And if he doesn't, he can come on out here and take on the shark himself, because I'll be gone."

Sheila held up her hands. "Okay, okay, just calm down."

"I am calm," Annja said. "I just want there to be no mistake. I am not going ahead with any plan to help Garin until I know the full extent of what's involved here. I tend to take a very long view of things when my own mortality is involved."

"I'll get Garin on the phone and talk to him. In the meantime, will you promise to keep this quiet?"

Annja frowned. "Who am I going to tell?"

"Hunter and Cole."

"You don't want them knowing you're in the clear?"

"Not yet."

"Why?"

"It will probably help flush out the real culprit if I'm still suspected of being the traitor."

"I can't keep it from them for very long."

"Just let them think that you've got me buttoned up and I'll get clearance from Garin. Then we can go see them."

Annja nodded. "Fine. I'm going to lie down. But move fast. I want more information than what I've got so far."

ANNJA GOT BACK to her quarters and stretched out on the bed, sinking into the mattress with relief. She felt butterflies in her stomach and did some deep breathing to relieve the nervousness she was feeling.

The idea of jumping into the ocean to do battle with the shark stalking the boat did nothing to make her pleased she'd agreed to come along with Cole on this trip. If anything, Annja only wanted to run home and lock the door.

At least in Brooklyn, she only had to worry about muggers, murderers and a variety of other scum. Sharks hadn't yet figured out how to settle down in any of the five boroughs.

Garin.

His face swam into her mind and Annja frowned. So Sheila worked for him. That was a surprise. More surprising was the fact that she knew plenty about Annja and was a decent match in terms of her combat skills. Annja hadn't met many who could go toe to toe with her.

Why was Garin recruiting his own operatives? The fact that he and Roux had once been mortal enemies hadn't stopped them both from moving around the world as it suited them. Sure, they kept reasonably low profiles, but why was Garin now so worried that he needed operatives in play for him?

She wasn't sure that made much sense and it had to be addressed the next time she saw him.

Then there was the whole notion that some rival was actively searching for the crucifix that had once belonged to Joan of Arc. Annja felt a twang in her stomach at the thought of the woman whose sword she now owned.

No, that wasn't it. Annja didn't own the sword. If anything, the sword seemed to own her.

Regardless, what type of organization was this? Did they know about Annja and the sword? Or were they only after the crucifix? Being granted immortality was a fantastic concept and one that Annja wasn't sure she could buy into, even knowing Roux and Garin had survived for centuries.

Of course, if someone had suggested that Joan of Arc's sword could manifest itself at will in her hands, she would have told them they were nuts, too.

She desperately needed sleep.

Annja stretched and let the pillow cradle her head as she took a few more deep breaths and sank further into herself. She let her mind go blank as she often did when she was tired and worn out. She could feel her awareness soften and expand as she took each subsequent breath.

Who is the traitor?

She heard a noise first and then turned sharply.

Someone was trying to open her door.

The knob moved one way and then the other. But Annja had been sure to lock the door when she'd come in. And that meant whoever was trying to get in would either have to pick the lock or kick the door in.

Or they could just knock.

Annja smirked. She didn't think they'd do that.

She slid out of the bed carefully and let her feet touch the floor before she shifted her weight any further. At least the floors don't creak, she thought as she stood and padded over toward the door.

The doorknob kept rotating back and forth. She heard another sound from the other side. Metallic.

She frowned.

What were they doing? She thought she could hear a vague clicking or scraping sound.

They were picking the lock. As far as she was concerned, that ruled out the idea that someone friendly was on the other side of the door. If they weren't knocking, then Annja wasn't happy to see them.

She crept closer to the door and put her ear to the surface. She could almost hear the breathing on the other side. She could visualize the face of the person picking their way into her quarters and see the exertion. She could feel their desire to get into her room.

But why?

No sense wondering, she thought. She turned the lock and yanked the door hard.

"Hi, there."

18

Sheila stumbled into the room, lock picks in her hands. Annja caught her and pushed her up against the wall. "Want to tell me why you were breaking into my room?"

"I didn't want to wake you."

Annja frowned. "If Garin told you about me, then you should have known that I'm a pretty light sleeper."

"You weren't yesterday when I clocked you. You were way out of it then. I thought I could creep back in here and you'd be none the wiser."

"At least until I woke up." Annja frowned. "You got in touch with Garin already?"

Sheila nodded. "He wasn't there, though. I had to leave a message."

"He knows you're on an operation and he's not there to pick up?"

"We have a set window of contact. This wasn't it. He won't be available until then. I'll have to call him back."

Annja nodded. "So, let's pretend that Garin says yes. Why

don't you go ahead and fill me in on the bad guys while we wait, huh?"

Sheila sat down on the chair in the room and faced Annja. "I really don't feel comfortable doing that."

Annja nodded, took a deep breath and summoned her sword. In an instant, it was in her hands, aimed right at Sheila's throat.

Sheila's eyes went wide and the color drained from her face. Annja smiled. "Pretty amazing, huh?"

Sheila nodded dumbly. "Garin told me it would be impressive, but I didn't expect anything like this."

"Yeah, most people don't." Annja kept the blade pointed at Sheila's throat. "You know, I don't really have a high tolerance for waiting. I'm much more of a 'let's get it all out in the open' kinda gal. So, we'll have a talk about these bad guys and not worry about what Garin might or might not say. How does that sound, hmm?"

Sheila's eyes were locked on the blade that seemed to hover just inches from the base of her throat. "There's really no need to bring that out and use it to threaten me."

"I'm not threatening you, Sheila." Annja smiled. "I'm just using this to illustrate a point—namely, that I don't like waiting. Especially when I know you have the answer to the questions I have."

"I feel like you're threatening me."

"I don't really care, to be honest." Annja pressed the sword at Sheila's throat. "See, I figure if you don't tell me, I'll just slice your head off and then tell Garin you had a horrible accident involving our pal the shark. Really an unfortunate turn of events, but that's the way it goes sometimes, huh?"

"You wouldn't."

Annja shook her head. "Don't even go there with me. You won't like the result."

Sheila glared at Annja. "You're serious."

"Deadly."

"I shouldn't do this," Sheila said. "I'd be violating one of Garin's rules that he ingrained in me a long time ago."

"Your choice," Annja said. "Makes no difference to me. Or to the sword I'm holding."

Sheila frowned. "This isn't how I envisioned our friendship developing, Annja."

"No?"

"I thought we had some sort of trust going."

Annja shook her head. Outside, she could see that clouds moving in had thwarted some of the afternoon sun. "That kind of went out the window when you picked the lock on my door."

Sheila sat quietly and then looked at Annja. "Fine. The organization is headed by a guy from Cleveland—"

"Cleveland?"

"That's what I said, why?"

Annja shrugged. "Never thought of a nefarious organization having someone in charge from Cleveland. Just doesn't seem right." She shook her head. "Whatever. Keep going."

"His name is Henderson. That's all anyone knows. He's supposedly one of these religious nuts who's obsessed with anything even remotely supernatural. Doesn't matter if it's from some other culture or what. If he hears about it, he wants it."

"And the crucifix fits in with his ideology?"

"Henderson's ideology is simple. If it's powerful, he wants it."

"To what end?"

Sheila shook her head. "Who knows? No one's ever really seen Henderson. He could be a complete flake. Or he could be a captain of industry. All we know is he has people everywhere, and when he hears about something unusual, he gets his fingers into it."

"Why didn't he recover the crucifix himself?"

"Henderson's never been much of a starter. He prefers swooping in after the work has already been done. He'll wait until the crucifix is recovered and then come and steal it. Easier that way."

Annja nodded. "Guess I can see how that might look attractive."

"He's on the hunt for this crucifix, Annja. He wants it very badly. The lure of immortality has always held sway over men."

"Women, too," Annja said. "Seems to me I can recall plenty of historical figures who spent their whole lives looking for something that would stave off the onslaught of age and death."

"Indeed. And Henderson is definitely one of those types. Garin's intelligence estimates his age at almost eighty."

"He wants the fountain of youth," Annja said.

"But he'll settle for something that keeps death away."

Annja eyed Sheila. "Who works for him?"

"Anyone he can pay. He recruits from every walk of life, knowing that money tends to make people very open to things like murder, deception and stuff along those lines."

"You're certain that he knows about the crucifix?"

"Absolutely." Sheila frowned. "He managed to plant someone on this boat. Apparently, Hunter's rather loose approach to hiring people worked out well for Henderson's organization. No background checks means they didn't have to work hard at positioning their people or supplying them with an extensive résumé prior to sending them out."

"Handy."

"And quite unlike Garin, who had me create an entire fictitious account of my life just so I could hold up under scrutiny."

Annja laughed. "Would have worked if you hadn't moved the way you do."

"Yeah."

Annja let the sword drop. "There, now don't you feel better having told me all of that? No sense bothering Garin at all. We'll keep it just between us."

"If you say so."

Annja stood, sending the sword back to otherwhere. "I'm still not sure how you think I can take out that shark. The idea of me fighting it—"

"You don't have to fight it, Annja. Just stab it with your sword or chop off its tail or something like that."

"That shark is forty feet long at least. That's big."

"I know."

"And that mouth. Did you see the mouth?"

"I wasn't on deck when you were."

"Miles of teeth. The thing's an eating machine. I mean, I've seen sharks close up, but this thing is beyond unreal."

Sheila nodded. "I'm not pretending that it's going to be easy."

"It will be for you. You're not going to be in the water. I will. It's my life on the line if something goes wrong."

"Nothing's going to go wrong, Annja. You just get in the water. When the shark approaches, you kill it. Very simple."

"You think so, huh? In that case, I'll lend you my sword and you can do the business yourself. How does that sound?"

"It won't work," Sheila said. "You know as well as I do that your sword won't transfer to anyone else. Like it or not, you've got to do this thing because there's really no one else who can."

"Maybe Hunter's got some guns on board. Maybe we can just shoot it and watch it sink to the bottom."

"The most powerful thing on this boat is a 9 mm pistol. That's not going to do squat against a forty-foot shark. Except maybe piss it off some," Sheila said.

"That's the last thing we need," Annja replied.

"All we've got to do is lure it to the cage where you'll be. Once it gets close, you can plunge your sword into its belly. Cut deep and fast and that should be a mortal wound. Once you do that, you can dispatch it at your leisure."

"Like when my heart calms down."

"Sure."

Annja sat back on her bed. "The whole idea sounds insane. There's got to be a better way, but damned if I can think of one."

"The problem is the size of the shark," Sheila said. "If it was smaller, we could try fishing for it. But with it being half the size of the boat, it will simply weigh far too much for us to try something like that. It has to be destroyed."

"Cole's going to love that," Annja said sadly.

"I can appreciate his sentiments on this. I'm not one to encourage wanton slaughter of animals, but there's no way around this. The shark is obviously interested in the boat since it's made a repeat appearance, even in the wake of Jock's death."

"So it's a rogue shark?"

"Could be."

Annja frowned. She knew a rogue shark was one that didn't behave like others of its kind. Its behavior was unpredictable and, because of that, trying to discourage it from staying around would most likely not work. Destroying the beast would be their only option.

"Okay," Annja said slowly. "You kept your word and told me about Henderson. I appreciate that. You didn't have to."

"Well, you did have a sword up against my throat."

Annja smiled. "I simply encouraged you to help me out with my distinct lack of information."

"Convincingly, I might add," Sheila said. "But Garin will kill me if he ever finds out, so you can't tell him about this, okay?"

"Sure. No problem." Annja leaned back and tried to relax. "When do you want to start?"

"It has to be soon. And it would be better if we can do it without anyone else knowing."

"Yeah, sure, that will be easy. We'll just wait until midnight so I can winch the cage into the ocean without anyone hearing me. Of course, it will be totally dark and I won't be able to see a damned thing." She glared at Sheila. "You're nuts. Of course people are going to have to know."

"The more people who know, the more difficult it will be to convince them that what we're doing is the right approach."

"Maybe we could just show them pictures of Jock's body. That might be enough to convince them."

"Maybe."

Annja knew she'd have to tell Hunter and Cole about this. It would only be with their help that she could even dream about pulling it off. "We'll talk it over around dinnertime, okay?"

Sheila nodded. "All right." She stood. "Are we finished here?"

Annja shrugged. "Hey, you were the one who came to my room, not the other way around."

Sheila smiled. "I think we're done." She put her hand on the doorknob and turned it. "Talk to you later."

"Not so fast."

Annja looked up at the sound of the new voice. Captain Jax stood in the doorway. She held a pistol in her hand, its black barrel aimed squarely at Sheila's chest.

"Seems to me," Jax said, "that we all need to have a serious talk. So, why don't we sit down for a few minutes until we get things cleared up."

19

Sheila backed into the room, her hands rising defensively. "Slow down, Captain. There's no need for any violence."

Jax frowned. "I'll be the judge of that." She looked at Annja. "Stay where you are, Annja."

"Why would I want to do that?" Annja asked. She could have the sword out in the blink of an eye if she could just keep Jax fixated on dealing with Sheila.

"Because I don't want to have to shoot you," Jax said. "But I will in order to get you to listen to me. You understand?"

Annja nodded but she was keeping her focus soft, ready to move if Sheila could help her gain an opening.

Sheila kept her hands up. "Why are you doing this, Jax? I thought we got along just fine."

"Appearances are deceiving," Jax said. "And frankly, I never cared for the way you carried yourself."

"Why not?"

"Too obviously disdainful of the rest of us." Jax smirked.

"Well, the joke's on you, isn't it? Nothing like having a gun barrel in your face to make you a little more humble, huh?"

Sheila shook her head. "This isn't necessary."

"I think it is. You've been trouble since I laid eyes on you. Time to take care of business since Hunter and Cole won't deal with it."

Annja frowned. Jax kept the gun steady on Sheila. She didn't seem motivated by anger. In fact, she seemed pretty calm. Annja looked at Sheila and there was concern on the woman's face. What was going on here? The presence of a gun in the mix didn't help matters.

As Jax focused on Sheila, Annja summoned her sword and went on the attack, drawing the blade high overhead and launching herself through the air. She heard a shout from Jax as she pounced.

But the captain dodged the blow and punched Annja in the side of her chest, sending a thundering strike rattling through Annja's body. Annja gasped, trying to get some air back into her. As she landed hard, Jax pivoted again and delivered a roundhouse kick to Annja's leg, sweeping it out and dropping her further.

Annja was down before she realized Jax had the pistol aimed at her chest. "Dammit, Annja, I told you not to engage!"

But then Annja saw a form hurtle across her field of vision as Sheila tackled Jax. Their two bodies fell across the mattress, toppling over backward beyond the edge of the bed.

Annja righted herself, still trying to get some wind back into her lungs, which felt as if they were spasming uncontrollably. That was some punch she'd taken from Jax. Who had taught her that?

She had more immediate issues, though. She could see a tangle of arms and legs as Sheila and Jax fought to control each other. Sheila was doing well, but Annja could tell that Jax was simply biding her time.

Sheila tried to disarm Jax, grabbing at the gun with both hands. Annja winced. That wasn't a good idea. Sheila should have gone for control on the hand and arm instead of the gun itself, which could be manipulated by her opponent.

Jax put that fighting tactic into effect, suddenly using her free hand to wrench the gun up and over Sheila's wrist, snapping it down sharply. Annja heard the bone break and Sheila cried out, bit back on the pain and punched Jax in the face.

Jax took the punch well, despite the sudden rush of blood, and kicked Sheila back and up, forcing her toward Annja.

Sheila rolled, got to her feet and clutched at her broken wrist. She turned to Annja. "You've got to stop her!"

And then she bolted for the door.

Annja shook her head and watched as Jax came crawling up, aimed the gun and started to squeeze off a shot. Annja lunged at her gun hand and the sudden shot went awry, the bullet burying itself in the wood paneling across the room.

"Annja! Dammit!" Jax punched her again in the stomach and Annja dropped. She tried to raise her sword. Jax stomped on her arm. Annja groaned in pain. When she tried to roll over with the sword, Jax pointed the gun right into her face.

"Drop that sword!"

Annja released the blade, her fingers clutching reflexively, not wanting to let go of her only protection.

Jax cast a look sideways at the door and frowned. She looked back at Annja. "I told you to stay out of this. Now I've lost her."

"You're the traitor," Annja said. "I guess I should have seen through the tough-gal demeanor."

Jax sighed and helped Annja to her feet. "No, you idiot. I'm Garin's operative on this boat. That one is the real problem. She's with Henderson."

Annja shook her head. "She just got through telling me all about Henderson and his organization."

"She just finished bullshitting you."

"Why should I believe you?"

Jax checked the slide on her pistol. "Because Garin told me you'd ask that question."

"And did he give you an answer for me, as well?"

"No, but he did tell me that if you gave me any trouble, I should just beat the crap out of you and be done with it."

Annja sniffed. "Sure sounds like him."

"He also told me that you were the one who billed your trip to Japan on his credit card."

"You could have found that out by hacking into a computer and getting his credit report. Give me something else."

"Antarctica. Sound familiar?"

"What about it?"

"You were surprised to find him there, right?"

"Maybe."

"And do you remember Bali? What you told him after you'd had a few too many glasses of wine?"

Annja frowned. She was sure no one else on the planet knew that. And Annja desperately wished she hadn't said what she had that night. But it couldn't be helped now.

Apparently.

Annja sighed. "So, who is she?"

"Sheila? Don't know if that's her real name or not, but she works for Henderson. She's one of his top people. Her specialty is acting like she's an amateur when, in fact, she's not. And she can turn people against each other. Us included."

"I nearly killed you."

Jax shrugged. "I try not to take things like that personally. It tends to happen a fair amount, and if I held a grudge every time it did happen, I wouldn't be the pleasant lass I am."

Annja smiled. "Pleasant lass?"

"It's a personality makeover as suggested by our mutual friend."

"I see. Did he pluck you out of obscurity, too, in order to train you to be his superspy?"

Jax frowned. "Do I look like I need any training other than what I got in the school of hard knocks? Garin can kiss my ass if he thinks he knows something I can't teach myself."

Annja chuckled. "I'd love to see his reaction to that comment."

"As long as he pays me, we get along fine. I know what side my bread is buttered on. You don't need to worry about me."

"But we do need to worry about Sheila."

Jax shrugged. "She can't go far. I broke her wrist."

"I heard it."

"She's probably gone running back to her room. There aren't a lot of other places she can go right now, are there? That's one of the benefits to being out on the ocean."

"A cornered rabbit can still put up a fight," Annja said. "What if she's got a weapon in there with her?"

"Like what? A pistol?" Jax shrugged. "She can use it on herself, if she wants. When the time comes to go in there and get her, I'll be happy to wrest it from her dead hands."

"I was thinking more in terms of explosives. She could blow up the boat."

Jax shook her head. "I already sent Dave to root through her junk. He knows what to look for and I don't."

"Is he clear?"

Jax nodded. "I trust him."

"All right, we've got to get to Hunter and Cole with this information. They need to know what's going on."

"Agreed."

Jax and Annja started for the door, but as Jax went through the doorway, Annja tripped and bent forward, bumping into Jax. Jax turned just as a bullet tore into the door frame.

Splinters of wood flew off and struck Jax across her cheek

as Annja realized that Sheila wasn't about to go quietly and cower somewhere. She hauled Jax back into her room.

"Dammit!"

Jax crawled to the door and stuck her gun through the opening. She squeezed off two rounds and Annja winced as the sudden explosion thundered inside her head.

Jax pulled back and brushed a hand across her cheek. It came away bloody. "I would have taken that slug if you hadn't bumped into me."

"That your way of saying thanks?"

Jax grinned. "Maybe."

She ducked and squeezed off another shot, then pulled back. Annja watched her. So far, they hadn't heard any return fire.

Jax frowned. "You think I tagged her on that first volley?"

Annja shook her head. "No idea."

Jax took a deep breath. "Well, no way to tell if we stay here."

"Just be careful," Annja said.

Jax got down on her belly and crawled over to the doorjamb. Annja frowned. "Wait."

Jax looked back. "What?"

Annja went to her bag and pulled a small compact out. She handed it to Jax, who took it with a grin. "Good idea."

She popped it open and used it to peer around the frame.

Annja braced for the impact of a bullet, but no gunshot came. After a second, Jax pulled back into the room and tossed Annja the compact.

"Seems secure."

Annja nodded and they crawled out into the corridor. Jax took the lead, her pistol ready to fire if need be.

They approached the turn in the corridor and Jax looked at Annja, holding a finger up to her lips.

Annja braced herself.

Jax spun around the corner and aimed her pistol.

The corridor was empty.

Annja let loose a pent-up breath and Jax's shoulders slumped. "So much for that."

"You think she's back in her room now?"

Jax frowned. "Doubt it. If she's acting like this, it means she's going on the attack. And that's not particularly comforting. We'd better hook up with Hunter and Cole and make sure that Sheila's not planning a hostage taking."

"Good idea."

They took the steps up toward the main deck, each time clearing the turns carefully. Annja half expected Sheila to pop out at any minute and squeeze off a few more rounds at them.

But nothing else happened. When they were close to the steps leading to the wheelhouse, Jax pointed topside. "Last I heard, Hunter and Cole are up—"

A sudden scream pierced the air.

Jax and Annja looked at each other and then ran for the steps.

20

Annja and Jax crested the steps, expecting to see something other than what greeted their eyes. At the stern of the boat, they saw Sheila holding a gun on Dave, who looked like he wanted to rip her head off. "Stay the hell back!" she shouted.

Sheila clutched another crew member Annja didn't recognize. The young man looked as though he might faint at any second. He didn't struggle and stayed right where Sheila had him pinned with her arm. The broken wrist didn't seem to be slowing her down nearly as much as Annja might have hoped.

"Get the winch and drop the dinghy over the side. Don't screw around or little Stevie here gets a bullet for his trouble."

Dave frowned, but made his way to the winch and secured the lead cable to the motorized dinghy that was strapped to one side of the ship. Once he had the cable secured, he fired up the winch.

"What's going on here?" someone said.

Annja held up her hand as Cole and Hunter came through

the doorway from inside the cabin. Hunter stopped short and then looked at Annja. "Guess you nailed it right."

"It's a long story," Annja said.

Hunter noticed Jax. "Where'd you get a pistol?"

Jax didn't take her eyes off Sheila. "I don't make a habit of going through life unarmed."

Annja could feel Jax tensing. She shook her head. "Don't do it," she said quietly.

"I can make the shot."

"You won't. And her finger is tight around that trigger. You might hit her, but she'll get the shot off before she dies," Annja said.

"You sure? I'm a crack shot with this thing."

"If you had a sniper rifle and could guarantee that you could take out the oblongata, then that would be a different story. But a pistol round won't stop the brain in time from sending the nerve impulse to shoot."

Jax glanced at her. "Okay, then."

Dave had the dinghy raised off the railing and was steering it over the side of the ship. He glared at Sheila. "Where do you want it, bitch?"

"Be nice," Sheila said. "Or I'll shoot you, anyway. Put the dinghy down right there."

Annja frowned. "You sure you want to be going out in that thing?"

Sheila looked at her. "Shut up."

"It's just that with that shark out there, you never know. It might show up looking for something to eat. And that dinghy's awfully small."

Sheila gestured with the pistol. "Back up, Dave. Over by the others."

Dave frowned and shook his head. "Let Steve go and we'll both get out of your way."

"You think I'm stupid? Jax will shoot me."

Hunter cleared his throat. "No, she won't. If you want to go, be my guest. No one's going to stop you. I'd rather you were off the boat, anyway."

Sheila eyed him. "I don't trust you."

Hunter shrugged. "Trust me, don't trust me. I don't care. But leave Steve alone."

Sheila nodded. "All of you, back inside the cabin and pull the door shut behind you. Once I see that, I'll let him go. But you stay inside until I'm in the dinghy and away from the ship. Listen for the motor and then you can come out. Leave before then and I'll shoot Steve."

Dave growled under his breath. "Why exactly are we letting this chick walk like this? I could close that distance and kill her."

"Too risky," Hunter said. "And Steve would die in the process. I promised his father I'd look after him."

"I still think she should die," Dave said.

"Agreed," Jax said. But she did as Hunter said. They all moved back into the cabin together. Annja could see Sheila struggling with the pistol and the weight of having to deal with a hostage. If they'd wanted to, they could have taken her. But Hunter didn't want to do that. She wondered why.

Sheila clambered over the side of the boat and eased herself into the dinghy. Steve fainted on the deck.

"Jesus," Dave said under his breath. "Someone get that kid a freaking spine."

Cole cleared his throat. "Most people haven't actually been in combat before, Dave."

He nodded. "I guess."

They heard the motor kick over and then they were all spilling outside onto the deck. Hunter ran to check on Steve and Cole helped him. Jax and Dave ran for the railing. Annja went with them.

Off the stern of the boat, already a hundred yards away, Sheila's dinghy was racing away at a good clip.

"Where the hell is she going?" Dave asked.

"Mainland," Jax said.

"Can she make it there in that thing?"

Dave nodded. "She's got two fuel bladders in the dinghy. That should give her more than enough gas to get there. I just wonder if she knows how to deal with the engine."

Annja turned to him. "Why's that?"

Dave looked at his watch. "Because it ought to be kicking out in about ten seconds."

Annja looked back at Sheila's dinghy. A thin trail of gray smoke steamed out of the small outboard motor. She grinned. "How the hell did you do that?"

"SEALs know a few things about how to make boats and motors work. Or, in this case, not work," Dave said.

"So now what?" Jax asked. "We just stand here and watch her float away on the current?"

Dave shook his head. "Nah, I'm sure a willful soul like Sheila will very soon come to a decision."

"What kind of decision?"

"As to whether she'll let the tide carry her into the mainland, or if she'll swim for it."

Annja frowned. "She's got a busted wrist. I doubt very much she'll decide to swim for it."

"Especially with that huge shark out there," Jax said.

Dave shrugged. "You'd be surprised what people will think about doing when they're faced with a big decision."

"I'd wait it out," Jax said. "Wait for someone to come and get me. No way I'd chance it against the shark."

Annja watched as the dinghy's motor sputtered and then coughed before completely dying. Sheila pumped the starter cord a few times and then slumped back in the boat. She glanced back at the *Seeker*.

Dave waved at her with a big smile. "Enjoy yourself!" he shouted.

Sheila aimed the gun in his direction, but no one aboard even moved. There was too much distance between them and the dinghy. The bullets would never reach their target.

"She just going to sit there?" Dave glanced up at the sky. "The sun's going to be setting soon."

Annja looked at the sky. Dave was right. The bright blue from earlier had given way to a darker sky stained with reds and oranges as the sun trekked westward on its daily route.

"I wouldn't want to be out there alone at night," Annja said. "That would just get a bit too freaky for me."

Jax nodded. "I'd start thinking of all those scenes in *Jaws*. I wouldn't be able to help myself. And then I'd really get scared."

Dave sniffed. "You know, it's not that bad. Sometimes the ocean at night can be quite peaceful. I remember being out one time in the South Pacific. A bunch of us in a Zodiac and it was kind of nice, actually."

"You weren't floating in waters where a forty-foot man-eating shark had been prowling recently."

"This is very true," Dave said. "And we also had a pretty impressive arsenal with us. There's nothing like overwhelming firepower to make things better."

"I don't think her 9 mm counts as overwhelming," Annja said.

Dave chuckled. "Not by a long shot."

Annja looked over her shoulder at Hunter and Cole. They had gotten Steve up and were giving him some water. "Is he okay?"

Hunter nodded. "Seems to be. A little shaken up, but I suppose that's to be expected."

Cole looked at Annja. "Good thing you pegged Sheila the way you did. That could have been ugly."

"Sheila lied to me," Annja said. "She had me convinced she was a good guy. It's Jax you ought to be thanking."

Jax waved her hand. "Forget about it. Just doing my part to keep the safety of the ship intact. Besides, I didn't like her, anyway."

Hunter grinned. "You'll get a bonus if this all works out."

"I'll take you up on that," Jax said. "And don't use 'if,' say 'when' instead. Makes me feel more confident."

"Holy crap," Dave said suddenly. "She's actually going to swim for it."

Annja spun. They could see Sheila standing in the dinghy. She seemed to be searching the water for something. She leaned over the edge.

"Careful," Dave said.

The stalled dinghy bobbed in the waves. Sheila fell over and into the water, kicking the dinghy as she did so. The little boat skidded away from her. Sheila came up spouting water and coughing.

Dave sighed. "Well, this shouldn't last too long. She doesn't look very comfortable in the water."

"It's probably pretty cold out there, too," Jax said.

"It is," Cole said, coming up next to them. "And I had a wet suit on at the time. She's in trouble if she stays in there long. She'll go hypothermic and that will be the end."

"I wonder if the shark likes Popsicles," Dave said.

"Oh, my God," Jax said. "Look!"

Annja looked where she was pointing, perhaps five hundred yards off the port side. The telltale silhouette of a triangular dorsal fin had risen out of the water.

The shark had returned.

"My God, that's a big fish," Dave said.

Jax leaned on the railing. "She'll never make it."

Annja watched as Sheila started swimming in the general direction of the mainland. But they were a good couple of miles from the coast. And even if Sheila had been an Olympian, she'd never make it in time.

Not when such a huge shark was on her tail.

Cole seemed restless. "I'm not sure if I can watch this. I feel like I ought to be doing something to save her."

"I don't know that she's seen it yet," Dave said. "She's seems pretty calm right now."

But then Sheila turned in the water and noticed the giant dorsal fin closing to within a few hundred yards from where she splashed through the water. She looked at the *Seeker* and shouted for them to help her.

"Even if we wanted to," Jax said. "There's nothing we can do. We'll never reach her in time."

"And should she be saved?" Dave said. "She almost killed Steve."

"And you," Annja said.

"I'm expendable," Dave said. He grinned. "Sorry, it's an old SEAL joke."

Cole turned away. "I can't watch this. Come find me when it's over, Annja. We need to talk some things through."

Annja turned back to the ocean. She didn't feel particularly compassionate toward Sheila. She'd deceived her and made Annja feel like a fool for trusting her. And now, Sheila was about to get her due. Still, no one deserved such a violent death.

"Not much longer," Jax said.

The dorsal fin cut through the waves, and seemed to be picking up speed. Annja thought it looked a bit strange. She frowned and had to remind herself that she was about to watch another human being be killed by a shark.

And yet, somehow she didn't feel anything deep inside her.

Annja frowned. Have I changed? she wondered. Have I

grown cold? Have I forgotten what it's like to feel the fear that Sheila must be feeling right now?

Sheila screamed again as the fin bore down on her.

"God," Jax said. "Here it comes."

There was a sudden explosion of movement as the shark's head reared out of the water. The massive form blocked everything from their view, but then, in an instant, it had clamped down and sunk completely back beneath the waves.

Sheila was gone.

21

Annja found her way to the galley for dinner. Tom was sitting at the nearest table eating toast and water. Annja nudged him. "Hey, how are you feeling?"

"Like shit," he said. "And I hear I've been missing out on all the excitement, which pisses me off to no end."

"Just a few gun battles, a giant shark, that sort of thing," Annja said. "Nothing you couldn't experience any day of the week."

"Thanks for rubbing salt in the wound."

Annja smiled. "I'm getting dinner. Will it gross you out if I sit with you?"

"What are they serving?"

"Looks like spaghetti and meatballs."

Tom blanched and bolted from the galley. Annja watched him dart past Cole, who had just entered, and shook her head.

"I'm guessing," Cole said, "that he's not actually all that well yet."

"Doesn't seem to be," Annja said. "Listen, sorry about earlier."

"About what?"

"Sheila and the shark."

Cole let a small grin play across his face but his voice was grim. "Sounds like a bad sea ditty they'd sing down at a dive bar."

"It does," Annja said. "But I don't want you thinking I'm some sort of bloodthirsty woman out for vengeance."

"I don't think that at all. I just couldn't stay to watch it happen. Maybe because it goes against everything I've come to learn about sharks. For me, seeing something like that would cause me to question everything I know." He shook his head. "It's crazy, right? I mean, here I am spending all my life studying this incredible fish and then we encounter this one. And it acts like a bad movie prop."

Annja shrugged. "All I know is it's big and seems utterly deadly and hell-bent on eating people."

"That's the thing," Cole said. "It's what I don't understand. I've seen other sharks in action attacking fish and whatnot. I've never seen something like this. Even the manner in which it attacked Sheila seemed wrong."

"I thought you didn't watch."

Cole looked sheepish. "My scientific curiosity got the better of me. I peeked from the wheelhouse."

"And what does your experience tell you about the shark?"

Cole shook his head. "To tell you the truth, I'm not so sure I'm ready to believe it *is* a shark."

"Sure looks like one to me." Annja helped herself to the pasta and then led them over to a table. "I mean, it's got the dorsal fin, the teeth, and moves like a plane through the water. Isn't that pretty much it?"

Cole bit into some garlic bread. "Remember when I

mentioned to you earlier that something hadn't clicked with me and I needed to mull it over some more?"

"Sure."

"Well, I've mulled. And what I've come up with is going to seem a bit strange to you."

Annja smirked. "Cole, you really need to spend a lot more time with me before you will succeed in shocking me. I can almost guarantee that anything you say won't surprise me."

"Genitals," Cole said.

Annja shook her head. "Okay, I was wrong. That's not exactly what I expected."

Cole smiled. "What I mean is that I'm not so sure I saw any genitals on the shark."

"No one did. All we could see was the mouth open and close down on Sheila. There wasn't much else, honestly," Annja said. "And it's probably better that there wasn't."

Cole shook his head. "I meant earlier. When the shark attacked my cage. Right before it rammed and I got knocked unconscious, there was a moment—a flash, really—where I could see the entire underside of the fish."

"And?"

"No genitals."

Annja chewed a meatball slowly. "I don't actually know what shark genitals look like, so obviously I'm going to have to take your word for it."

Cole held up his hand and formed it into a blade. "They're kind of like these claspers that the sharks use to hold on to each other prior to fertilization. It's quite fascinating, actually, when you see them in action—"

Annja stopped him. "Shark porn is not going to do a damned thing for me. Like I said, I'll take your word for it. If you say you didn't see any genitals, then that's enough."

Cole fell silent for a moment and then looked back up at Annja. "Of course, that begs a fresh question."

"What's that?"

"If it's not a shark, then what in God's name is it?"

"Another species of fish? Some type of underwater mammal?"

Cole shook his head. "Can't be a mammal. It would need to surface to breathe and we haven't see any incidents of that. No, can't be a mammal."

"How about a reptile? Maybe something like the Loch Ness Monster?"

Cole frowned. "I don't see it. This thing swims like a fish, and acts like a fish to some extent. I've got to assume it *is* a fish. But the lack of genitals is truly bizarre. How would it procreate?"

"Are you sure it would?"

Cole fixed a stare on Annja. "You're kidding, right?"

Annja leaned back. "I'm just saying that it's a big fish. Maybe it's the last of its kind. Maybe it doesn't reproduce because there are no others like it."

Cole shook his head. "I can't buy into that. It had to come from somewhere, right?"

"I guess." Annja went back to eating her pasta while Cole chewed on the same section of garlic bread he'd been gnawing on since they sat down. She regarded him for a moment. She could see he was going to stew about this for the rest of the night.

"I already know what you're thinking," Annja said.

He looked at her. "And what is that?"

"You want to get back in the water with it."

Cole smiled. "You're right. That's exactly what I want to do. I have to be sure about what I saw. And there's only one way to do that. I've got to get close to the shark."

"Hunter is going to freak out."

"Then maybe we shouldn't tell him."

"Oh, great, you want an accomplice. Hunter will get pissed

off at me, as well." Annja swirled some of the spaghetti strands around her fork. "We'll both be in the doghouse."

"At least we won't be lonely."

"And when are you thinking about revisiting your friend the shark?"

"How about after dinner?"

Annja looked at Cole. "You're not serious. Tell me you're just joking about this."

"I'm not."

Annja laid her fork down. "Okay, so allow me to point a few things out here. First, there's the whole nature of getting back into the water with that thing. And bear in mind that I only recently saw it devour Sheila, so I'm not especially keen on a repeat performance."

"Granted," Cole said with a vague smile on his face. "Go on, please."

"Well, the next thing is kind of obvious. Or at least it seems to me it damn well ought to be." She eyed Cole. "It's night. In other words, it's dark out there. And I'd imagine it's going to be pretty dark underwater. Just how are you supposed to be able to see anything?"

"I've got a flashlight. More of a spotlight, actually. It should do the business well enough for me to see what I need to."

"The genitals."

"Or lack thereof, yes." Cole wiped his mouth with a napkin. "Listen, I know it's crazy. I'm not trying to convince you otherwise. Odds are I probably need to get my head checked. Any normal person wouldn't even dream about doing this. I understand that. But I also understand that unless I settle this question, then the fear of this thing is going to immobilize everyone in this entire situation."

Annja leaned back in her chair and took a breath. "You know, I thought we'd all agreed that we wouldn't worry about the wreck or the possibility of treasure until we got to the bottom of who was sabotaging the ship."

"I pretty much thought we'd laid that question to rest with the discovery of Sheila and her subsequent demise."

Annja shook her head. "I was under the impression there was someone else."

"Why?"

"Well, because—" Annja stopped. "Well, Sheila told me there was."

Cole nodded. "So much for that."

Annja frowned. "She did admit that she'd attacked me in my room yesterday. Even after I asked if there'd been someone else. She said it was just her." Annja sighed. "All right, maybe we *are* safe now."

"Which means we can talk about diving again," Cole said. "The main purpose for us coming here."

"I thought that was the shark," Annja said.

"Well, yeah, but it's all connected." Cole took a bite of a meatball and chewed. "So, are you with me on this? I could use your help."

"If I say no, you're probably going to do it, anyway, aren't you?"

"It will take me a lot longer if I have to do it alone," Cole said. "There's the whole winch thing and clambering into the cage. It's not a very easy process working alone like that. Especially if I'm trying to do it on the sly."

"Like when everyone else is asleep?" Annja said. "I think that would probably be the smartest move, if you could even say any of this is smart."

Cole thought that over. "All right. We can wait until later. I don't think it will really affect the lighting situation. It's going to be dark any way we look at it."

"And this light of yours will work underwater?"

"Professional rig," Cole said. "I've used it before off the coast of South Africa…" He frowned.

"What?"

He looked up. "Huh?"

Annja pointed at him. "You frowned and your voice trailed off. What is it? Did you just think of something?"

Cole's frown deepened. "I guess I did."

"Please share with the rest of the class." Annja rested her chin on her hands. "Hopefully, it has something to do with not going through with your desire to dive into the pitch-black ocean."

"No such luck, toots." Cole took a drink of his soda. "Another thing just struck me about our friend the fish."

"Yeah?"

"The manner in which it attacks."

"What about it?"

Cole shook his head. "Doesn't make sense. It's not natural."

"What are you talking about?"

Cole pointed at her. "Remember when it attacked my cage?"

"Sure, I was there."

"But *how* did it attack my cage?"

Annja shook her head. "What exactly are you getting at? It rammed it. You know that. You felt it, I'm sure."

"Yes, that's what I wanted to hear. It rammed the cage. From a horizontal level. Right?"

"Well, yeah, its dorsal cut through the waves like it did when it attacked Sheila just a little while ago."

"It attacked horizontally." Cole nodded. "There is definitely something wrong with this picture."

"Then could you explain it to me, please? Because I'm not following you."

"It has to do with how most sharks track their targets. Most of them—not all, but most—will stay close to the bottom and use the light from above to silhouette their targets against the surface of the ocean."

"Okay."

"Once they've gotten a bead on the target, they will accelerate and attack vertically. They do it by coming up from below and biting. They don't attack from the side usually."

"But this shark does."

Cole nodded. "Right. Which is one more thing that just doesn't ring true about the nature of this beast. Great whites—which is what I think this fish is related to—are known for their vicious attacks from below. They will literally breach the water in South Africa. I've seen them decimate seals that way. But it's always the same thing—they attack from below. That way, the victim has little chance of seeing them. It's a sneak attack that has devastating results."

"Maybe this shark is different."

"Oh, it's different, all right. And that's what we've got to find out. Because, as I've told you all along, sharks are remarkably intelligent. They don't want to go into battle and risk injury to themselves. They choose the path of least resistance, attacking so suddenly that their prey has little time or ability to fight back."

Annja nodded. "So, then why does this shark attack differently."

"I don't know," Cole said. "But I intend to find out."

22

Annja crept out of her quarters and made her way down toward the stern deck. The luminous hands on her watch read twelve-fifteen and the dark turtleneck she wore with black pants helped her blend into the shadows.

At the entrance to the deck, she paused to make sure everything was clear. She knew Jax would be in the wheelhouse keeping watch. She and Hunter had come to an arrangement about that. And Hunter had made no secret that he intended to turn in after what he called a "long and exhausting day."

The coast seemed clear. Annja made her way out on to the deck. Cole had planned to arrive about twenty minutes before Annja, to get things ready for his descent into the inky water.

Annja waited. She saw Cole skirting the edge of the deck by the rail. He had the cage righted and clasped to the winch line. Annja could also make out oxygen tanks and the rest of Cole's diving gear. She took a calming breath. He certainly seemed ready to go through with his plans.

Annja walked over to him. They couldn't be seen from the

wheelhouse unless Jax stepped outside and heard noise. She'd still have to come down the stairs in order to ascertain what was going on.

The chances of that seemed remote.

"You all right?" she asked.

Cole nodded. "I'm almost set to go here. Just need to get the winch fired up." He put a hand on Annja's shoulder. "We won't have much time when we start that up. The noise is bound to draw attention. But I've got to do this, so whatever happens, try to stall them from hauling me back, okay?"

"I'll do my best."

"I know you will." Cole pointed at the cage. "I'm going to do it a little differently this time."

"How?"

"I'll be in the cage when you winch it overboard. I don't want to take a chance of missing the opening in the dark. It's safer that way."

Annja almost laughed. "I think this is the first time I've heard you suggest that you do something that qualifies as 'safe.'"

"Maybe I'm changing."

"I doubt that."

"Me, too."

Annja watched Cole scramble up the cage and sit on the top as he cinched down his weight belt and tanks. He gave her the thumbs-up and then lowered himself through the opening. He dropped in lightly, without making much noise.

"Let's do this," Cole whispered.

Annja moved over to the winch and fired it up. The noise of the hydraulics hissing seemed incredibly loud compared to when they weren't sneaking around.

Figures, she thought. Things are always noisier when you're doing something wrong.

She pressed the winch into action and watched as it extended and started to lift the cage off the deck. Cole grabbed onto the bars and nodded at Annja. With the regulator in his mouth, he looked like some type of alien. Annja smiled and waved once as she directed the winch over the edge of the boat.

The cage touched the murky blackness of the ocean and started to slide beneath the depths. When it was buoyant, the top of the cage rested just below the surface.

Annja slid away from the winch and walked toward the side of the boat. She watched as Cole switched on the brilliantly bright spotlight and started shining it through the water.

Now it was just a matter of waiting.

Annja leaned on the rail and tried to peer through the darkness. There was no way she could see what was coming until the last minute. She imagined that huge fin cutting through the darkness, headed straight for Cole's cage.

Her stomach cramped up at the thought. What would she do if it went bad? What if the shark was able to ram its way into the cage? How would she save Cole? She could try to winch him out, but if the shark bit down, she'd be dealing with its weight, as well. And that would cripple the crane.

Cole would be on his own.

She wondered if he'd gone through all those scenarios in his head prior to embarking on this craziness. Annja sighed. She'd met a lot of men in her time that she considered a few sandwiches shy of a picnic. But Cole, as much as he seemed crazy, was also rational. He was trying to sort through this problem—the questions he had about this shark—and he was determined to do whatever it took to get the answers.

She found that admirable.

I'd probably like it even more if it didn't entail him risking death to do it, she thought.

The spotlight cut through the water in all directions. She wished that Cole had radio contact with her. It would make the wait a lot less tense. It would probably have been nice for him, as well, she thought.

But they didn't have the radios. And they had to wait. Annja on deck and Cole in the water.

They could have prepared some chum for the shark. A few fish heads and assorted bloody goop in the water would draw it in nice and fast.

She glanced down and frowned. What was Cole doing? He had one of his gloves off.

That water looks terribly cold, Annja thought.

She saw a flash of metal.

Cole took his knife and cut into the palm of his hand. The ambient light from the spotlight showed an immediate cloud of dark blood mixing with the ocean water. Annja shook her head. He must have had the same idea about the chum line. And not to be too concerned, he cut his own palm and waved it around in the water trying to attract the shark.

She wondered if it would work.

"What the hell is going on down here?"

Annja turned and saw Jax descending the stairs. She looked over at the winch and then at the water. "Oh, shit. Don't tell me the nutty professor is down there trying to attract the shark."

"He is."

"You helped him?"

Annja shrugged. "He raised some interesting questions."

"Like what? How he'd taste to the shark after it chews him up? Jesus, Annja, you realize this is completely nuts?"

Annja nodded. "Yeah. I'm not crazy about it. But he would have done it, anyway, if I hadn't helped him. Cole's like that. At least, this way, I can be here if something goes wrong."

Jax shook her head. "You mean *when* something goes wrong. Because looking at this situation, I can already see that happening." She took a breath and sighed. "Garin warned me that you sometimes made decisions that left him speechless."

"That was nice of him," Annja said. "Are you going to stay here and tell me how bad I am for helping him?"

"Nah, but Hunter's going to go into a conniption fit when he hears about this."

"Now why would he hear about it?"

Jax looked at her. "You want me to pretend I don't know what's going on? When I'm on the bridge and manning the wheelhouse? That would cost me a hell of a lot with Hunter."

"But it would gain you a powerful ally in me."

Jax shrugged. "I don't need a powerful ally. I've already got one of my own and his name is Garin."

"Garin doesn't have the sword."

"No, but he does have a lot of other stuff." Jax smiled. "A lot of other stuff that I can certainly find a use for."

"So you'd sell me out for that?"

Jax sighed. "Probably not. But if it happens, it happens. I can't explain it, Annja. I've been on my own a long time and watching out for numero uno is the way I live my life."

"I know a lot of people like that. Most of them are incredibly selfish and lack any sort of compassion or ability to see things from another perspective," Annja said.

Jax frowned. "If you're going to stand here and insult me all night, I'll go back to the bridge."

"Maybe you should."

Jax spun and climbed the steps to the wheelhouse. Annja watched her go, trying to figure out what made Jax tick. She sighed and turned back to the cage floating in the darkness.

She could see Cole down below. The bleeding seemed to have stopped on the cut he'd made on his palm. Annja wondered how long it would take for blood to dissipate and work its way down the current to where waiting sharks could smell it?

Cole's spotlight continued to move back and forth in all directions. She wondered if he was trying some sort of visual experimentation. Not being able to talk with him was a real disadvantage.

Maybe Annja could have even helped if she knew what to do.

She frowned. Somehow Cole would have to figure this one out for himself. And Annja hoped he wouldn't regret his decision.

Coming from some distance away, she thought she heard a splash. But it was a small sound compared to the wind that had suddenly whipped up around her and made her shiver despite the warm clothes she wore. I could have done with adding a sweater to my outfit, she realized.

The waves lapped against the ship and the *Seeker* lolled slightly in the current. They'd stayed at anchor, Hunter not willing to move off this particular stretch because of the proximity to the *Fantome*.

She wondered if their position had something to do with the shark's interest in them. Where do sharks go when the sun sets? She knew that some sharks hunted at night, but otherwise, where did they go? Did they even sleep?

I don't know enough about these things to even pretend I'm stupid, she thought with a grin. She decided to ask Cole about that when he got back topside.

Annja jerked her head around. Something else had splashed far out in the water beyond the range of Cole's spotlight.

She'd definitely heard something.

She peered into the darkness. She couldn't see a thing.

A quick glance down told her that Cole was still okay and, judging from his body movement and the way he floated in the ocean, that nothing had drawn his attention.

But something was out there.

Annja felt certain of it.

She tried getting Cole's attention, but his mask wouldn't give him much peripheral vision. He wouldn't notice her unless he happened to look up and see her waving at him.

And that didn't seem likely.

Dammit. Annja frowned and turned back to the direction where she'd heard the noise. It's out there, she thought. Out there and waiting. Maybe it's just toying with Cole. Maybe it will make a surprise attack.

I can't let him down.

She heard a rush of movement from behind her and turned around. Jax was coming back down the stairs.

Fast.

"You back to make amends?" Annja said.

Jax shook her head. "No. That damned fish is. It's on the scope. If Cole wants to have an encounter with that shark, he's going to get his wish. Real soon."

23

Annja looked down at Cole bobbing in the cage. She could tell that he'd seen the shark by how his body had stiffened. His spotlight was shooting straight behind the stern of the boat, tracking something in the water some distance away. Annja could just make out the slow-moving shape as it cruised in toward the cage and then broke away to the left.

She frowned and understood why Cole was puzzled with the shark itself. He was right that it seemed to behave unlike the other sharks she'd seen when she went diving with Cole off Montauk.

Cole tracked the shark with his light as it prowled the waters. It was still a good distance away and Annja had trouble making out any details.

As for Cole, Annja thought he seemed more relaxed now. She could see him floating and keeping himself locked on the shark. Every now and again, the dorsal fin would break the surface of the water and then it would submerge again. The effect reminded Annja of a seesaw and it was another difference that she found vaguely disturbing.

Jax came to stand next to Annja. "If he gets killed, Hunter is going to feed us both to the shark."

Annja nodded. "I don't think that's going to happen."

"Why in the world not? That thing's huge. And it seems to be sizing him up, if I'm seeing it properly."

But Annja shook her head. "I can't place it, but something is not right. Cole knew there was something strange about it and that's why he wanted to get back in there. I hope he's getting his answers now."

Jax looked at Annja. "I hope so, too, because Hunter's on his way out here."

Annja turned and saw Hunter running down the steps. "Is he out there with that thing?" he shouted.

Annja nodded. "It's not what you think it is."

"Suicide? No? Then tell me what it is, Annja. And tell me why you both felt the need to go behind my back on this."

"Cole thinks there's something, well, fishy, about the shark."

Hunter stopped. "What are you talking about? That thing killed Jock and then it killed Sheila. What the hell is left to figure out? It's deadly and he shouldn't be in there with it."

"True. I tried to talk him out of it, but you know how he is when he gets his mind on something."

Hunter sighed. "Yeah, I know. He's pretty much unstoppable. Guy's obsessed about stuff."

"Yeah, seems as if you both get like that," Annja said.

Hunter came to stand by the stern of the boat. "How's he doing?"

Jax pointed. "It's still cruising around out there, maybe fifty yards to the port side. It hasn't approached the boat beyond thirty meters. I can barely see a thing except this occasional shape in the water."

"Cole's doing better under the water," Annja said. "His spotlight's got a bead on it."

"At least he can't be surprised," Hunter said. "That's a positive, I suppose."

Annja watched Cole's beam of light. It was just catching the dark gray shape moving through the water. The shark seemed content to merely observe right now.

"Maybe it's still full from earlier," Jax said. Then she blanched. "That came out sounding a lot worse than I meant it."

"How did he ever attract the damned thing?" Hunter asked.

"Cut his hand open," Annja said. "He waved the blood in the water and a few minutes later the shark showed up."

Hunter groaned. "You're joking."

Annja shook her head. "Nope. You know he'll do whatever it takes to accomplish his objectives. That apparently extends to include mutilating various parts of his body."

"Wonderful," Hunter said.

"Where'd it go?" Jax's voice held strains of tension. "I just had it and now it's gone."

Annja peered into the darkness. But the shape in the water seemed to have vanished. "Is it gone?"

Hunter shrugged. "I could barely see it to begin with."

Annja glanced down at Cole in the cage, but even he seemed unsure of the shark's position. His spotlight cut back and forth through the water. He must have lost it, too, Annja thought.

"Great," Jax said. "How can something that big simply up and vanish?"

"It must know these waters," Hunter said. "That gives it an immediate advantage over us."

"We didn't have an advantage, anyway," Annja said. "After all, we're on the boat and it's in the water."

"I'm staying on the boat," Jax said. "Things get out of hand, you can jump in the water if you want, Annja."

Hunter frowned. "Why on earth would she do that?"

Jax bit her lip. "No reason. Just in case she felt like helping Cole."

"By sacrificing herself?" Hunter shook his head. "That's ridiculous. No one's worth dying for like that."

Annja kept scanning the waves but didn't see anything. She frowned. This wasn't going down the way Cole had predicted it would. Annja felt uneasy at the thought of Cole in the water. She wondered whether it was because something was wrong or just stress over the situation as a whole.

"It's gone," Hunter said. "I can't see it moving around anywhere out there. Maybe it got bored or sensed that there really wasn't any food at all, but that Cole was baiting it."

"I wouldn't think a shark cage would deter a forty-foot shark," Jax said. "Especially considering that it attacked it once before."

"Maybe that's why," Hunter said. "Maybe it didn't have such a good time ramming it."

"Cole has always insisted that they're very smart creatures," Annja said. "But I wish we'd seen it retreat or swim away rather than just vanish. I don't like that."

"Hey."

They looked back down at the cage. Cole was poking his head out of the top.

Annja waved. "You okay?"

"I guess." Cole glanced around, shining his spotlight all over the top of the water. He frowned. "I guess it's gone."

"Did you get a good look?"

He frowned. "Not really. It stayed too far away for me to see its underside."

Hunter sighed. "And why would you want to do a thing like that? It's not enough to see it barreling straight at you?"

"Genitals," Annja said.

"What?"

"Cole couldn't remember seeing any genitals on the fish earlier and that had him concerned."

Hunter looked at Annja and then stared at Cole. "You're risking your life just so you can get a closer look at a shark's 'nads? That's a new one even for you, bro."

Cole waved him off. "I'm not sure what I saw. I didn't see anything this time around, though. It seemed to stay deliberately far away. It was frustrating as hell. I wanted it to come in closer."

Annja nodded at the winch. "You planning on staying in there and getting hypothermia or do you want me to winch you out?"

Cole frowned. "Guess I'll come out. It must have gone someplace else that I couldn't see."

Annja nodded and walked to the winch. "Probably better this way. That water's awfully cold."

"Fish 'nads," Hunter said. "That's almost unbelievable."

"That's why we couldn't tell you ahead of time," Annja said. "He knew you'd laugh at the idea and then not let him go out."

"Yeah, like I could ever stop him. One thing about Cole, he doesn't take no for an answer," Hunter said.

"I've seen that," Annja said.

Hunter nodded at the winch. "You want some help?"

Annja frowned and pressed the button to start the winch. But nothing happened. "That's weird. It doesn't seem to have any power."

The lights on the boat went out.

"Shit!" Hunter bumped into Annja. "We lost power."

"How did that happen?"

"I don't know, but I'd better get the backup generator online. I don't want Cole left out there."

"What's going on?" Cole's voice floated back to them.

Annja felt her way to the back railing. "Power's out. Hunter's gone to fix it. Can you hold on?"

"Do I have a choice?"

"Not really."

Cole's spotlight cut through the darkness and illuminated the back of the boat. Annja could see him almost sitting on top of the cage. She frowned. "Are you sure you want to be positioned like that?"

Cole nodded. "I just checked again. The shark's gone. No idea where." He sighed. "I didn't get what I needed, Annja."

"I guess that means you'll be going back out tomorrow, huh?"

"Yep."

Jax looked at Annja. "I'd better get back to the wheelhouse."

"Can you find your way there in the dark?"

Jax frowned. "Good point." She turned toward Cole. "Can you shine that thing on the stairs so I don't kill myself?"

The spotlight beam suddenly illuminated the back steps and Jax walked off, making her way carefully up and then disappearing beyond.

Annja turned back to the ocean. "Nothing moving out there, huh?"

Cole shook his head. "Just bobbing along here. How long do you think it'll take Hunter to fix the lights?"

"No idea, why?"

"I need to go to the bathroom."

"Can you hold it?"

"Water's cold," Cole said. "I might just go in my wet suit. At least it'll warm me up a little."

"That's gross," Annja said. "Try to hold it."

"I'm trying."

The lights on the back of the boat flickered and then went out again. Annja frowned and wondered if this was more sabotage that Sheila had set up or if it was a genuine problem with the *Seeker*'s electrical system.

"Hey, Annja?"

She turned back toward Cole. "Yeah?"

"I was thinking about something relating to what we were discussing earlier at dinner."

"And what's that?"

"Remember when I was talking about the way the shark seemed to attack? How it didn't come up from below but made a more horizontal-style ramming attack?"

"Yes?"

"Well, I think I have it figured out."

"Figured what out? Why it attacks like that?"

"Yeah."

Annja spread her arms. "Well, go ahead and explain it to me. I'd be very interested to hear why."

"I think the shark is—"

Annja had just enough time to catch her breath as a massive shape suddenly blotted out her view of Cole and the cage. She heard a terrible sound of crunching metal and splashing water as the shark thundered into the cage.

"Cole!"

There was another explosion of water jetting into the air, spraying the back deck of the *Seeker* and Annja as it came back down.

And then everything was silent.

"Cole!" Annja screamed.

The lights returned to the *Seeker* a moment later. Annja scanned the ocean, her eyes coming to rest on the dented and battered shark cage still floating lopsided in the water.

But there was no trace of Cole.

24

Annja stood on deck paralyzed. She didn't say anything. And she didn't move. After five more minutes rolled by, she heard movement behind her and knew it would be Hunter coming back from the engine room.

"Where's Cole?" he said. But then he saw the mangled cage floating half in and half out of the water. "Jesus," he shouted. "What happened?"

Annja shook her head. "When the power went out, we couldn't see anything. Jax went back to the wheelhouse and Cole, well, he was waiting for you to get the power on so I could winch him out. And then…" Her voice trailed off as she struggled to describe the explosion of motion that had suddenly occurred and taken Cole.

Hunter stayed quiet for a moment. "I don't think there's anything you could have done, Annja."

"I should have persuaded him not to go out there."

"You wouldn't have been able to talk him out of it. I know my brother. And believe it or not, I think he'd tell you that he's happier going this way than if he hadn't been doing what he loved."

Annja shook her head. "Doesn't make this any easier to take. He was a good friend."

"He was my brother," Hunter said. He shook his head. "I can't believe he's gone."

Annja watched the water sway back and forth against the cage. Then she walked over to the winch. "No sense keeping the cage out there."

Hunter nodded. "Let me help you."

Annja fired up the winch and watched as it took in the slack and then started to ease the cage out of the surf. As it did, both she and Hunter could see the full effect of the incredible ramming attack that had shredded the wire bars like they'd been made out of straw.

Hunter gasped. "I've never heard of anything that could cause that kind of destruction."

"Me, either," Annja said. "And yet here we have the proof right in front of us that something can do just that."

The winch slowly brought the cage back over the side and Hunter eased it into position on the deck. As the cage came to rest, Annja moved around it, examining it. The bars had simply given way under the assault. But otherwise, there was nothing to suggest that Cole had even been there. "The ocean must have washed the blood away."

Hunter cleared his throat. "Or he might just have been swallowed whole. Given the shark's size, it's entirely possible."

Annja shuddered. "It's too horrible to even think about." She couldn't imagine what that would be like—to be swallowed completely and then crushed under the jaws while those serrated teeth ripped through wet suit and then flesh and bone.

"My God," she said quietly.

"We need to destroy this fish," Hunter said. "I don't even care about the treasure sitting beneath us. I just want this thing dead and gone. If for no other reason than pure and unadulter-ated vengeance."

Annja looked at him. "At least you're honest about it."

Hunter shook his head. "I wouldn't even try to conceal the fact that I want this thing dead worse than anything I've ever felt before in my life."

"But how?" Annja leaned against the back railing. "How are we supposed to kill it when we can't even get out there?"

"I don't know," Hunter said. "But we've got to do something. It's better than just sitting here and doing nothing. And we owe it to three memories to try, anyway."

"Maybe we should call in the Navy or something."

Hunter smirked. "What, and ask to borrow a few torpedoes or depth charges to blow the thing up? As if they'd even bother with us. No, we're on our own dealing with this creature. And we will definitely deal with it. Mark my words."

Annja watched him walk past the cage and lay a hand on it for the briefest of moments before climbing the steps toward the wheelhouse. She turned back to the ocean.

Her heart ached. I knew this would happen, she thought. Why did Cole have to go out there and risk his life trying to prove something?

And what had he been about to say? The shark is...what?

It didn't make any sense to her. And then she heard the splash. She turned abruptly toward the sound on her left side.

Was someone out there?

"Cole?"

Her voice trailed off, drowned out by the strong breeze that had kicked up. And then she saw the triangular dorsal fin just within the range of the deck lights. The fin cut its way through the waves.

Damn you, Annja thought. You took one of my friends.

The fin swerved away from the boat and then cut a course

a few degrees off the starboard side. To Annja's eyes it looked as if it was zigzagging back and forth.

Is it going to attack the boat? If it did, it could do a lot of damage. And that would mean a really big problem for the crew. If any of them went into the water, the shark would devour them.

Was that its goal? Did it want the boat so badly damaged that everyone would have to abandon ship and go into the water? She looked at the waves lapping against the side of the boat and wondered how cold it was. Would death come from the hypothermia or from the shark? Which would get to them first?

The shark is…

Annja pondered Cole's words. Is what? Big? That was obvious. Along with being dangerous and deadly and to be avoided and pretty much everything else Annja could think of.

What had Cole been about to say before the shark had attacked him?

Maybe he'd been trying to tell her something critical that he thought she needed to know in case he was attacked. But what? Had Cole been able to see the shark on a collision course with him? Was he trying to save Annja from it?

It was possible, she supposed, but it didn't make any sense. Cole had seemed utterly relaxed as he bobbed atop that cage. She frowned. Anyone else would have been terrified.

But not Cole.

Was he simply courageous beyond any shadow of doubt? Or did he know something?

Annja thought back to the first time when she had seen the shark. The head had lifted out of the water, that immense enormous maw filled with those serrated teeth.

And yet…

Jax came down the steps behind her. "Hunter just told me."

Annja shook her head. "It happened way too fast for me to do anything."

Jax shrugged. "What were you supposed to do? Dive in and fend it off with the sword? How well would that have worked?"

"I have no idea. I've never done anything like that before."

"Exactly," Jax said. "That's the thing. You always have to remember to look out for numero uno. That's you. If you couldn't help without risking your own life, then it's not worth it."

"He was my friend. I owed him more than I tried."

"You didn't owe him crap," Jax said. "You know how many people I've had tell me that I owed them something? Tons. I don't owe anyone anything. Where I'm at in my life is where I got myself."

Annja looked at her. "Yeah, but doesn't that seem a little selfish to you? Not exactly compassionate of your fellow human beings."

"What—it's selfish to look after yourself?"

"I didn't say that."

Jax pointed at the ocean. "Look, Annja, I don't know what sort of thing you and Cole had going on, if anything, but the fact of the matter is, he's gone. There's nothing you could have done to protect him even with that gift you have."

"Doesn't feel like a gift right now."

Jax nodded. "Yeah, I know that feeling."

"Do you?"

"Well, not exactly in your context, of course. I think there's only one sword and you've got it. But I can grasp the idea that something that's supposed to make you better, able to do more, suddenly feeling as though it's the worst thing to have to bear."

Annja nodded. "Yeah. You're right."

"I'm making some coffee. With a bit of whiskey in it. You want a cup?"

Annja pointed at the ocean. "There's nothing left of him. No trace of his body anywhere."

Jax nodded. "Well, yeah. That's good, though, right?"

"Why would you say that?"

"Well, it's just that you don't want to have body parts floating on the waves. You'd have to collect it all and try to get it back ashore for the funeral. In a way, it's almost better this way."

Annja stared at her. "Go make that coffee."

"Just saying," Jax said. But she turned and walked away. "I'll let you know when it's done."

Annja watched her go and then turned toward the ocean. She heard another splash and then saw the huge dorsal fin cutting back and forth in front of her. She frowned and wanted to scream at it.

She felt as if it was taunting her. Swimming out there like that, it looked as though it would stay just at the edge of the lights, so she couldn't get a precise fix on its location.

Why was it coming back again?

Did it want more? Could it see her from where it swam? Did it feel the fury she felt at losing Cole to it?

The fin drifted away and then came zipping right back toward the boat. Twice more it did this and, each time, Annja wondered if she would need to brace for the impact of its body slamming into the hull of the boat.

But just as she thought it was going to impact, it would veer away and travel off on another tack.

Annja's heart hammered in her chest. She wanted to kill that beast, the monster that had brought so much death in the short time she'd been on board the *Seeker*.

"Come a little closer," Annja said quietly. "And I'll happily cut you to ribbons with my sword."

But the fin only drifted away from her and continued on its never-ending zigzag.

What the hell was going on here?

Annja willed the sword to manifest itself. Immediately, it

was in her two hands, its shimmering blade casting off a pale luminescence in the ship's light.

Annja felt strength flow into her limbs and she took a few practice swings with the sword, feeling the surge of energy in her system from holding it.

The fin cut by close again. Annja took a halfhearted swipe at it and then she laughed abruptly. "You're damned lucky you're out there and not on dry land. Otherwise, we'd be having a different conversation."

She looked at the length of the blade in her hands and swung it overhead.

She felt the power of the sword as it sang through the air, cutting at wisps of nothing in the night sky. Annja spun the blade around and flipped it over. Somehow, she felt utterly indestructible.

The shark fin again came close to the ship and then veered away.

Annja watched it.

"Damn thing," she said.

She wanted vengeance as badly as Hunter did. Annja saw the fin turn to head straight back at the ship.

Power flowed through every cell of her body. She felt electric.

Annja gripped the sword in both her hands, squeezing the hilt until she felt there was nothing that could wrest the blade from her grasp.

She leaped into the air, clearing the railing and the dive platform. She looked down and saw, for the first time, the entire length and girth of the massive shark.

And then she was plunging down faster and faster, through the air, directly at the back of the mighty beast.

She readied herself to drive the sword straight into its black heart.

25

At the last second, the shark veered, almost as if it could sense the attack coming at it from above. Annja tried to redirect herself but splashed down a second later. The abrupt shock of the cold water almost made her convulsively suck in water. But she surfaced and sputtered.

Annja bobbed in the waves, spinning around and searching for her target. She still held the sword in front of her, but she was immediately aware of how utterly exposed she was. Whenever she'd fought before, she'd only had to worry about people in front of her, behind her or to her sides.

Now she had to worry about being attacked from below.

And she could barely see anything in the darkness. The moon and the ship's lights gave limited visibility.

Where was the shark?

Annja spun around in the water and kept checking herself. So far, the shark hadn't attacked.

There was something different about this creature and

Annja was determined to find out what it was. Right after she killed it.

She heard a splash to her right and she turned again, searching the darkness for the source of the noise.

She held the sword aloft and scanned the surface of the water. Annja saw the triangular dorsal cutting back and forth in the waves a hundred yards or so away from her.

She bobbed in the swells and considered her options. She could wait for the shark to notice her, if it hadn't already.

Or she could attack it.

Annja paused for a moment, wondering how she had ended up in such an incredible situation. But the hell with it. This shark had already taken the lives of three people. And Annja was determined that no one else would die in its jaws.

She returned the sword to the otherwhere and swam through the waves toward the shark. Her strokes were broad and powerful and Annja cut her way through the current, almost oblivious to its pull on her.

Her legs fluttered like a motor and Annja gained on the slow-moving shark.

But then the dorsal fin turned.

The shark headed straight toward her.

Annja stopped and treaded water. "Yeah, that's right. Come and get me, you bastard."

Annja summoned the sword and held it up in front of her, its point up, the blade between her body and the approaching shark.

Her heart hammered in her chest, but she felt no fear. Not this time. She was done being scared. And she would see this creature dead by her hand.

The fin bore down on her. Annja had estimated the distance from the dorsal to the shark's mouth at about fifteen feet. She knew she had about three seconds to ready herself.

The head reared up out of the surf, the massive gaping maw

widening and showing the serrated teeth that had shredded three other humans.

Annja gripped the sword as the blackness of the maw seemed to suck all the light out of the surrounding area.

It's even bigger than I thought, Annja realized. In an instant, the mouth swept over her, blocking the night sky. Annja almost closed her eyes but then forced herself to dive forward and down the gullet of the fish before the teeth could start to shred her.

She had no idea what was happening. She'd expected it to stink of rotting flesh. But it didn't.

She realized she could see some sort of light somewhere ahead of her. How was that possible?

Then she heard a sound. Like a motor.

Behind her, she felt the mouth close and the outside world vanished. Annja was inside the shark.

But this was no shark.

Ahead of her, Annja could see very little, but a dim red bulb gave off light. She could breathe. Oxygen was being pumped into the area. She could almost sit up, but stayed on her stomach, aware that there was a small amount of water on the floor of the belly of the shark. Not that she cared. She'd already been soaked when she jumped into the ocean.

She almost laughed. So this was what Cole was trying to tell her.

"The shark is fake."

Or something like that. It didn't really matter at this point. Annja knew that she had nothing to fear from this machine. She even twisted around and felt her way back toward the opening of the mouth and ran her finger over one of the teeth. They were made of heavy-duty rubber.

But what was the point of this thing? Who would go through the incredibly complex and expensive process of building this machine? And why would they resort to using it?

Annja leaned back in the holding compartment and listened

as the engine sounds changed. They were revving up and she felt the shark start to turn and then descend, vanishing from close to the surface.

We're going deep, she thought.

Wherever this led, Annja wanted to be ready for anything, so she kept the sword with her. There wasn't much sense in going into the unknown unarmed. She'd already had enough surprises thrown at her.

"At least I'm not dead," she said quietly to herself. Considering it all, she was amazed at what had come over her. What made her think she could jump overboard and take on a forty-foot shark that had supposedly killed three people?

Insanity.

But she decided it was simply a matter of being tired of the stalemate that existed. Coupled with the sudden violent loss of Cole, it had just been too much for her to put up with.

Drastic times call for drastic measures, she thought. She glanced around. Although this thing might be the most drastic of all.

Her ears started to pop from the increasing pressure. Annja swallowed reflexively and the pressure dissipated momentarily. She felt the shark level out and the engines seemed to kick up another notch. Wherever they were headed, they were going fast.

Was this what happened to Cole earlier? If so, then surely he had to be alive. She hoped that was the case. It would be tragic if she let herself get excited only to be let down again.

And what about Sheila? What had happened with her? Had she been swallowed up whole by this machine, as well, and carted off somewhere? That meant there would be at least one person at the other end of this trip who would not be friendly toward Annja.

And if she still had the gun in her possession that meant Annja might have to be ready for an immediate fight.

She patted the sword, relieved that it went anywhere with her. She certainly couldn't use it now, it was too tight a space in the shark's hold. But whenever she reached her destination, she had to assume there'd be more space.

She looked around, marveling at the airtight structure of the machine. A steady volume of oxygen filtered in from two holes on either side of her, cooling and providing her with air to breathe. Meanwhile, all of the gaps had been sealed to be watertight, save for whatever happened inside when the shark's mouth opened.

Clearly, the machine was not designed to kill anyone, but rather to carry them away to some unspecified location.

But where?

There had to be a point sooner or later where they would stop. To go far would require fuel, and food and water for the passengers. Annja decided that they would be getting to the destination soon enough.

She tried to relax and enjoy the ride. It was a smooth sensation and she had no sense of direction aside from going up or down. She reasoned that it would be good to rest and be ready for whatever greeted her next.

She sat up and leaned back, letting her head rest against the wall of the holding compartment, with the sword across her lap. In the dim interior, the gray luminescent light contrasted with the red bulb and provided enough light for Annja to see, but aside from the oxygen holes, there was nothing to observe. The walls were featureless.

Fascinating, she thought. She couldn't wait to find out who owned this machine and why they'd had it built. She could only guess what the reason might have been.

Dave Crosby had been with the SEALs. Was he still working with them in some undercover role on Hunter's team? If so, why? Was someone aboard the *Seeker* a terrorist?

Would SEALs even have access to this type of technology?

She knew they had smaller submarines they called SDVs—
swimmer delivery vehicles—but they looked nothing like this
and they were nowhere near as technologically advanced. The
SDVs she'd seen looked like oversize steel torpedo casings that
let SEALs squeeze inside and travel a distance to their targets.
Compared to the SDVs, Annja was riding in a Bentley.

No, there had to be something else to it all. And she felt
certain it had something to do with the HMS *Fantome* and
its treasure. Hadn't Hunter mentioned rival treasure hunters?
Could this machine be a tool of those rival hunters? Were they
purposefully trying to scare the *Seeker* and her crew off the
dive site so they could take it for themselves?

It almost seemed too fantastic to be true and yet Annja had
no other possible explanations for what was happening.

Maybe I should just stop thinking and rest, she thought.

She leaned back and closed her eyes, taking deep breaths
that made her eyelids feel heavy.

The shark started to ascend. Annja opened her eyes. We're
going up. But where?

The engine started to slow down. Wherever they were going,
it was definitely on a final approach. To Annja it almost sounded
like when a plane is approaching a runway and the flaps start to
come down while the engine revs up and then throttles back.

She wondered if the shark had landing gear.

More oxygen started coming out of the holes and the breeze
made Annja shiver just a little bit. Why would they be pumping
more air into her now? Did they want her to wake up in case
she'd fainted or fallen asleep?

Annja gripped the sword. Wherever they were, Annja fully
intended to jump out just as soon as the mouth opened to let
her escape.

She yawned suddenly, aware that she was seeing small spots
in front of her eyes. Spots? She started to feel very heavy and
relaxed.

She bit her tongue and felt blood flow.

Dammit!

They were going to knock her out prior to getting her out of the shark. Annja tried to cover her nose and mouth with her clothes, but it didn't help. Annja spat out a bit of ocean water and felt even more tired.

She tried to concentrate on the sword, willing it to help her stave off the effects of the gas.

But it was no good.

I can't be found with the sword, Annja thought. And as much as she hated to do it, she closed her eyes and the sword disappeared. At least they wouldn't find her with it and she could use its surprise factor to her advantage when she woke up.

If she woke up.

Annja considered the possibility that they were drugging her now so she wouldn't give them trouble and they could calmly and methodically kill her at their leisure.

She frowned. No. If they'd wanted her dead, she already would be.

Wherever she was going, they wanted her alive.

And as Annja drifted off to sleep, she found herself wondering what she would see when she woke up.

26

When Annja awoke she was covered with a thin, threadbare blanket made of coarse fibers that poked into the exposed bits of her skin. She shivered and realized that she was in a dank cell. A steady dripping sound of water told her that she might be underground or even below the waterline.

Where the hell am I? She got up and walked the expanse of the ten-foot-by-ten-foot holding cell. The walls were made of smooth stone and small rivulets of water cascaded down, only to disappear into a small drainage hole at one end of the room.

Annja had no memory of being taken out of the shark when they'd arrived, but of course, that would be due to the gas she'd breathed in. She wondered what was so top secret that they couldn't afford to let her know where she was. Or perhaps they knew about her sword?

She thought about Sheila. Sheila had been well briefed on Annja. That meant there was a leak somewhere. Annja tried to figure out how they could have learned about the existence of the sword. Did Garin have a leak in his organization? Or had Roux sold her out?

Annja frowned. If that had happened, then she would see to taking care of Roux herself.

Light came from a single bare bulb burning overhead. A small pull chain dangled from it and Annja tested it. The light shut off when she pulled and went on again when she repeated the process.

So they weren't necessarily looking to deprive her of sleep. She nodded. That was good news.

She sniffed and smelled the salt clinging to the air. They were at least near the ocean, but where? Or were they in some sort of massive underwater lair?

She wondered if Henderson was a reality instead of some story Sheila had told her. Annja tried to picture an old guy using his power to wield influence over the world by devising some mechanical shark that could terrorize people. She almost laughed. It sounded like a bad movie on the Sci Fi Channel.

She paced off the cell again just to get some blood flowing and tried to examine the walls. She wondered if they had any type of surveillance in the cell. But after checking the walls for what seemed like an hour, Annja couldn't find a single camera—pinhole or otherwise.

"Hello?" she called out.

Hearing her voice made her feel better at least. But she sounded hoarse. Some water would be good. She looked around and saw nothing but the crappy blanket they'd given her to ward off the chill.

She sat down and tried to figure out what was going on. Was Cole being held in another cell like this? Did he know what was happening? Or had they killed him?

And what about Sheila? Had she known about this before she jumped or fell into the ocean? Was it all part of some elaborate hoax designed to get the *Seeker* to move away from the *Fantome* so they could swoop in and claim it?

Annja thought of the story Sheila had told her regarding the crucifix of Joan of Arc. She wondered if that was true. Was there another relic of Joan's that could affect the vulnerability of the wearer?

Immortality.

She whistled to herself. Imagine what people would go through to get that. Anything, she concluded.

And that made this situation all the more dangerous.

She closed her eyes and checked on the sword. It hovered in the gray mist, ready for her to use. Annja opened her eyes and felt the wall closest to her hand. No, she thought; there would be no sense in trying to hack her way out of the cell.

She realized that she'd completely ignored the door to her cell, which was carved out of stone just like the rest of it. She could see no locking mechanism and figured it must have been bolted on the other side. A small slit cut into the door opened out beyond, but had a shutter on it.

Annja scampered over to it and tried to push the shutter back so she could look out.

It was locked.

She slumped back. So they were doing their best to keep as much information from her as possible. That was smart, Annja reasoned. If she had prisoners, she wouldn't want them knowing anything about their surroundings, either.

But it frustrated the hell out of her. She wanted to know what was going on. And for that, she needed information.

Annja's throat ached. She needed some fresh water. She glanced at the walls and the water running down them. She took a sniff and then put her lips to it.

She spat the water out when she tasted the salt in it. As tempting as it would be drink the salt water, she knew it would kill her. If she took in too much of it, her liver would shut down and she'd die within a day.

Annja sat again and tried to calm herself. She began doing some deep-breathing exercises.

She had no idea how long she sat that way but eventually she heard a noise. Footsteps approached her door, echoing along the length of the corridor.

She heard a click and the shutter was drawn back. She saw a hand slide a tray of food and a container of water into the room.

Annja dashed for the door, but the shutter slammed shut.

"Wait!" she called out.

The footsteps receded, but Annja could hear that they had gone to the right. At least she knew something. If she escaped the cell, she would go right instead of left.

Annja looked down at the tray of food. A simple ham sandwich with lettuce and cheese. An apple sat next to it. And the container of water was a small sixteen-ounce bottle.

Annja grabbed at it and tore the cap off. Her subconscious registered that there was no safety seal on the bottle and Annja froze.

What if they had drugged the water? What if they needed to keep her doped up for some reason?

She frowned. She needed the hydration. I'll have to risk it, she thought. And then she drank deep, feeling the cold liquid slosh down her throat. Another two gulps and she gasped as she brought the bottle away from her lips.

Thank God.

The water hadn't tasted funny, which buoyed her spirits some. She looked at the sandwich and then lifted the slices of cheese to see if there was a hidden surprise.

Nothing.

Annja tore into the sandwich and chewed it up while washing it down with more of the water. She would need to save some for later, knowing that it was never a good idea to simply assume that if your captors fed you once they would do so again.

But the food tasted wonderful and the apple was juicy and helped replenish her, as well. Annja chewed it slowly, welcoming the cleansing effect it had on her mossy teeth.

Before long, her meal was finished and Annja felt content at having ingested water and food. She tried to snuggle up to one of the dry parts of the wall and wrapped the blanket around her. She shivered and started to doze off.

As she relaxed deeper, she could hear other ambient sounds that drifted to her, bouncing from wall to wall. She thought she could hear the sounds of machines humming somewhere far off in the distance.

She wondered if they were generators or other machines designed to keep the drains flowing. If she was underwater in some sort of weird cavern, then they would need to keep the water under control or else the entire place would flood in a second and kill them all.

"Did you eat well?"

Annja's eyes snapped open. There was no one else in the cell with her.

"Who said that?"

"I did."

She frowned. The voice had an accent but one she couldn't quite make out since the speaker's volume seemed deliberately hushed.

Annja scrambled to her feet. Where was it coming from? She'd gone over every inch of the cell, and yet someone was talking to her, presumably through a speaker of some sort that she must have missed.

"Why am I here?" Annja asked as she continued searching for the source of the sound.

"You're here because you threaten our plans."

It seemed to be coming from near the roof of her cell. But

there was no way Annja could reach the ceiling to check it out. From where she stood, it appeared to be smooth stone, uninterrupted with any cracks or holes that would permit an intercom system from being installed.

"And what plans would those be?" she asked as they searched.

"All in good time."

"Tell me now."

There was a long pause. "No. I can see that you're busy trying to find the speaker system, so I'll leave you to that. Don't want to make it too easy for you, now do I?"

Annja frowned. It had to be some place in the roof of her cell. Did they have a camera up there, as well?

"How long are you going to keep me in here?"

"As long as is necessary."

Annja slumped back down against the wall. "Well, if you're planning on holding me here for any period of time, I hope you have the whole bathroom thing worked out because I'm going to need to use it soon."

She heard the lock release on the shutter and saw a pail come through before the shutter slammed closed again.

"You can use the pail."

Annja frowned. So much for modesty. "You've got to be kidding me. Don't you have a bathroom around here?"

"Of course we do. You do not, however. So I suggest you use the pail. We'll empty it during your meal breaks."

"This is disgusting."

"No one told you to get involved. Now you're simply living with the consequences of your own decisions."

"Go to hell," Annja said.

"As you wish."

Annja heard a click as the speaker system switched off. So she was under surveillance, after all. And she had to use a pail as a bathroom.

Fantastic.

She looked at the walls again and wondered if the sword would be able to cleave the rocks enough to get her out.

It might just be worth attempting if they didn't clue her in on what was happening soon.

Next meal, she thought. If I don't have some answers by then, I'll take matters into my own hands.

But what if the stone shattered the blade?

Well, that would mean she might be free of the sword. She could go back to living her life the way she wanted to.

Wasn't that a good thing?

She frowned. Who the hell knew anymore.

She pulled the blanket around herself and started to fall asleep. Then she opened her eyes again. They could still watch her.

Annja got to her feet and reached for the light cord. With a pull, she plunged the cell into darkness.

"No free shows," she said aloud.

But it didn't seem as if anyone was listening.

27

Annja woke up and switched the light back on. She figured that at least several hours had passed since she had fallen asleep. She drank the last of her water, but Annja felt refreshed and energized. She couldn't detect any trace of narcotics in the food or water, nor did she feel the sluggishness typical of having been drugged, so it seemed fairly certain they weren't trying to keep her doped up.

Just a prisoner.

Within the confines of her cell, Annja had no way of knowing what time it was. She could only guess, but it seemed that another food break should be coming soon. Nothing had happened since the mysterious voice overhead had started speaking to her, so Annja decided that it might be time to get herself out of the cell.

If she could.

First things first. She had to figure out where the surveillance was. If they saw what she intended to do, they might be able to send people to stop her. And Annja didn't want her party interrupted by those she hadn't invited.

The voice had come from above. But where? She stared at the ceiling, trying to scan it in-depth. But even so, the ceiling was at least three feet above her. And that meant she couldn't get her fingers onto the surface to check for possible hiding spots.

Her eyes went past the lightbulb and she stopped.

Was it possible to conceal something in a light fixture? She peered closer. The lightbulb screwed into a socket that was embedded in the stone ceiling. But as Annja tried to peer past the brightness of the light, she thought she could see something there. A small grill wrapped around the base of the socket.

It was a speaker. Definitely. She stopped looking at it and smiled. All right, she thought, I know where the sound comes from. But how are they watching me?

Would it make sense to house both the intercom system and the video camera in the same socket fixture? Maybe, but the real problem would be the light. It would make it hard to see much of anything happening in the cell.

Ideally, they'd have the camera positioned elsewhere. That way they could take advantage of the light source to get a good feed and picture of Annja.

But where would they put it?

And what if it was infrared or thermal? It wouldn't matter if Annja shut the light off. They would still be able to see what she was doing.

She went to the door and ran her fingers all over the surface and the jamb. She figured it would make the most sense to house it somewhere near there. They'd have a clear shot into the room and be able to see her from all angles.

Annja missed it the first time, but on the second round, her fingers felt a small nub that jutted out of the stonework. She went back and saw that it looked like a small half dome of acrylic.

So they had a pinhole with a fish-eye lens to see the entire room clearly.

Wonderful.

"What are you doing?"

Annja looked up at the lightbulb. "Excuse me?"

"You seem to be expressing a lot of interest in how your cell has been constructed. Take it from us, you can't get out of there until we want you out."

"I'm not thinking about escaping."

"Oh?"

Annja shook her head. "But I don't like being kept under surveillance. It annoys me. So I was looking to see where you've got the intercom system."

"And you found it?"

"In the lightbulb socket. Made the most sense, I suppose."

"Good girl."

"And the pinhole over the door."

"Ah, you found that, too, eh? Brilliant."

Annja frowned. "Is it really necessary?"

"Absolutely."

"Why don't you just tell me what it is that you want from me."

There was a pause. "You'll know when we tell you and not a moment before, Annja."

She frowned. They knew her name, as well. She wasn't all that surprised, but it was one more thing that annoyed her. She didn't like the other side knowing everything about her and her not knowing a damned thing.

"Time to eat again, Annja. Enjoy it."

She turned as the shutter went up and the tray and a fresh bottle of water came through the opening.

The shutter closed again. She had underestimated them.

They knew that being a prisoner she'd try to make her escape during mealtimes. And they'd kept her distracted while this one was delivered.

Annja looked at the plate of beef stew and French bread. There was a chocolate-chip cookie for dessert.

And the water.

Annja devoured her dinner. She was ravenous and realized that her body might be overcompensating for the stress and pressure of being held captive. She knew that there were a lot of different physiological reactions that could occur when a person was taken prisoner. Her system always seemed to demand food.

But Annja wouldn't let herself get duped again.

She finished the stew and the last piece of bread, using it to mop of the bits of gravy and small pieces of beef and carrots that had been left on the plate. She chewed slowly, relishing the last bite of the meal, which, she had to admit, was pretty damned good for prison food.

The chocolate-chip cookie had obviously been made recently and it was soft, her favorite. Annja frowned. Hello Stockholm Syndrome, she thought. I've been here less than a day and I'm already starting to find myself grateful to them for cooking me such nice meals.

It wasn't the exact definition of Stockholm Syndrome, but Annja knew that they were toying with her mind.

Fine, she decided. Let them. The next time mealtime comes around, I will get the hell out of here and find out what is really going on.

Heaven help them then, she thought with a smirk.

After dinner, Annja used the pail for the first time—after she shut the light off. It was an awkward and humiliating experience, but necessity demanded it.

She dozed for an hour or two, keeping herself partially primed to any sounds that might signal a change in procedure.

She expected it, since they would know she might have figured out their initial routine by now.

If they were going to alter things, then she wanted to be ready for it. And this time, she'd have the sword out when they came with her food.

Still in the dark, she crawled back to the door and used her hands to explore the shutter. Even though it was locked shut, she could tell it opened to the other side of the door. That meant that the shutter could be lifted up and the meal tray slid through.

But this time, Annja would be sliding her sword through instead.

The trick would be to grab the hand as it came through the shutter and then use that to gain leverage.

She frowned. But what then? She couldn't very well hold them in place and tell them to open her door at the same time. In order to do that, she'd have to give up her control and trust that they would.

And why the hell would they do that?

Annja slumped over and sighed. There had to be a better way.

She looked back at the shutter. It was large enough to accommodate the pail but not by much. Annja was slim and lithe, but she wouldn't be able to wriggle through that opening.

She had to make it bigger.

Annja summoned her sword and set to work on the shutter. She expected that it would probably have been locked with just a simple bolt. But she had to be careful. If they heard any noise in her cell, she would have visitors soon enough.

And she didn't yet know if they could turn the lights on and off without her consent.

She had to risk it.

Annja braced the tip of the sword at the edge of the shutter and then stabbed at the opening. The blade striking the metal shutter produced a loud metallic clanging sound that made Annja wince.

They had to have heard that, she thought.

But nothing happened and no voice came over the intercom. Maybe they weren't paying attention to her cell right now. Maybe they were preoccupied with someone else.

Annja bent back to the door and rammed the sword blade at the shutter. She heard a clink and then the bolt snapped off and the shutter flew open.

She dropped to her knees and peered through the shutter. The corridor outside was dimly lit with bulbs set into the stonework at intervals of maybe thirty feet. They cast long shadows and Annja couldn't see much beyond the range of their light. As it was, her head barely fit through the opening.

But it had been a glimpse of the outside world. And she felt stronger now that she'd managed to get something they didn't want her to have.

I have to get out of here now, she thought. Even if they didn't hear her, they might get suspicious if I sleep for too long.

She looked at the edges of the opening and saw that the stone seemed solid enough. But she figured if she could enlarge the opening perhaps by a few inches all around, she'd be able to squirm through and then get the hell out of Dodge.

It was worth a try.

It hadn't been that long since her last meal. That meant the time to act was now.

She pressed the sword's blade on a stone edge and started almost shaving the stone away. At first, nothing happened, but once Annja used her shoulder to put more weight on the blade itself, small flecks of rock started flaking away.

She started sweating. This was going to be a long haul.

But Annja had little time to consider the exertion required. She kept working on the stone on all sides, using the blade to whittle away at the opening. A small pile of stone and dust started building up both within her cell and on the floor of the corridor outside.

She sighed. It would have been so much easier if she could have somehow accessed the bolt that held her door locked. But she couldn't reach that high and the shutter restricted any movement above based on how it had been positioned.

No, Annja would have to finish this or die trying.

As she cut deeper into the stone, larger chunks started coming off. She was worried that the constant chipping sound would alert her captors, but they hadn't yet interrupted her. And Annja was determined not to give them any breaks.

She coughed once and thought she heard something, but after a second, she resumed her work. Another large bit of stone came away in her hands and she saw that she'd actually made a bit of progress.

Annja laid the sword down and tried to squeeze herself through the opening. She had to force one of her shoulders through first and then awkwardly bring the other one along.

It was risky at this point because if anyone came down the corridor, she was trapped.

But no one did.

Annja got herself halfway out. She used her feet still in the cell to give her more leverage to push her hips through. Her butt was squeezed up against the top of the jagged opening and she was worried her pants might get caught.

She pushed as hard as she could and fell out into the corridor.

She was free.

Annja reached back into the cell and grabbed her sword, pulling it out into the dim light of the corridor.

She glanced left and right and remembered that the noises earlier had all originated from the right side.

Time to go find out what this is all about, she thought.

She headed off, sword in hand, to do just that.

28

Annja stalked down the corridor, expecting at any moment to hear an alarm go off. If her captors could control the lights and switched them on, they'd see she had escaped.

There was also the expectation that another meal would be coming. She might well run into the person who fed her.

What a nice surprise that will be for them, she thought.

The corridor sloped upward at a gentle angle. Annja noticed that there seemed to be a constant stream of water running down sections of the walls. Where the walls met the floor, small troughs had been carved to help funnel the water down and away, presumably to some sort of drainage system.

But it made Annja wonder exactly where she might be if there was so much of it running throughout the complex. She figured she must have been in some underwater cavern.

She tried to remember if she'd ever heard of underwater caves off the Nova Scotia coast before and couldn't. But then again, she'd never really wondered if there were any. For all she knew, there could be vast amounts of them.

Her sword gleamed and Annja kept moving, preferring to stay close to the walls rather than out in the middle of the corridor. She tried to keep her shadow behind her, but with each light she approached and then passed, her shadow would move.

She stopped suddenly.

Ahead of her she could have sworn she heard something out of rhythm with the rest of the ambient noise in the corridor.

Annja checked her position. The corridor curved around to the right and she was in a good position to surprise anyone coming at her. The next light was about twenty feet in front of her and cast her shadow behind her body. There was nothing that could give her position away unless she did something to make noise.

Annja stilled her breathing.

She heard the sound again.

There was definitely something up ahead of her. But who? Or what?

She knelt down and risked a quick peek around the corner. She saw a shadow and ducked back. In the glimpse, she'd made out someone about six feet tall. And he was armed and walking toward her.

He wasn't carrying a meal tray.

Annja waited until the very last possible second and then as the muzzle of his submachine gun came around the curve, Annja grabbed it and jerked him forward.

The man went with the momentum and tucked himself into a roll, bringing the gun up across his body to protect it and simultaneously get a bead on Annja. Annja came cutting down at him with the blade.

He pivoted and used the gun to deflect her stroke. Annja tried to recoil and bring the blade back up and across at his chest, but he scrambled away, coming up on his feet as the hilt of Annja's sword bounced off his gun.

She heard something clink on the floor, and as the man tried to bring the gun up level with her, he squeezed the trigger and frowned.

Nothing happened.

Annja didn't wait for him to correct the problem. She slashed down at him. He gave up trying to fire the gun and used it to knock her blade away from him. Annja's sword went flying across the floor. The man punched Annja in the stomach. Annja fell back gagging and retching.

She couldn't get any air into her lungs.

The man was a highly trained fighter. He aimed a kick at her head and Annja barely had a second to dodge it before he caught her with another one in the lower back. Annja felt the steel toes of his boots sink into her kidneys and she grunted.

But then she rolled back, trapping his legs and lifting to toss him onto his backside. She came up, still trying to catch her breath. He punched at her but Annja brushed his strikes away, going for a sharp knee to his groin. She caught him and he grunted, knocking his head against Annja's upper lip. Annja felt the lip balloon into some swollen mess. She reached for her sword blade, which was still about ten feet away.

He tackled her around the waist and then dragged her away from it. Annja scrambled to get her feet under her, looking for any purchase she could find on the damp floor of the corridor.

She felt his hands clawing at her and then managed to get one foot under her. She drove off her other leg and fell forward as he refused to give up the fight.

Annja turned around and raked his face with her fingernails. He winced as blood streamed. Annja kicked again and, this time, he backed off a little.

Annja summoned her sword to her and at last wrapped her hands around the hilt. She sensed movement behind her as the man came up with his submachine gun and fumbled with it for a moment.

Annja dived to the right as the explosion of bullets swept across the corridor, ricocheting off the stone walls.

Annja threw the sword and heard the sudden intake of breath as it sank into the man's stomach and pierced his vital organs.

He coughed and spit blood across the wall.

The shooting stopped.

Annja's ears rang and her head screamed in protest at the horrible noise. But she quickly drew out her sword as the man sank to his knees and then toppled forward, dead.

A pool of blood spread out from his body and then ran into the trough on the left side, quickly mixing with the water and sliding away toward the drainage area.

Annja wiped her brow and took quick stock of her own injuries. Her lip was a swollen mess and her kidneys hurt like hell, but she was alive.

Apart from the sudden barrage of gunshots, there'd been little noise during the entire fight aside from the grunts and sounds of exertion. It always amazed Annja how little noise occurred in hand-to-hand combat. No one screamed or yelled or did any of the craziness that happened in martial-arts movies.

Usually it was quick, dirty, sweaty stuff that left one person dead and the other alive, for better or for worse.

Annja hefted her sword and used some of the water running down a nearby wall to wash the man's blood off.

She dragged her victim's body behind the curve where she'd waited for him before the fight. It wouldn't do for long, but it might keep his corpse concealed for a few minutes.

Of course, the entire complex had probably heard the gunfire and knew something was wrong. The fact that more people hadn't come rushing had her somewhat confused. Annja had expected instant backups to fly at her from wherever the corridor led.

But no one had.

She wondered if the sound had even reached them. Perhaps due to the construction of this facility, sound didn't echo or bounce along as it might elsewhere? She didn't know. Acoustics weren't something she knew much about. One thing was certain. She had to reach the end of the corridor and see where she was. Annja took off again, walking up the slope toward a dim light she could see at its summit.

It took her three more minutes of fast walking to reach it, but as she came abreast of the zenith, she started hearing more noise. She picked out loud machines that hummed and heavy industrial gear from the sound of it.

Annja paused and sank down to her knees to get a better picture of what was going on beyond.

Bright light greeted her, making her blink rapidly. Her eyes had been so used to the dim light that the sudden rush of illumination hurt her head. Annja looked back and blinked to further acclimate her eyes.

What she saw amazed her.

She was overlooking the vast expanse of a stone cavern that was filled with all manner of machinery. One of the things she thought she recognized was a huge drill that seemed to be boring right into the base of a giant stone.

In the lower part of the cavern, Annja could see scores of people working on a variety of geological contraptions. Across from them, she saw a dock and, floating in water, she spotted several submarines and two giant sharks.

Two of them?

Annja frowned. Where the hell was she? And whatever she'd stumbled upon, it was obviously well financed. To get this type of machinery and gear down here, let alone employ so many people in whatever processes were ongoing, would take enormous sums of money.

Who had that kind of financing available to them? Sheila had mentioned Henderson. Was she lying or was there really a man named Henderson who was fronting this entire operation. Surely this wasn't just about some crucifix. They wouldn't need resources like this just to recover a sunken relic.

No way.

Annja looked around and saw more armed guards on patrol overlooking various parts of the cavern. But the machinery noise was so loud, Annja wasn't surprised that the guard she'd killed hadn't attracted any notice. No one would have heard the gunfire from the main cavern.

The area where Annja knelt opened onto a ledge that seemed to run all the way around the cavern. It was on this catwalk of sorts that Annja spotted the other guards.

And across from her, she could see a glass-enclosed control room. She noticed a series of monitors and computers.

If she was going to get any answers as to what was happening here, she would have to reach that spot.

But what had happened to Cole? Was he here? Were there other cells back where she'd been held?

Annja wanted nothing more than to go and check, but her gut instinct told her that Cole wasn't back there. Something inside her insisted that he was still alive, but where?

She saw soon enough.

A break in the machinery din caused her to look down and to the right when she thought she heard a laugh. As she did, she saw Cole strapped to a board, arms and legs akimbo.

A guard nearby held a long wand that crackled at the end. Annja recognized the Taser and wondered why they were torturing Cole when, to her knowledge, he had no idea what was going on.

She saw the guard touch the device to Cole's chest and

watched as Cole arched his back in agony. The voltage was not enough to kill him, but they could make him suffer for hours until he mercifully passed out or had a heart attack as his body gave up.

I've got to get to him, she thought. But a quick glance around the catwalk told Annja that reaching Cole would entail her taking on half a dozen armed men who were presumably very well trained if the first guard she'd encountered was any indication.

Those weren't good odds for Annja.

She leaned back and took a deep breath. Could she possibly reach the control room? That would mean she'd have to expose herself.

She looked around and tried to figure out how people were able to get down to the lower levels. Clearly, this area led up to the catwalk, but what about going in the opposite direction? Would that lead Annja down to where Cole was?

She had to try.

Annja ran back the way she'd come. She wasn't worried about running into anyone there. Her feeling was the prisoner cells were positioned so that someone could get to them from either the top level or from the bottom.

Annja ran past her cell, relieved that no one appeared to have visited her since she escaped. She kept going along the corridor. It started to slope downward pretty fast and Annja had to slow her pace or risk falling forward from her own momentum.

She skidded to a stop twenty yards away from another doorway. This time the noise was much louder than it had been up on the catwalk. Annja could hear all the different machinery.

And, along with those sounds, she could hear Cole screaming.

I have to get to him, she thought.

But she couldn't risk running out and getting them both killed. She had to sneak out there without anyone knowing.

But how?

Annja crept up to the doorway and risked a look, hoping that the answer would reveal itself to her.

29

The first thing Annja spotted was a group of workers in coveralls heading out of a room that hadn't been visible to Annja from the catwalk. One of them was still zipping up the coveralls and Annja suspected that there might be more sets in what she hoped was a changing area. Judging by the makeup of the group, which included three women, Annja felt a surge of hope.

She waited until the group passed her spot and then she cautiously crept toward the next doorway. She could see a polished stone floor that gleamed from the constant dampness that seemed to pervade every aspect of this complex. Just beyond the doorway, she spotted a series of metal lockers set against the stone wall and beyond them another doorway where Annja heard what sounded like flushing toilets.

And they gave me a pail, she thought. The bastards.

She checked the first locker and found it locked but then spotted a bin full of used coveralls. Quickly, she grabbed one and stepped into it, zipping it up to her neck and effectively covering her body.

Fortunately, the coveralls had booties and Annja hoped that her absence of shoes would be hidden from view.

She wished the people wore masks but that didn't seem a likely event, so she took a deep breath, checked to make sure the sword was ready to pull out if she needed and then stepped out of the changing room just as two more workers entered.

"Hey," one said, barely even looking at her.

Annja smiled at the one that spoke to her. "Hey."

And that was the extent of the exchange. Annja took a breath and tried to remain nonchalant. Clearly, not everyone here knew who she was or even what she looked like. That was good news.

Outside the changing room, she looked around and spotted Cole still hung up on the wooden board. She started making her way over to where he was.

The guards near Cole seemed not to even notice her as she drew closer and closer. Annja's heart hammered, but she had to commit to this. She had no idea how they were going to make it out of there, but judging from how Cole screamed, he wasn't going to last much longer if they kept shocking him the way they were.

She closed the distance to ten feet and was ready to jump the closest guard when she saw a new guard come down from a circular stone staircase cut into the back of the rock. He pointed at the Taser holder and shook his head. "That's enough now. There's no sense in killing him. At least, not yet."

Cole's head slumped forward and Annja saw sweat running down through the muscle valleys on his body. She frowned and bit back the surge of anger she felt coursing through her veins.

"Get him down and take him back to his cell."

The guards complied and Cole fell forward into their arms. As he did so, his eyes fluttered open and he saw Annja.

Annja winked at him and she saw the immediate reaction of relief in his body. But he checked it and nodded toward the area by the staircase.

Annja looked over and saw something she hadn't seen before. A video camera was stuck on a rotating pole that covered that particular part of the lower cavern. No doubt its feed led back to the control room she'd spotted from the catwalk overhead.

Cole was still staring at her so she nodded once and then he slumped forward again. Two of the guards dragged him away and Annja was relieved to see that they headed back the way she'd come down from her own cell.

The relief was short-lived, however. She realized that if they got Cole back to this cell, they'd see that Annja's own door was a mess and she was no longer in her cell.

She turned and started working her way toward where the guards were carrying Cole.

"You there."

Annja's heart sank. She turned. "Yes?"

"Are you supposed to be over here?" It was the guard who had stopped the torturing of Cole. But he didn't look even remotely friendly. The submachine gun slung over his shoulder wasn't at the ready, but it was close to his hands. And the expression on his deeply scarred face was a portrait of evil and hatred.

"Aren't I?" Annja said.

He shook his head. "All drill workers are supposed to be over in that area there." He pointed in the opposite direction that Annja was headed. "Get over to where you need to be. You don't want the boss looking for you and I don't need any extra bother today."

Annja smiled. "Great, thanks." She started walking in the

same direction that she had been heading. She was close to the opening. Just six feet to go.

"Did you hear what I said?"

She nodded. "Yep, I just have to check on something over here first," she said.

Four feet away from the doorway, she heard the ratchet of the submachine gun's charging handle slammed into place. The guard had a round ready to fire into her back if he wanted to. "Doesn't seem like you heard me," he said.

Annja considered her options. If the guards got Cole back to his cell, she was finished. If she took this guard out, she was finished, as well. There was no other option left but to make a messy scene.

As she came abreast of the doorway, she grabbed a small rock she'd noticed on the ground and wheeled around, aiming with perfect accuracy at the guard's head.

Before the man had a chance to react, the rock struck him between the eyes and he slumped to the floor. Annja grabbed him and his gun before they could draw attention and dragged him into the changing room. She struggled and heaved until she stuffed the body in the laundry bin and then stripped off her coveralls.

Annja grabbed the gun and raced toward Cole's cell.

She turned the corner and came face-to-face with one of Cole's guards heading back at a run. She could see the body of the guard she'd killed in the distance.

Annja collided with the oncoming man and they both went down, their respective guns clattering on the stone floor.

Annja had the faster reaction and instantly shot her right leg out toward the guard's head. He saw the kick coming but didn't have enough time to block the savage blow that snapped his head back. He lay still.

Annja scrambled to her feet and grabbed at the two guns, slinging one of them on her back and running for Cole's cell.

As she ran, she wondered about the absence of radios on the guards, but quickly dismissed it as a nonissue. Probably due to the solid rock that surrounded them, radios were unreliable.

She went up the slope toward the row of cells and saw the second guard examining the entrance of her cell. Cole was nowhere to be seen.

The guard saw Annja and started to aim his weapon at her. "Hey—"

Annja's trigger finger twitched and the gun recoiled in her hands as three rounds tore into the guard's chest, shredding his black turtleneck and splattering blood across the walls.

He dropped and Annja knelt next to his body, grabbing his keys off the belt he wore. She called out, "Cole!"

"Annja?"

She raced to a door past her cell and fumbled with the lock. She got the door open and saw him struggle forward. He collapsed into her arms. "So it really *was* you. I hoped, but couldn't be sure."

"It's me, you big jerk. Now come on, we've got to get you out of here."

She wrapped her hands around him and took his weight. He was heavy and outweighed her by a great deal. Annja took a breath and propped him up.

He tried to stand by himself. "Let me go. I can manage."

"You sure?"

He nodded. "I feel like shit, but if we can get the hell out, I'll fake it long enough to escape."

Annja took the submachine gun off her back and handed it to him. "It's going to get messy before we're clear."

They headed out into the corridor. Cole looked down at the dead guard and scowled. "I wanted to kill that guy myself. Talk about a sadist."

"No need now. We've got to get out of here. I've taken

out three guards so far and my actions won't stay hidden for long."

"You got three of them? You've been busy."

They headed toward the lower level of the cavern. Annja led the way. "I saw a submarine from the catwalk. And there are two sharks. They must be submarines, as well."

"Of a type," Cole said. "But I think they're here specifically to scare the hell out of anyone who stays in this area."

"You have any idea what's going on?"

Cole shook his head. "Not a clue. For some reason, though, the gas they used didn't completely knock me out, so I was pretty aware when they unloaded me from the shark."

"You must have been surprised when the shark swallowed you up only to find that it wasn't real."

Cole almost chuckled. "You could say that. I imagine you were the same way, obviously." He frowned. "But how the hell did you get swallowed up?"

"Long story," Annja said. "Let's just say that after I saw you presumably killed, I was more than a little bit upset with that shark. The next time it came around, I decided to take it on and that's when it happened."

"Take it on?" Cole shook his head. "You make it sound like it was some back-alley fight."

"Yeah, I know. Pretty insane, right?"

"Sounds like it." Cole smiled. "I'm glad you're here, though."

"Well, we're not out of the woods just yet. We need to get one of those submarines and disappear before someone finds out that we didn't think too highly of our accommodations."

They passed the second guard Annja had killed with the kick to the head and Cole whistled. "Impressive."

"Necessary," Annja said. "Let's leave it at that if we could. I'm not what I would consider a bloodthirsty woman. But if need be I can do the deed."

"Remind me never to get on your bad side," Cole said.

"Done."

They ran down the slope toward the lower level. Annja thought she heard noises behind them, but she couldn't risk looking back.

"Something tells me that our advantage of surprise may be up," Cole said.

"You might be right." Annja felt certain she heard footsteps pounding the stone corridor behind them. No doubt reinforcements had come in from the catwalk. "Dammit," she said.

"What?"

She stopped running. "Your cell."

"What about it?" Cole asked.

Annja shook her head. "I can't believe I forgot. You were probably under surveillance just like I was. They had a camera in there. And the light was on. They know you're out and they know I'm out, too."

"That's not good." Cole looked behind them. The sounds were growing louder. "How do you want to handle this?"

Annja checked the magazine on her gun and saw that it was full. She slapped it back and pulled the charging handle. "Only one way to play it as far as I'm concerned. I wasn't born to be someone's prisoner."

Cole nodded. "Good. Let's do this."

Annja pointed behind them. "We'll be sandwiched between two sides if we keep going to the lower level."

Cole nodded. "Then let's do what they don't expect. Let's meet these guys head-on and hit them before they can do the same to us."

"Good plan," Annja agreed.

They turned and ran back up the slope. The sound of boots tramping down the corridor was clear. Annja saw shadows coming at them. Three by the look of it.

She waved Cole to her side and they both dropped to their

stomachs. From the prone position, they would at least have a small advantage.

The guards rounded the corner.

"Now!" Annja said.

She and Cole opened fire.

30

The bullets struck the three guards running down the sloped corridor. By the time they recognized the ambush, it was already too late. Annja fired tight, controlled bursts the way she'd been taught by an old friend who had served in special operations. She raked the three guards and noticed that Cole seemed equally adept with his gun.

The guards went down under the hail of gunfire.

Annja was up and checking them to make sure they wouldn't be able to somehow squeeze off another shot, then she and Cole headed away.

Cole was breathing hard. "Now what?"

Annja eyed him. "You okay?"

"Yeah, just winded. I think that last Taser session took a lot more out of me than I thought."

"If you need a break—"

"What I need is to get out of this place. So don't even think about leaving me behind. I can hold my own. Just point in the direction you want me to shoot and I'll get it done."

"I noticed."

Cole shrugged. "Boy Scout camp."

"Right."

"Okay, I took an auxiliary police course one time. The highlight was getting down on the ranges and going full-auto. Guess it stayed with me." He nodded at Annja. "What's your excuse?"

"Classified," Annja said. She pointed back down the slope. "We need to get back there now that we've eliminated this threat."

"You think they'll be waiting for us?"

Annja nodded. "I'd bet on it."

"Great."

Annja held his arm. "If we get down there and fight our way through, we head for the dock across the way. It won't be easy, but if we can make it, then we can get on board and escape."

"You know how to pilot a submarine?" Cole asked.

Annja tried to grin. "How hard can it be? As long as I'm surrounded by metal and bullets can't get to me, I'll be happy to learn as I go."

"Stick with me," Cole said. "I'll get us out of here. Or at least into the water. I have no idea what direction to head once we do that."

"We'll figure it out." Annja slowed her pace as she came around a shallow curve in the corridor. Noises drifted up to her. She motioned for Cole to stop.

Cole came closer and whispered in Annja's ear. "Did you hear that?"

She nodded. "Probably the other half of our welcome party."

"Now what?"

Annja shook her head. "What option do we have? We can't wait here all day and risk them getting more reinforcements or sending another party down behind us."

"Best defense is a good offense?" Cole said.

Annja nodded. "I'll take the lead. You come second."

"Right behind you."

Annja ducked down and slid out into the straight portion of the corridor that opened up on the lower level. She could see a stack of wooden crates near the doorway. This contingent was obviously smarter than their brothers on the upper level.

As soon as they saw Annja, they opened up and sent a volley of bullets shrieking at her and Cole. Annja barely had enough time to register what she saw and push Cole back before the first rounds slammed into the walls near them and ricocheted up the corridor.

Cole fell down next to her. "Shit!"

Annja frowned. This wasn't good. The longer they were trapped there, the better the chances of them getting captured again. She had to do something to break the stalemate or it would be all over for her and Cole.

She looked at him. "You trust me?"

Cole frowned. "What—I have to prove that to you now? Of course I trust you. Why wouldn't I?"

"Because I'm going to do something that will probably seem pretty damned crazy."

Cole smirked. "So, business as usual apparently."

She rolled her eyes and then handed him her submachine gun. "Here, take this."

He frowned. "What? You need this. Why give it to me?"

"Be quiet, Cole." Annja summoned her sword. Next to her, she heard Cole gasp.

"What th—?"

She put a finger to his lips. "Not a word. I don't have time to answer any questions right now. If this doesn't work, then don't bother asking anyone about it. No one else knows."

Cole's eyes were wide but he accepted her response and nodded dumbly. "All right."

"Here's the plan," Annja said. "I'm going to charge their position."

"With that?"

Annja smiled and looked at the sword. "You'd be surprised what this blade can do."

"Or where it came from," Cole said. "But I won't ask."

"Thanks." Annja smiled. "When I charge them, they're going to be a bit surprised."

"You don't say."

"That's your opportunity to get some good fire on them. See if you can take out as many as possible in the short span of time the surprise will give me. It won't be long if these guys are any good. They'll switch back on and start shooting at me. And I don't think I can block bullets with the sword."

"All right."

Annja took a breath. "Isn't this fun?"

"I prefer diving with sharks."

Annja nodded. "Welcome to my world."

"Is it really like this?"

Annja thought about it for a second as another volley of bullets echoed off the corridor walls. She looked back at Cole. "With an almost startling regularity."

"Wow."

Annja squatted and prepared herself. She took a few deep breaths to fully oxygenate her blood and then nodded at Cole. "Here we go." She looked back at him. "Make sure you don't shoot me in the back."

She ran out from around the bend and screamed as she ran straight at the stacked crates, her sword held up in front of her.

Please, she thought, just let me close the gap in time for Cole to take them out.

As she'd predicted, the guards stopped short when they saw

her and froze for a moment. Annja heard sporadic gunfire from behind her.

The guard closest to her took two rounds in his throat and toppled backward with a bloody gurgle. A bright spout of crimson erupted from the base of his neck.

That's one, Annja thought.

The second guard took a close stitch of bullets across his chest and slid sideways with the force of the impact, streaking red across the wooden crate.

Two.

The third guard brought his gun up on Annja but then took a single well-placed shot in the shoulder that spun him around just as he squeezed the trigger. His gun went off and stitched one his fellow guards.

Annja kept running. Three and four.

A single shot came at her as she dived forward, twisting her body out of the bullet's path. She reached the crates and scrambled over them, coming down on the other side and finding herself within striking range of the next guard.

She backstroked and cut him down with a quick slash across his abdomen. He clutched at his stomach and fell. Annja kept moving and slashed another guard who was trying to draw his pistol and shoot her in the close confines of the space.

Annja cleaved him with a single stroke.

She whirled and caught the final guard with a slash that barely creased his throat over his voice box. The bright red smile that she scored across his neck melted in a bubbling fountain of blood and he clutched at his neck as he fell.

Annja leaned against one of the crates and took a deep breath. She heard footsteps and brought her sword up just in time to see Cole come running toward her.

"They all dead?"

She nodded. "Nice shooting there, pal."

"Glad it worked out." He shook his head. "I've never seen

anyone move like you did. I thought you were dead. I heard that one shot and then you just, I don't know…moved at the perfect moment."

Annja shrugged. "Like I said, the sword does some amazing things."

"That wasn't the sword," Cole said. "That was you."

"We can debate it later," Annja said. "For now, let's get the hell out of here."

Cole looked at the lower level. And Annja noticed that there weren't any workers down there. The roar of machines continued unabated, but there seemed to be no one else around.

Annja frowned. "This place was crawling with people just a little while ago."

"I know," Cole said. "What do you suppose happened?"

"Well, we did." Annja glanced up at the catwalk but she couldn't see if there were any guards there. "They probably sounded some type of alarm that we didn't hear. They got everyone out of here so they could take us on without risk to the workers."

Cole pointed across the way at the dock. "There are the subs."

"Yeah," Annja said. "And you notice how there doesn't seem to be anything in our way?"

"What do you mean?"

"It's wide-open. No guards, no real obstacles. Just a nice easy walk in the park for us."

Cole frowned. "I take it that means something?"

"Yeah, it means they're planning to ambush us somehow. It's a trap. And I hate traps."

Cole sighed. "What choice do we have? We have to get out of here. And we still don't even know what's going on."

Annja nodded. "All good points." She craned her neck and searched the catwalk. She couldn't see anyone up there. Even the windows on the control room had been shuttered. It looked as if the complex had been abandoned.

But Annja knew it hadn't been.

She took a few moments to really scan the area.

"Cole."

"Yeah?"

"Keep watch and stay quiet."

Cole nodded.

Annja relaxed and crept outward. She sat and listened.

She realized the first guard was directly above their position on the catwalk.

He would be difficult to get past. He could wait until they were exposed by other guards and then fire down on them.

They'd be dead before they knew what hit them.

Annja carefully charted the positions of the other guards she could detect. They had the area well covered. Whoever they'd been dealing with thus far, these guards seemed to have a coherent strategy in place.

And Annja fully expected that they would be shooting to kill, regardless of what their boss might have told them.

She looked back.

Cole was scanning the area. "What do you think?" he asked her.

"I know where they are."

"If you say so."

"But it's going to be tough," she said. "We might not make it."

Cole smiled. "Has there been one thing about this entire mess that's been easy?"

"Not a damned thing."

He nodded. "Exactly. So why don't you tell me what you need me to do and let's stop wasting time."

31

Annja headed back along the corridor and took one of the submachine guns from the fallen guards. She then collected the magazines from the other guns so she and Cole would have enough ammunition. She slapped home a fresh magazine and Cole did the same thing.

Cole kept his voice hushed. "You think they have any idea what we're doing down here?"

Annja shrugged. "We have to assume that they do. I always try to imagine myself in their position. That tends to keep me honest in my plans."

"So, what now?" They worked their way back to the opening.

"Our biggest problem is the guy above us. He's up there waiting for us. I think they're planning to let us get out into the open, then have two shooters pin us down from the front. He will then pick us off from behind. It's a neat and efficient way to take us down without exposing any of them to any degree of threat."

"So how do we get out of this?"

"They hold the high ground," Annja said. "Strategically, that gives them the advantage. But if we can throw a wrench into their plans, then we have a chance."

"And what's our wrench is this instance?"

Annja smiled. "I don't know yet."

Cole frowned. "That's not the answer I was hoping for."

"It's not the answer I hoped to give you."

Cole nodded. "Why don't you leave this one to me?"

"You're in bad shape. There's no way I'm letting you take the lead, not when you're injured."

"I'm not that badly injured," Cole said. "And I need to do this. If it doesn't work, we'll try something else."

Annja shook her head. "I hate to tell you this, but we're only going to get one chance. If we don't pull this off, they'll just come down on us and that will be it."

Cole nodded. "Even more reason to let me try."

"I don't know…"

"Look, you risked your life the last time we got bogged down. It's only fair that you give me my shot, as well."

"I had the sword."

"And I have my incredible sex appeal."

Annja looked at the blank expression on his face and then broke into a grin. "Wow, all right, you can go for it."

"I get points for saying that with a straight face, right?"

"Definitely."

"See?" Cole grinned. "I can die happy now."

"Well, don't say that," Annja said. "You'll make me reconsider my decision."

"Team work, Annja." Cole readied himself. "Now, just wait until I clear the way and then come on out and give me some covering fire from the guys in front of us."

Annja frowned. "What in the world are you planning to do?"

Cole pointed at a small dolly. "Can you grab that for me?"

Annja got the dolly and Cole took it from her. "This should work." He glanced at the catwalk above them. "You said he was up there? Directly above us?"

Annja nodded. "Yeah."

Cole looked out into the open space before them. "Looks like a clear shot."

"What does?"

"The lay of the ground."

Annja shook her head. "What exactly are you up to?"

Cole lay down on the dolly. "Just watch."

And before Annja could say anything, Cole jumped on the dolly and used his legs to push off out into the open. From the position he was in, he was looking back and up at the catwalk above where he had been with Annja.

As he rolled out, Cole brought up the submachine gun and aimed the barrel at the guard above them. Cole fired three times and then came to a rest out in the wide-open part of the cavern.

Annja immediately started firing up at the two guards in front of them, at the ten-o'clock and two-o'clock positions. She made it to a crate in front of her and waited until Cole got down next to her.

"Another stalemate," he said. "What side do you want?"

"Ten," Annja said. "We need to get through this fast or they'll reinforce and chop us up."

"I'm on the two," Cole said. He leaned out and fired off three rounds. Annja did the same.

"We need to catch them reloading," Cole said. He nodded toward the area under the catwalk on the other side. "If we can make it there, they won't have the drop on us anymore and we should have a clear run to the subs."

Annja nodded. "I like it." She leaned out and drew more fire from above before responding with her own.

Cole fired his bullets and then they waited for return fire. Annja heard something that sounded like an empty magazine dropping. She pulled on Cole. "Now!"

They darted from behind cover and zigzagged across the space toward the underside of the catwalk. Annja could hear the fresh magazines being slapped into place and pulled Cole down behind a tall stack of machine parts. Bullets exploded off the wall closest to them.

Cole blanched as a shard of rock cut his face. He drew his hand away wet with blood but nodded to Annja. "I'm okay. How much farther?"

Annja pointed. "If we can make it twenty feet, we should be okay."

"Twenty feet's a mile in this game," Cole said. "You think we can do it?"

Annja smirked. "We've already gotten farther than I would have given us odds on."

"I love the optimism," Cole said. "Let's get going. I'm tired of being shot at. It really sucks."

"Tell me about it."

"How the hell do you get used to this?"

Annja looked at him and then checked the expanse in front of them. Another bullet rebounded off the metal parts in front of them. "You never get used to it, actually."

"Good to know."

"You ready?"

Cole nodded. "Another volley?"

"Yeah, on three." She counted off and they both fired at the same time. Annja nudged him. "Fire on the run."

She knew it wouldn't be accurate fire. That was almost impossible for anyone to do while they were running and dodging bullets being fired at them. What Annja hoped to achieve was to just get them ducking down and not worrying about firing back at her or Cole.

She fired upward as she ran and was ten feet away from the safety under the catwalk when she tripped and fell. Cole didn't notice and kept running until he made the safe area. Then he looked back and saw Annja scrambling to her feet.

She held up her hand. "Stay there!"

Bullets exploded around her. She needed cover fast.

Annja jumped up and dove for the minor safety behind another open crate. She could tell the wood was flimsy and wouldn't stop any of the bullets being shot at her.

She ducked down and checked her magazine. There were only two rounds left so she dropped it and slapped another in its place.

"You okay?" Cole called to her.

"Yeah."

She risked a look out and almost got her head blown off for her troubles. "Can't make it." The open ground was too exposed.

"I'm coming back."

"No!" she shouted. "Stay there. If I can't make it, get out of here and tell someone about this place. Come back for me with the cavalry."

She heard nothing in return. She knew he wouldn't like it, but if he tried to come back for her, they'd both get killed. And that would be useless.

"Cole, don't think about it!"

Annja ducked out and squeezed off a single round at the two-o'clock position. A rain of lead answered her back, the withering fire reducing the top of the crate to Swiss cheese. Splinters of wood showered down on Annja's head.

"Dammit!"

She couldn't stay there. She wondered how far she would have to throw her sword to score a hit on the guard above her at ten o'clock.

No time like the present to find out, she thought.

The first thing she did was lean out and lay down a rain of fire at the two-o'clock position. Then she dropped the gun and summoned the sword. She rolled out and came up into a crouch before hurling the sword like a javelin up at the catwalk.

She ducked and rolled back behind the cover again, laying her hands on the submachine gun. Annja came up and fired two rounds at the two-o'clock position, barely aware that the firing had stopped from the ten-o'clock position.

She risked a look and saw that her sword had impaled the guard. He was dead, with the sword jutting out of his chest.

Another volley of bullets made her duck back down.

It seemed there was only one guard left.

Annja came up again, fired long and then ran for the safety of the overhang. She rushed into Cole's arms, almost tackling him as she did so.

"Jesus, Annja, you okay?"

"Yeah."

"I saw you throw the sword. Incredible."

"Save it for later," Annja said.

He stopped her. "But what about the sword? Don't you need to get it back? You can't just throw it away like that."

Annja laughed. "Don't worry about the sword. It takes care of itself and always comes home. Kinda like a boomerang."

"Interesting."

Annja eyed the expanse of open space in front of them, and scanned it carefully, but didn't see anything that would bar their way. "I think we're clear," she said.

"You sure?"

Annja nodded. "I think that was the last major obstacle. What sub do you want?"

Cole hesitated. "I'd opt for the normal-looking one, actually. Too many bad memories of being swallowed by a shark. I don't think I'd enjoy the ride back home."

Annja nodded. "Okay, let's go for it."

She and Cole dashed for the dock. They made their way down a set of metal steps that led to the mooring area. Annja could see the detail on the two sharks as they drew abreast of them. Floating as they were in the water, they didn't seem nearly as frightening as they did when they were actually moving through the water.

Incredible, Annja thought. "That's damned impressive," she said.

"Maybe we can get one as a souvenir," Cole said. "I don't see any guards anywhere."

"Neither do I," Annja said. "Let's get aboard and get this thing started."

She climbed aboard and started untying the ropes that held the submarine to the dock. She heard the engine start up and then switch off.

Annja's stomach knotted.

Not now, she thought, don't tell me we're having mechanical difficulties. That's the last thing they needed.

"Cole?"

He didn't respond and Annja heard the engine start to turn over again and then fall dead.

She finished untying the moor lines and scampered over to the conning tower entry point. "Cole?"

Annja climbed over the edge and then dropped down into the main portion of the sub itself. She heard noises from the engine room and moved through the hatchway. "Everything okay now?"

Cole was nowhere to be seen.

But two guards aimed their guns at Annja.

Behind them, in the captain's chair, sat an older man with white hair tinged with red streaks. He looked pleased.

"Welcome, Annja Creed. It's so nice to have you here with

us." He smiled at her. "Now, listen to me very carefully. I won't hesitate to shoot you, but I would prefer not to. If you stand very still you might even live to enjoy the next few minutes of your life. Imagine that."

32

Annja looked at the man and frowned. "You must be Henderson."

He smiled. "Thornton Henderson III at your service. And I must say it is my pleasure to make your acquaintance."

"Where's Cole?"

"You mean the lad who came scrambling down here with the intent to steal one of my submarines?"

"Yes."

"He's a bit tied up at the moment," Henderson said. He snapped his fingers and one of the guards moved to the side just enough so Annja could see Cole on his stomach with his hands tied behind him.

She looked back at Henderson. "You shouldn't have done that."

"Oh, dear me, did I do something to annoy you?" His smile widened and he leaned forward. "Tough."

Annja looked around the area. The submarine was about half the size of a normal attack sub that she'd seen once in Groton,

Connecticut, but still had an impressive array of electronics and instrumentation. If she'd known it would be this complicated to run, she might have insisted they take one of the mechanical sharks instead. "This is some sub."

"You like it? I bought it from the same firm that makes unconventional platforms for special-operations commandos. I had them do a little custom job on it for my purposes. They did marvelous work."

"I'm sure they'll happily use your testimonial in their next sales brochure."

Henderson frowned. "That might be difficult as it seems the entire company has ceased to exist. Someone planted a rather large bomb at their production facility on the same night their corporate offices endured a horrendous fire. Tragically, anyone connected with this submarine seems to have perished. One of those strange coincidences I guess. Shame about that."

Annja didn't waste time berating Henderson for killing anyone who could talk. He didn't seem the type to give a damn. "So, since you've been in such a rush to meet me, suppose you tell me what this is all about. You can start by telling me why I was kidnapped."

"Kidnapped?" Henderson chuckled. "You left me no alternative, my dear girl. After all, it seemed it was your intention to do battle with my creation. I couldn't very well let you have your way with my shark and be able to maintain its terrifying characteristics, now could I?"

"Why have the sharks?"

"They serve a very concrete purpose. One I think you've seen in action over the past several days since you arrived."

"Terror."

"Indeed. There's nothing like the prospect of coming face-to-face with a giant killer to keep people from doing what they set out to do. In this case, I needed you all on that boat of yours and not down in the water."

"Why?"

"Because I have interests there, as well. And to be frank, your little treasure hunt was going to interfere. I couldn't allow that. So I took steps to ensure you wouldn't become a problem."

"The shark attack on Jock."

"Yes."

"And Cole's first encounter with it."

"The cage was a marvelous idea, by the way," Henderson said. "We had to reinforce the shark's nose after we had that little run-in. We knew the cage would come back in the water and we wanted to get to it without giving ourselves away. Fortunately, we've got quite the ingenious workshop full of creative minds."

Annja leaned against the hull. "So, where exactly are we?"

Henderson shrugged. "Where do you think you are, Annja? Have you figured it out yet?"

"I think we're underwater. In some cavern that you've somehow managed to make habitable."

He clapped his hands. "Marvelous. Tell me how you arrived at that conclusion."

Annja frowned. "It wasn't hard. You've got a plumbing issue here. There's water everywhere."

"Well, not everywhere. We've come light-years from where we were when we first located this place. The water level had to be reduced significantly before we could get people down here. But it's all worked wonderfully. I think you'd agree that this is quite a technological achievement."

"I guess. But to what end?" Annja looked around. "You've got a submarine and two mechanical sharks to keep people away from this place. But why? What are you up to?"

"I'm not here to steal your paltry little treasure wreck, I assure you," Henderson said.

"That's not what Sheila said."

Henderson smiled. "Sheila told you exactly what she was supposed to tell you, Annja. As well as give you all some worry about sabotage when the screw was found. You see, it's little things that are sometimes more effective than some grand statement like blowing you up. By planting small doubts, we distracted you just enough."

"And the shark?"

"Insurance in case the little stuff didn't work."

Annja nodded. "And how is Sheila doing? Last I saw her, she had a broken wrist."

"She's fine. All bandaged up and doing quite well. I think she's looking forward to some alone time with you once she recovers. Not sure I'd be anxious about that if I were you. Terrible temper, that one has."

"I handled her once before."

Henderson nodded. "Yes, it was quite a fight, I'm told. But Sheila is a very good actress. I wouldn't count on having such an easy time with her next go-around."

"I'll keep it in mind." Annja pointed at him. "So, you've got an underwater colony of sorts and all this mechanical drilling equipment. What's the deal? You trying to find some lost store of oil?"

"Oh, I've already found it, my dear. And we're sitting on it right now." He shrugged. "Well, not literally, of course."

"Of course."

"But under this part of the Atlantic there lies an incredible store of oil reserves. Enough to make what they've drawn from the sands of Saudi Arabia look like a wad of sputum."

"Colorful."

"Enough to turn me into the world's first trillionaire." Henderson clapped his hands together. "It's never been done before, you know. When this is all said and done I will have more money than most of the nations on this planet."

Annja frowned. "If there's so much oil, then why hasn't anyone else tried to tap into it yet?"

Henderson sighed. "Well, there's the rub of it, you see. Some people apparently have the notion that drilling here would result in the destruction of this particular ecosystem. Some such silly notion like that. They've cited studies on the marine life in this area and make all these excuses that basically put the animals ahead of humans."

"The nerve," Annja said. "And of course, you couldn't stand for that silly sentiment."

"Exactly. So I had to take steps to liberate that conventional thinking from its prison."

Annja frowned. "And how the hell did you do that?"

"Well, I haven't yet, my dear. You see, that's why I need this place to myself for a while. Can't have any nosy people around wondering just what all these submarines and mechanical sharks are doing prowling in the waters up here. Do you know how difficult it is moving crew of workers around without anyone noticing? It's quite the logistical feat, I'll tell you."

"But to what end? If you can extract the oil without anyone knowing, then why not just do that?"

"I need to get to the oil first. And it's buried under several hundred feet of bedrock. The cost of drilling that far down would be prohibitive to the job at hand. After all, I'm a capitalist. I like my ventures to earn me money. If they get me some fame, then that's nice, as well. But money is my main goal."

"That's great," Annja said. "Another human being motivated solely by greed. Like we don't have enough of those already."

Henderson frowned. "There's no need to be rude, young lady."

"So what's the plan," Annja asked. "You going to drill or not?"

"I'm not going to drill for the oil," Henderson said.

"But you just said—"

"I said that drilling for it was cost-prohibitive." He leaned back in his chair. "There is an alternative that I personally find a lot more enjoyable."

"That being?"

Henderson smiled. "Come over here, Annja."

Annja hesitated but Henderson waved her on. "No tricks. I want to show you something. It's easier this way than having me explain it. Come on, then."

Annja walked over and stood next to Henderson. He smiled at her. "Now watch." He turned in his seat and started typing on a keyboard close by. On the monitor attached to it, a map of the North Atlantic blossomed on the screen.

Henderson pointed at Nova Scotia. "Here's where we are right now."

"Yeah, I got that."

Henderson clicked the mouse and the screen zoomed in to the exact spot where Annja figured the *Seeker* floated. Then the screen changed again, this time showing depths and lines like Annja had seen before on undersea charts.

"This is our position, here." Henderson jabbed a stubby finger at the screen. "We're currently in a cavern about three hundred feet down. Not bad, huh? Ordinarily, you would have been killed by the pressure by now, but one of our feats was to pressurize this cavern while we worked here."

"Impressive," Annja said.

"Thank you," Henderson replied. "I'm quite proud of the accomplishments my people have made." He winked at Annja. "But then again, money is truly such a motivating factor. It amazes me what people are capable of when they suddenly have almost unlimited funds in front of them."

"I guess so." Annja pointed at the screen. "So, what's this thing here?" She was pointing at a line that ran jaggedly down one part of the monitor.

Henderson nodded. "I'm so glad you noticed that. That is a previously undiscovered fault line."

"A fault line?"

"Tectonic plates, my dear. You know, the earth's crust jutting up and against other parts? Rather like the human skull on a newborn infant. Not all of the plates have fused together yet. Surely you have some basic grasp of earthquakes?"

"I get it," Annja said. "But what's the big deal about it?"

"The best way to access the huge reserve of oil hidden under that immense bedrock is to induce a rather neat opening in the bedrock."

"How are you planning to do that?"

Henderson smiled. "We'll be introducing a seismic event of grand proportions. That should do the trick nicely."

"You're going to create an earthquake."

"Exactly."

"How?"

Henderson clicked away from the undersea chart and over to a new screen. Annja watched as a series of graphics displayed and immediately saw where Henderson was headed with his plans.

And she didn't like the look of any part of it.

"Rather creative, wouldn't you agree?" he asked.

"You'll kill hundreds of thousands of people if this goes wrong," Annja said. "I don't think that's a very good plan."

Henderson took a breath. "Given the nature of human society these days, I think that a little apocalypse isn't such a bad thing."

"I disagree."

"You're not in a position to argue that point," Henderson said.

"Not currently."

"Not ever," Henderson replied. He jabbed at the screen. "Once we implant the small nuclear device into the hole we're drilling at the top of the fault line, the resulting explosion will enable us to get a pipeline straight into the oil reserves and begin siphoning it to the underwater processing facility that we're building."

"Radioactive oil?" Annja frowned. "You can't be serious."

Henderson shook his head. "There will be no radiation in the oil. Due to the exact nature of the controlled nuclear detonation, we can contain the radiation and keep it from contaminating the supply." He frowned. "Sadly, the marine life in this area will be sacrificed, but that's how it goes."

"And the resulting tidal wave? That will kill thousands of people."

Henderson shrugged. "They might have some warning."

"Probably not."

He smirked. "Yes, probably not. But I can't be bothered with it. And neither can you. Your destiny lies elsewhere."

"And where would that be?"

Henderson pointed over his shoulder. "With your friend Cole there. You two will have seats at ground zero. Imagine that."

33

Annja couldn't believe what she'd heard. "And what about the rest of your workers? Are you going to kill them, too, now that they've served their purpose?"

Henderson shrugged. "There's plenty of time to finish evacuating them. We've already started, in fact." He looked at his watch. "In the meantime, I believe the moment has come for you and your friend Cole to get situated."

"Where are you putting us?"

"Outside by the hole we drilled that leads right into the mass of bedrock." He smiled. "I'll tell you what, I'll even leave the cavern pressurized and full of oxygen for you and Cole to talk about your final time together while we count down to the explosion from a very safe distance away."

"Just how big is this nuke?"

Henderson held up his hand. "Not that big, actually. You wouldn't believe the trouble it is to get any weapons-grade plutonium these days. Even for a man of my wealth. We might have had an easier time just hijacking some old Soviet-era surplus submarines, but they were always so unreliable. Bloody thing might have gone off on us, and that wouldn't be any good, now would it?"

"Yeah, that would have been a real shame." Annja looked at the guards. "So, are they going to shoot me?"

"Not unless they have to. I'd much rather you anticipate the countdown in the opposite way I will be."

"Why have you got such a grudge against me?"

Henderson shook his head. "My dear, I don't have a grudge against you or your friend. This is simply business. You two wandered into an area where you shouldn't have and regrettably, you must pay the price for that curiosity."

Annja frowned. "You could always let us go."

"And have you tell the world what I've done here?"

"As soon as that bomb goes off, the rest of the world is going to know what you did. How else will you explain your sudden appearance on the scene to tap into the oil reserves hidden here?"

Henderson smiled. "By the time the officials of the United States and Canada get their act together, I will already have sucked this particular reservoir dry and moved it to another site in international waters where I can claim that I struck the reserve myself using my money. And then I'll simply start selling it at such a bargain price that the OPEC countries will find themselves teetering on economic collapse. I'll have a line of countries wanting to do business with me for my low prices, and before anyone realizes what's happening, it will be too late. The oil will be gone, I'll be rich and no one will be the wiser."

"You've made that sound far too easy. There's no way that will ever work and you know it," Annja said.

"I'm not hearing any convincing arguments from you, Annja. If you've got a point to make, I'll entertain it, but if you're just stalling for time, I'm afraid you're working on the wrong man."

Annja shook her head. "They'll take you out. You won't have a safe haven anywhere in the world. You'll be hunted down like a dog."

Henderson laughed. "You do have a very simplistic view of the world's politics, don't you? In reality, no one will care. The elected officials will be happy that they suddenly have access to oil at remarkably low prices. They can bulk up their strategic reserves and have enough for at least a half century without buying anything from the Middle East."

"And you expect those countries to collapse?"

"Why wouldn't they? Nothing but a bunch of sand dwellers who happened upon the world's bulk of oil. Not very equitable, is it?"

"I don't know," Annja said. "Considering a lot of their real estate isn't arable, I'd say it's almost a fair trade."

"They're barbarians," Henderson said. "And they should be treated as such. When I release the oil and they have no customers, they'll wither away and die. There will be a rush to try to sustain themselves in some other economic fashion, but it will be far too late for most of them." Henderson rubbed his chin. "Although the United Arab Emirates might do all right. Ingenious bastards, that lot. Those folks in Dubai are wizards."

"That's acceptable to you?"

"Oh, I believe we can have a Dubai in the world and not lose much sleep over it."

"Your actions will simply spawn a new era of panglobal terrorism. Tons of innocent people will die. And it will all be because of you."

Henderson shrugged. "Perhaps."

"And you can sleep at night with that hanging over your head?"

Henderson laughed. "Actually, I sleep very well indeed. But I thank you for your deep concern. It's almost touching."

"You're a maniac."

"Undoubtedly."

Annja stopped. "It's not too late to stop this."

Henderson shook his head. "I'm getting tired of this conversation, Annja. I'd hoped you might be rather more amusing than this. But instead of giving me any original thought, you simply tell me not to do it. Disappointing."

"Well, jeez…"

"I'm not one to abandon a project after I've already committed almost fifty million dollars to it. Fifty million, Annja. Do you have that kind of cash available? Would you like to pay me off so you can save your precious lives and this area of the ocean?"

"I don't have that kind of money and you know it."

He shrugged. "Well, you never know. There was a fantastic article in one of the magazines I read about the unglamorous millionaire next door. That might have been you."

"Where will you go?"

"After I leave you? Off to our processing facility. It's even more impressive than this station. I wish you could see it, Annja, but I'm afraid the time has come for me to leave you in the very capable hands of my guards."

The first guard started toward Annja while the second guard brought his gun up and leveled it on Annja's head. He was too far away for Annja to smack it off-line and she had little choice but to accept the handcuffs that the first guard put on her wrists.

"This isn't the last you'll see of me," Annja said.

Henderson nodded. "Yes, I know. You've got that dying urge to tell me how you'll hunt me down and get your vengeance. Wonderful. Well, I look forward to it. And so, too, does Sheila, I'd expect."

"What about these guys?"

Henderson nodded. "They'll be fine." He addressed the guards. "After you get her and the man positioned, take the second shark and rendezvous with me at the processing facility."

They both nodded and then led Annja back up to the ladder and forced her to climb out of the submarine. The act was considerably tougher with her hands restricted, but fortunately, they'd cuffed her hands in front of her rather than behind.

The first guard nodded back at the sub. "He's going to be harder getting out of there."

"It was your idea to cuff his hands behind him," the second guard said. "Have fun hauling his ass up here."

The first guard left. Annja looked at the second guard, who stood next to her on the submarine. "Not very smart that guy, huh?"

"Shut up."

"Just making small talk."

"I said be quiet or I'll shut you up."

Annja nodded. "All right, then. I just can't believe you guys are going along with this. All this destruction. People are going to die."

"What the hell do I care?"

"I don't know, why *don't* you care?"

The guard looked at her. "You know what kind of life I had back in the States? I came home from Iraq and my government forgot about me. I lost my house and my car. Then my wife. It all went to shit because all I was good for was holding a gun and killing terrorists. No one cared. At least with Henderson there's a chance of getting ahead."

"But you're still just toting a gun."

"So what? I don't care anymore." He looked at her. "Now shut up. I don't want to have to punch you in the face, but I will if you talk to me anymore."

"All right, fine." Annja fell silent and watched as a submarine she hadn't noticed before drifted down a tunnel. "Is that the rest of the workers?"

"I said be quiet, lady."

"Just wondering."

"Yeah, okay? That's them. That tunnel leads out of the cavern. And that's where we'll be heading once we finish strapping you and your friend to the bomb that Henderson had built for him."

"Who built it?"

The guard chuckled. "Some Pakistani scientist who thought he was working for al Qaeda. It was actually pretty funny. Imagine his surprise when Henderson killed him after he took delivery of it."

"Just a trail of bodies in Henderson's wake, huh?"

She heard a noise and saw the top of Cole's head appear out of the conning tower. The second guard helped him out and then the first guard emerged huffing and sweating after the exertion. "Well, that sucked," he said.

"Help me get them ashore so Henderson can leave." The second guard elbowed Annja. "Let's get a move on."

Annja walked over toward the gangplank, amazed that the sub had stayed close to the dock despite none of the ropes still holding it there.

As she came abreast of the gangway, Annja spotted a familiar face. Sheila was walking toward her. And the smile on her face was anything but friendly.

"Hiya, Sheila, sorry about the wrist."

Sheila punched Annja in the gut. Annja retched and bent over, trying to get her wind back. When she came back up, Sheila was in her face. "I wanted to kill you myself. But Henderson insisted. Here's the good news, though. I'm going back to the *Seeker* and I'm going to kill everyone on that damned boat. Hunter, Dave, Sammy, all the rest of them. And then I'm going to have a real nice time playing with Jax."

"Isn't that going to be a little tough with a busted wrist?"

Sheila shrugged. "I've had worse injuries."

"What about the explosion? It might destroy them all before you have a chance to," Annja said.

Sheila thought about that for a moment and then shrugged. "The hell with it. As long as they die, I'm good."

Henderson's head popped out of the conning tower. "Sheila, darling, are you coming?"

Annja glanced back at Henderson and then at Sheila. "So, that's the deal, is it? You guys shacking up on the sub ride back to the processing facility. That's sweet."

Sheila punched Annja in the gut again. "It's nothing like that at all."

"Okay." Annja gasped and sucked in a breath. "Well, have fun, anyway. He looks like he might need his diaper changed."

Sheila frowned at the guards. "Make sure you put the bomb right between her legs. I want no chance that she can survive."

The first guard cleared his throat. "It's a nuclear bomb. Don't think there's much chance she's going to survive."

Sheila stormed off.

Annja glanced at the guards. "She's really a big fan of mine."

"Yeah, we can tell."

They led her and Cole off the gangway. Cole kept his head down and basically had to be carried by the first guard. Annja hoped he was okay, but she had no idea what they'd done to him before she got into the submarine.

"What happened to him?" she asked finally.

The first guard shrugged. "Probably lingering effects from

the Taser session he had earlier. Maybe all the fight's gone out of him. He's ready to die."

"That makes one of us," Annja said.

"You don't have a choice," the guard said. "Give us any grief and we'll just shoot you. Play your cards right and you and the quiet man here can have some valuable alone time before the bomb blows."

"Nothing like going out with a bang," the second guard said with a laugh.

"Oh, that's hysterical," Annja said. "Henderson really does hire the brightest boys he can find, huh?"

They walked up the slope toward the lower level and Annja heard the submarine's engine switch on. The guards stopped long enough for her to see the submarine head off down the tunnel toward the cavern's exit.

"That's it," the first guard said. "Now it's just us left."

The second guard nodded. "Let's get this done and hightail it out of here. I don't like being left behind. I've been expendable before and it's no fun."

"Good point."

Annja let herself be guided to the lower level into a section that she hadn't seen before. She could see the shaft that led down to the bedrock that Henderson wanted blown up.

At the bottom of the shaft, she could see a yellow circular case with the international symbol for nuclear material on it.

She looked back at the guards. "That's it?"

"Yeah."

Annja nodded. "You know, come to think of it, I don't really want to die in this place."

34

Annja summoned the sword and it appeared in her hands in the blink of an eye. She slashed down on the first guard's gun, knocking it from his hand. The second guard brought his gun up but, at that moment, Cole's head snapped up and he kicked the guard square in his crotch.

"Annja, my hands," Cole said.

Annja cut the chain between his cuffs and then turned back to the first guard, who had backed away from Annja after seeing a mystical sword appear out of thin air.

"Still thinking about blowing us up?" she said.

He held up his hands. "I was just following orders."

"Of course you were." Annja advanced on him and he stumbled over a crate. He landed hard but then rolled backward. As he came up, Annja saw that he had unholstered his pistol and was bringing it to bear on her center mass.

She slashed down and the guard fell under her blade.

Annja swung back to Cole, who was busy wrestling with the second guard. She saw the second guard score a kick into

Cole's stomach and Cole fell toward the shaft. Annja leaped forward and steadied him with the flat of her blade before he could topple over the edge.

As she guided him from the edge, the second guard grabbed his gun and turned it on them.

"Stop!"

Annja froze, her sword held horizontally by her right side. "All right, just take it easy."

The second guard backed away to check on the first guard. Annja shook her head. "I wouldn't do that if I were you."

The guard looked and blanched at the sight of what Annja's sword had done. He stared at her. "Where did you get that thing?"

"What thing?" Annja asked.

The guard didn't hesitate and raised his gun. As he did so, Annja flicked her hands toward him and sent the sword spinning right at his head. His neck spouted a fountain of blood before he fell forward, a spreading pool expanding outward toward the shaft with the nuclear bomb.

Annja helped Cole to his feet.

"Are they dead?" he asked.

Annja nodded. "Yeah, the sword saw to that," she said as she willed the sword back to the otherwhere.

"Good. The bastards." Cole looked around. "Can we leave now? I'm tired of being here."

Annja smiled. "I wish. We've got to take care of some other business first."

"What business?"

"First, my handcuffs, then the bomb."

Cole grabbed a set of keys from one of the dead guards. He freed Annja's hands and then removed the broken cuffs from his own wrists.

Cole shook his head. "I must have missed some of the details after they knocked me out. What did you say about a bomb?"

Annja pointed at the shaft. "You see that?"

"Yeah, you saved me from falling down there. What about it?"

"Take a look at what's inside." Annja waited until Cole crawled over to the lip of the shaft and looked down. The color drained from his face and he stared back at Annja. "Is that what I think it is?"

"Unfortunately."

"That's a nuclear device, Annja."

Annja nodded. "Yep. That's what Henderson is using to open up the reservoir of oil that's buried beneath the bedrock in this cavern."

"You're joking."

"I wish."

Cole frowned. "So, we're sitting atop a nuclear bomb right now. Any idea when it's going to go off?"

Annja frowned. "Don't know. Those two were supposed to put us down there and then take one of the mechanical sharks to rendezvous with Henderson at another facility."

"He's waiting for them?"

Annja shrugged. "Maybe."

"Why maybe?"

Annja sat down on the lip of the shaft and dangled her legs over the side. The bomb sat thirty feet below her. "Depends on how much you trust Henderson's word."

"And you don't?"

"The guy's a fruitcake. Banking on his word would make as much sense as trusting a politician. What I think is going to happen is Henderson is going to get a safe distance away and then trigger that bomb. If the guards are gone, well and good, but I don't think for a moment he really gives a damn about them."

"Which means we don't have a lot of time," Cole said.

"Exactly."

Cole cleared his throat. "I don't mean to sound insensitive, but why the hell are we staying here instead of getting out?"

Annja pointed at the bomb. "Because if that thing goes off, then hundreds of thousands of people might die."

Cole frowned. "The bomb's not that big, Annja."

"Henderson's got this thing positioned atop a fault line. As in earthquake fault lines."

"So it will cause an earthquake."

"What it might do is precipitate a massive quake that would result in a tsunami that could take out part of the eastern seaboard of the United States and Canada."

Cole's eyebrows shot up. "No way!"

"We've got to stop that thing from going off."

"Just like that?"

Annja faced him. "Got a better idea?"

"Hey, my specialty is sharks. Bombs weren't on my course electives, Annja. I'm fairly useless in this situation."

"Well, you can always amuse me with your comedic gold routines."

"Great."

Annja looked at the walls of the shaft. The drilling had left a series of pockmarks that Annja thought could make decent hand- and footholds. She lowered herself over the edge and found her way onto the first one close to her feet.

"Jesus, you're really serious about this," Cole said. "You think you can do something?"

"I don't know. But I've got to try." She looked up at him. "Look, it's not fair for me to ask you to stay. Why don't you take that shark and get out of here?"

"Don't tempt me," Cole said.

"I'm serious."

Cole nodded. "Yeah, I know you are. But what good will it do me if I run? Even if I get out of the cavern, there's no guarantee I'll make it out and back to the *Seeker*. And if this thing is below the ship, then the *Seeker* and my brother might be in mortal danger, too. That's not cool."

"Agreed."

"I'll stay."

Annja continued climbing down, using the holds until she at last made it to the small ledge sitting next to the yellow container. She looked at the top of the container and saw the variety of symbols, all of which were clearly designed to scare the bejeezus out of anyone who got too close.

Annja took a few deep breaths and looked at the four claps securing the lid to the main body of the bomb. "I screw this up and we're going to glow in the dark," she said.

"You screw that up and we won't have to worry about glowing," Cole said. "There won't be enough pieces of us left to glow."

Annja nodded and released one of the metal clasps. It popped back and Annja heard a vague hiss of escaping air. Cripes, she thought, have I already released radioactivity into the air? Was she already breathing contaminated air? I have no clue what I'm doing here, she thought.

"How's it going?" Cole asked.

Annja shrugged. "Here goes another clasp." She undid the clasp and heard another hiss of escaping air.

"That sound freaks me out," Cole said.

"You and me both," Annja replied. She released the third clasp. She took a breath and sighed, trying to stay focused. A line of sweat broke out along her hairline and she wiped some of it away before turning back to the device.

"Fourth time's the charm?" she called out.

Cole laughed. "Let's hope so."

Annja bent back and looked closely at the device. All right, she thought, just one more to go and then maybe I'll get a better look at what this thing is all about.

She undid the fourth and final clasp.

Another hiss of air escaped.

"I'm ready to lift the lid off," Annja said.

"Go slow," Cole said.

Annja looked up at him. "What makes you say that?"

He shrugged. "Every movie I've ever seen they always say that. Maybe bombs don't like being rushed. Damned if I know."

Annja tuned back to the bomb and lifted the yellow lid off. She stood and threw it up at Cole. "Hang on to this, will you?"

He caught it and set it down next to him on the lip of the shaft.

Annja peered down at the wiring and the digital display on top of the bomb. To the right of the display, a small remote receiver with a wire sticking out was situated next to a bunch of wires.

"It's rigged with a remote," she said.

"You sure?"

"Yeah." Annja examined the rest of the area. "There must be a hundred different colored wires twisting this way and that all over the place." Annja peered closer and saw a metal cylinder in the center of the device. She tried to remember any facts she might have come across relating to nuclear bombs.

She couldn't think of a single one.

She took another calming breath and started touching the various wires, trying to see if there was a single one that looked as if it might initiate the reaction that would trigger the bomb.

"What do you see, Annja?"

"I don't know what I'm looking at. It could be any number of things here. There are so many wires. It's confusing as hell. It probably takes an atomic scientist to make sense out of this thing."

"Well, you'd better hurry up or it won't matter anymore."

"I need a knife to cut these wires."

Cole frowned. "Annja, don't you have, like, the biggest knife in the world, in that sword?"

Annja laughed. "That's a bit like using a hatchet for surgery."

"Sometimes a hatchet does this job," Cole said. "And I don't think anyone's going to complain about your bedside manner as long as you get results. Like, soon."

Annja nodded. "Good point."

She drew the sword again.

"I'm going to cut the wires," she said. "First for the remote and then for what I think is the timer."

"Go for it," Cole said.

Annja eased the tip of the blade through the mass of wires closest to the remote receiver. "If this is the receiver and initiator, then I'm hoping this takes it out."

"And if not?"

"Then we're screwed."

"Well," Cole said. "Good luck. Here's to choosing right."

Annja nodded and carefully started slicing into the mass of wires. The sword divided them one after the other until she'd cut through a dozen of them. Annja removed the sword and leaned back.

"Did it work?"

The display suddenly flashed and a digital readout lit up showing a rapidly dwindling clock.

"Damn."

Cole's voice floated down to her. "What's that mean?"

Annja looked up at him. "I think it means that I made the wrong decision when I cut the wires."

35

"Are you sure?"

Annja nodded. "As soon as I cut the wires leading from the receiver into the center of the bomb, the clock sped up."

"How much time is left?" Cole asked.

Annja looked at the clock. "Two minutes."

"Two minutes?"

"Yeah."

Cole said nothing for a moment. Then he cleared his throat. "Well, that's not much time to do anything except hope that there is an afterlife, huh?"

Annja smiled. "Pretty much."

"Nice knowing you, Annja."

"Likewise," Annja said. But she kept peering at the clock. What if she cut the wires leading from the clock? Were they booby-trapped? Would that simply initiate the detonation? She frowned. They had so little time left that if she chose to cut the wires it wouldn't make much difference if she was wrong.

"I'm going to cut some more wires," she said.

"You always face death this calmly?"

Annja shrugged. "Maybe I'm just used to it."

"That's really sad."

"Tell me something I don't know." Annja bent over the timer with her sword and saw where the wires came away and led into the metal cylinder. If I can just get those cut before the clock runs out, she thought, then there might be a chance to stop this.

She eased the blade below the wires and watched as it sliced through them cleanly. Then she leaned back and checked the clock.

The display still showed the clock running down. She frowned. There must have been a secondary power supply for the clock. But would it still initiate the detonation if it wasn't connected? She didn't know.

"What's going on?" Cole called.

"I cut the clock's wires, but the timer's still counting down."

"So, what's that mean?"

"I have no idea. A nuclear scientist I am not," Annja said. "I think this is going to be one of those times when we have to do a wait-and-see."

"Well, climb the hell back up here and hold me until we either die or live," Cole said. "I'm feeling very vulnerable just now."

Annja smiled and scrambled back up to the top of the lip. Cole held out his arms. "I know this flies right in the face of the extremely macho persona you're used to with me, but dammit, I need a hug."

Annja wrapped him in her arms and felt him squeeze her back. "You're adorable when you act like a little kid."

"Oh, great, thanks," Cole said. "That's a fair thing to go off to the afterlife with, huh?"

"I could have said worse things."

"Forget about it. How much time is left?"

Annja looked down and checked. "Ten seconds."

Cole looked at her. "It's been fun. Seriously."

Annja looked into his eyes. "Likewise. Thanks for the good times." Then she bent forward and kissed him on the lips, feeling him press back into her with whatever emotion he had running through his heart at that moment.

They stayed that way for far longer than ten seconds. Annja finally broke away from Cole and took a breath. "Wow."

Cole frowned. "Shouldn't we be dead?"

Annja nodded. "The clock should have finished running down by now." She peered over the lip of the shaft and saw that the clock read nothing but zeroes. She glanced back at Cole. "Clock's finished."

"And no boom."

"No."

Annja came back up and sat beside Cole. "Well, that's interesting."

Cole took a deep breath. "I don't know if I want to ever come that close to being blown up again."

Annja looked at the lid of the bomb. "What the hell is that?"

"What?"

Annja pointed. "On the underside of the lid. Looks like an envelope."

Cole scrambled over and pulled the small envelope off the inside of the lid. It had been taped down securely. Cole held it up. "Think we ought to read it?"

"Well, yeah."

Cole ripped open the envelope, read the note card inside and then a big smile broke out on his face. "Well, this is interesting."

"Give it here," Annja said.

Cole handed it over to her and Annja read the few lines.

I knew you would double-cross me. So, instead of giving you a nuclear bomb, I've given you a big dud. If you're reading this, then I'm dead and you think you got the better of me. You didn't. See you in hell.

Annja shook her head in disbelief. "I love it. Henderson thought he was pulling one over on the guy who built this, and instead, he got cheated in the process. Fantastic."

"That whole thing is just a big dud?"

"Seems to be."

Cole laughed. "Well, that's the first bit of good news we've had all day. How about that?"

Annja looked around and took a deep breath. "We're not out of the woods yet."

Cole groaned. "Oh, don't tell me that, Annja. You're spoiling the good mood I'm in."

Annja shrugged. "Can't be helped. Henderson thinks he's getting a big bang. And when he doesn't, you know what that means."

"He'll give up his life of crime and go raise organic vegetables or something?"

"Not a chance. He'll come back here to find out what went wrong."

"So, let's get the hell out of here, then. We can leave now, right?"

Annja frowned. "I don't know. If Henderson comes back and we're not here to stop him, then he might get away and be free to just do this all over again someplace else. And this time he won't let himself be fooled."

Cole sighed. "So, you mean we have to stay here and take him down, huh?"

"We should."

"Why can't we just let the cops handle this?"

Annja shook her head. "People like Henderson don't get captured by the police. They've got too much money to ever do any time no matter how heinous their crimes. Henderson will get his high-powered attorneys to bail him out. He won't serve a bit of time despite almost killing thousands."

"Well, when you put it like that." Cole frowned. "How long until he comes back?"

"I'd guess within a few hours."

"He'll have a lot of people with him, won't he?"

"I'd guess," Annja said. "He won't come back here alone. And if he thinks we're still alive, he'll want to make sure we don't make it out alive."

"We need help," Cole said. "It's too much for us to handle by ourselves."

Annja nodded. "Take the shark and get back to the *Seeker*. Tell Hunter, Jax and Dave what's going on. See if they have any ideas."

Cole stood. "You'll be all right by yourself?"

Annja nodded. "I've got some things to get ready for our visitors. Just don't waste any time. Get up there and get back. We might have the element of surprise right now, but it won't last if Henderson comes back first."

Cole nodded. "I'm leaving." But he leaned in and kissed Annja again. "Just in case."

She kissed him back. "Who knew shark guys were such good kissers?"

Cole smirked. "I'm the exception to the rule."

Annja watched him hurry away and then turned back to the shaft. She would try to get the bomb to look as if it hadn't been tampered with. That way, it would draw them all over to the shaft. She could count on that much at least.

But she knew the surprise would be short-lived. Once they got the lid off they'd know what was going on. And then they'd be even more on guard.

Annja tossed the lid down and then scampered back into the shaft. In two minutes, she had the lid secured tightly again and climbed out. Looking down, it seemed as if nothing had been touched.

She turned back to the two dead guards. She had to dispose of their bodies. She dragged them into the corridor where the prison cells were and hid the bodies there. Then she tried to mop up the blood and gore as much as possible.

She set about exploring the rest of the facility. The control room turned out to be a big letdown. The only thing inside was surveillance equipment for the prison cells. Aside from that, there was very little. They didn't even have a radar screen set up so she could see if Henderson was on his way back to the cavern or not.

Annja spent the rest of her time setting up several choke points leading away from the dock. If she could funnel Henderson and his men into a variety of kill zones, then they stood a chance at making this work.

She ran around the complex collecting guns and ammunition. She'd need it for the rest of her crew when Cole brought them.

But how long would it take Cole to get back? She had to imagine that once he got out of the cavern complex, he would be able to find his way to the surface and then locate the *Seeker*.

But how would they take to seeing him again? They might even have pulled up anchor and gone back ashore.

Annja tried not to focus on that possibility. If she was going to be the only one facing Henderson and his gang, she wanted to make sure she had the maximum advantage possible.

To that end, Annja positioned guns and ammunition at each of the choke points. She created a series of fallback options. She could stage closest to the dock and take out a few of the guards before giving that up and falling back to the next control point. By staggering her attack that way, she hoped to whittle their numbers down until she would eventually have to close in and do close-quarters battle with them using her sword.

The ammunition wouldn't last forever.

And they might get a lucky shot off.

Annja would need all of her skill and cunning if she was going to make it out of there alive.

She thought about Cole. That had been some kiss. But had there been any real feeling behind it, or had it just been a function of almost dying together? They'd never really had much of a relationship before and to think that a simple kiss would change that seemed a bit naive to her.

But then again, she'd enjoyed the kiss.

And, in retrospect, she supposed there might be some potential. If she wanted there to be.

Annja frowned. First things first, she decided. There'd be plenty of time to ruminate on whether she and Cole had a future once Henderson and his gang of thugs had been dispatched.

Until then, Annja had to keep her head on straight.

She fully expected Henderson to show up at any time. More than an hour had passed since Cole had taken the mechanical shark and traveled back to the *Seeker*.

Annja wasn't convinced there was enough time for Cole to get reinforcements down there before Henderson returned.

This was going to be up to her.

Again.

She heard a noise down by the dock. A motor sound was coming from the interior part of the cavern.

Someone was coming down the tunnel.

Annja moved to the first position, picked up a submachine gun and yanked the charging handle to put a round in the chamber.

Showtime.

36

Annja watched as the submarine motored into the mooring area. She couldn't see anyone on the conning tower, but that would have been too much to hope for. Besides, she wanted to let them all get out of the submarine before she started firing. If she attacked too soon, they'd simply retreat in the submarine. Henderson would abandon the complex and live to destroy mankind another day.

Annja couldn't let that happen.

She watched the submarine idle up to the dock. She heard a hatch open and watched as four men emerged, weapons at the ready. Two of them secured the submarine to the dock while the other two covered them.

Annja waited.

The four guards made their way to the gangway and then crossed over. One of them held a radio and Annja heard him mutter something into it.

A moment later, Annja saw Sheila's head poke out of the conning tower. Henderson and three more guards followed her.

Annja frowned. Nine-to-one odds were definitely not in her favor. But she had to hold them off for as long as possible.

Henderson strode onto the gangway. "I want this area secured. Find the other guards and Annja Creed. Kill the woman on sight, but I want them all found. Drag their bodies here if you have to."

The guards started up the slope while Henderson, Sheila and the other three guards remained behind.

Annja opened fire.

She took out one of the guards on the first volley, but the others returned fire a lot faster than she expected them to. She had to remind herself that they were primed for action and knew they were probably coming into a hostile situation.

The return fire obliterated her cover behind the crates. Annja fell back to her second position amid shouts from the guards and Henderson to flank her.

Annja took out another guard at the second retreat point, her bullets ripping him across the chest. He went down and started to get up again until Annja squeezed another double-tap that caught him in the middle of his forehead.

But the others were gaining on her. The two remaining guards of the first patrol split up and got positioned on either side of her in a pincer movement that would cut her apart if she let them.

She opened fire on her right flank and then charged the guard positioned there. She caught him flatfooted and, as he realized his mistake, she squeezed the trigger.

But nothing happened.

Annja didn't waste time trying to get the gun to fire. She dropped the weapon and jumped on the guard, using her elbows and knees to pummel him. He fought back, scrambling to punch her and drive her away so he could use his gun, but Annja refused to be thrown. She got her hands around his throat, squeezing as if she was holding on to a rope for dear life.

The guard's eyes bulged out and he gurgled, fighting desperately to get her off him. Annja held on until his body went limp.

A shot ricocheted off the wall close by. Annja rolled and grabbed the dead guard's gun, bringing it up and squeezing off rounds as she rolled over.

She caught the approaching guard across his thighs as he bore down on her. His feet were blown out from under him and he went down hard, his own gun firing as he dropped. Annja winced as one of the bullets grazed her forehead and she felt the flow of warm blood down her face.

With no time to look after herself, Annja got to her feet and fell back to her last defense position. She dropped the magazine out of the gun and checked it. Seeing only a half dozen rounds, Annja picked up the last remaining magazine she had and slapped it home.

She heard movement and poked her head out. A single bullet exploded near her eyes and Annja jerked back, blinking away tears and the splinter that had lodged under her eyelid.

"Did I get you, Annja?"

Sheila was obviously back.

"No."

"That's a shame. I won't miss again."

"Maybe that broken wrist is slowing you down some. Maybe you should just walk out into the open and let me finish you off," Annja called out.

"Keep dreaming, sweetheart." Sheila laughed. "And I'm a crack shot with only one hand, anyway."

"How nice for you."

Annja took a deep breath and tried to figure out from which direction Sheila would come at her. Annja could see off to her left. A stack of crates there would give Sheila cover. But the pile of machinery on the right would also offer a good vantage point. Sheila wouldn't be able to advance until she knew for certain where Annja was. And if she suspected that Annja might move, it would make things tougher on her.

But Annja didn't have anywhere to retreat to. She'd built three fallback positions, thinking that she and the others would have had plenty of opportunity to destroy the attackers before it got to this point.

Annja on her own, however, was at a far greater disadvantage than if she'd had help.

Beggars can't be choosers, she decided.

She poked out and squeezed off a single round at the area where she hoped Sheila was hiding.

There was no return fire.

"Oh, I'm not over there," Sheila said. Her voice floated around the cavern and Annja frowned. She couldn't get a bead on where she might be.

In the next instant, gunfire raked the back of the crate Annja huddled near. She dived and rolled out from behind it, her body taking over so her slower conscious mind didn't waste time trying to consider all its options.

How did Sheila get behind her?

Annja rolled and came up squeezing off two more rounds. Annja saw Sheila duck and run across the catwalk for cover.

There must have been another way to get up to the second level without being seen. And of course, Sheila knew all about it, Annja realized.

If she stayed up there, Sheila would be able to get the drop on Annja and this thing would be over far sooner than Annja anticipated.

A gunshot from behind her told her that the remaining guards were now advancing on her. Idiot, she thought. Sheila had distracted her while they got into a better position.

Annja caught movement out of the corner of her eye and instinctively fired at the retreating shadow. Her bullets scored a hit and the body of one of the guards went sprawling out all over the floor.

"Not bad, Annja." Sheila seemed to be laughing at her. "You're a better shot than I gave you credit for. I won't make that mistake again."

"Why don't you come down and play? No guns, just the two of us," Annja said.

Sheila laughed. "You forget that I'm handicapped. Only one good wrist. I can't throw a punch right now. Besides, I like shooting at you better."

Annja twisted as the rounds bit into the area just above her head. If she hadn't already been moving, she would have died.

But she ran for the corridor that led to the prison cells. If Sheila was on the upper level, Annja planned to be there, too.

She scooted past the bodies of the guards she'd killed earlier. She gained the upper level and ran into Sheila coming down to meet her.

Sheila fired first, her bullets raking up from the floor and cutting across Annja's body. But Annja was already diving for the wall and, as she did, the rounds struck her gun, splintering it into several pieces.

Annja tucked, rolled and came up with her sword in hand, already charging Sheila before the startled attacker could gather herself for another offensive strike.

Annja leaped high and brought her sword straight down.

Sheila did the only thing she could by bringing her own gun up and trying to deflect it. The blade bit into the submachine gun and Sheila got her back behind the block. Annja gritted her teeth and the two of them stood there, locked together.

"I won't be easy to kill, Annja." Sheila's face broke into a sweat and she tried to push forward.

Annja grimaced. "I never expected you would be." She put

her own weight into her move and grunted as she tried to jerk her sword blade free of the gun barrel.

"You're trapped. Give up the blade and we'll go unarmed," Sheila said.

Annja stepped and used her hands to throw the sword and the gun away. But as she did so, Sheila whipped out a Bowie knife and slashed across Annja's abdomen. Annja clutched at her stomach, but knew the cut was very shallow.

It still hurt like hell.

"Did I say unarmed?" Sheila laughed. "I must have forgotten to tell you about my knife skills."

Annja backed away from Sheila and scowled. "I never trusted you, anyway. Your word means nothing."

"Unfortunately for you, it seems like you're out of time." Sheila stepped in and slashed high at Annja's face before ducking low and stabbing right at Annja's heart.

Annja brought her leg up to block the thrust and just barely managed to do so. Sheila spun away, bringing the knife back up in front of her.

"Enough of this," Annja said. She had the sword manifest itself back in her hands.

This time, Sheila gasped. "How did you do that?"

But Annja was already attacking, cutting in and slashing upward at an angle to Sheila's hip. To Sheila's credit, she managed to use the Bowie blade to block the initial cut and parried it, but that just led Annja into her next attack and, this time, the blade bit deeply into Sheila's hip.

Annja watched as her sword cut in and then streamed through Sheila's upper torso, cleaving as it went.

The air exploded with the stench of blood and gore. Sheila started to scream but that was choked off by the upsurge of blood rushing from her mouth.

She died as she fell, staining the floor in front of Annja and her sword.

Annja spun as another volley of bullets exploded in front and behind her.

The other guards!

Annja was pinned down and had no options. Her own gun had been shattered and Sheila's gun was damaged. Annja's only option was the sword.

She could see the shadows of the advancing guards as they came at her from two opposing points—one from the upper level and one from the lower.

Annja stepped out into the center of the corridor.

They reacted as she'd hoped they would. Both of them brought their guns up and opened fire while Annja tucked and dived for the side of the wall.

She heard two shallow grunts that told her both guards had hit what they had aimed at.

Each other.

Annja crawled out and saw they were both down.

She collapsed and took a moment to get her breathing back to normal. Sweat poured down her face and she was still bleeding steadily. She checked herself over and decided she would live.

But she needed some help. And soon.

Annja got to her feet. Henderson was the only one left to deal with.

She emerged on the lower level and kept her sword up in front of her. There was no telling what Henderson might try if he knew he was the only one left alive.

In the distance, Annja thought she heard something.

A motor? Was Cole finally on his way back in?

Annja hoped that he had brought the cavalry with him.

"That's far enough, Annja."

She turned and saw Henderson standing behind her. The gun he held was aimed right at her heart. He shook his head.

"Don't think about it. I'm quite the marksman and I assure you that I will shoot you if you even so much as blink."

Annja heard the motor clearly now.

So did Henderson. He gestured with the gun. "Now, then, I'd imagine those are your friends come to rescue you. So let's not be rude, shall we? Let's go have ourselves a nice visit."

37

Annja walked carefully back down to the dock area, aware as she did so that Henderson stayed just far enough behind her to be out of reach if she chose that moment to attack. And the fact that the hammer was cocked on his pistol meant that he was fully serious about shooting her if he needed to. But right at that moment, he wanted Annja alive.

"Just keep moving. I don't want this to take any longer than is absolutely necessary," he said as they started down the slope to the mooring.

Annja saw the mechanical shark idle up next to the dock and then Cole emerged followed by Jax, Holly and Tom. Annja frowned. Where were Hunter and Dave?

Cole's face initially lit up when he saw Annja, but then he caught a glimpse of Henderson. "I see you weren't entirely successful," he said.

Annja frowned. "I got all the rest of them, for crying out loud. Give me some credit, why don't you?"

Henderson cleared his throat. "If you two would stop the

idle chatter, I'd very much appreciate it." He gestured with his gun. "Just so you all know, I've got a dead bead on Annja's heart from back here so please don't do anything that would precipitate me pulling the trigger. I assure you that I am quite capable of doing so. Even if you manage to get to me, she will die before that happens."

No one moved. Finally, Jax spoke up. "So, what would you like us to do now? Just stand here?"

Henderson spoke quietly to Annja. "She's not very much on decorum, is she?"

"Depends on what you define that as," Annja said. "She doesn't take bullshit too lightly, though. Better just tell them what you want."

Henderson grunted. "Very well. What I want is to get out of here intact. Seeing as I am currently outnumbered, that means a strategic retreat."

"I didn't think that word was in your vocabulary," Annja said.

"It's not normally," Henderson said, "but I am a prudent fellow. And since you have the strength of numbers right now, I can see the writing on the wall and it is definitely time for me to leave."

"Great. Feel free to get going," Cole said. "No one here will stop you, you have my word."

Henderson chuckled. "If only it was that easy. You see, I need something that I left here."

"And what's that?"

"My nuclear bomb."

Cole glanced at Annja. Annja grimaced and hoped he read that as "Do not say a thing about the fake bomb."

Luckily, Cole seemed to get the message and just nodded. "So, go ahead and get it. We won't stop you."

"Yes, well, I am a bit long in years and no longer possess the strength needed to move it. That said, I'd appreciate it if you and that fellow there could help move it onto the submarine. Then I'll be on my way."

Cole glanced at Tom and shook his head. "My friend isn't feeling too well. Choose someone else."

"I choose *him*," Henderson said. "Now he either helps you or else I'll put a bullet in your friend's heart. Your decision."

"Well, when you put it like that." Cole looked at Tom. "You up for it?"

Tom shrugged. "What choice do I have?"

"That's the spirit," Henderson said. He nudged Annja. "If we could just move closer to the dock while the rest of your party comes up the slope and away from me, then I'll know there's no monkey business about to take place."

Jax, Tom, Holly and Cole moved past them while Henderson kept Annja between them. Then Henderson backed down the slope and stood on the dock with Annja still in front of him.

"There, that wasn't so difficult, was it?" He turned to Cole. "Now, you and the young man there go and fetch my bomb. Stow it aboard and I'll be off."

Cole and Tom headed to the lower level. Annja shifted a little bit.

Henderson poked her in the back. "Stand still, Annja. I don't want to shoot you just yet."

It took Cole and Tom just over twenty minutes to bring the yellow case back down the slope, grunting and heaving as they did so. Henderson chuckled as they struggled with it. "Be careful. I assure you that cost me a great sum of money to have built."

"I hope you got your money's worth," Annja said.

"Actually," Henderson said. "I didn't. As you could obviously tell, it didn't detonate. So now I'll have to take it with me and have someone examine it to find out what went wrong. I'm assuming you didn't tamper with it?"

Annja sniffed. "I'm a dirt digger, not an atomic-weapons specialist."

"Indeed." Henderson called out to Cole. "Can you and the young fellow get that on board?"

"We'll have to come down there," Cole replied.

"Do so, then."

Cole looked at Tom and nodded. They hefted the bomb and carried it farther down the slope. At the dock they stepped onto the gangway and then eased the bomb up and through the conning tower hatch.

Annja watched them while Henderson kept her in front of his body as a shield. Cole and Tom emerged a few seconds later.

Cole looked at Henderson. "We left it on the bridge."

"That's fine. All the easier to get off when I reach my people again."

Cole flexed his hands. "All right, we did as you asked. Now let Annja go and get the hell out of here."

Henderson shook his head. "It's not that easy."

"Seems like it would be to me," Cole said. He took a step and Henderson shot him in the thigh.

Cole screamed and went down to one knee. Annja started forward to help him but Henderson's voice was sharp in her ear. "Not so fast, Annja. Stay where you are."

Blood poured out of Cole's leg. Annja wondered if the bullet had struck the femoral artery. If it had, then Cole needed immediate medical attention. Tom hadn't moved.

Henderson turned to Jax. "You and the other girl can see to your friend. I expect he'll need a great deal of pressure to stop that wound."

Jax and Holly moved to Cole and got him off the deck of the submarine. He grunted as they laid him down on the dock. Jax examined the wound and her face looked pale. "You nicked his artery by the look of this."

"Shame, isn't it. You see what happens when you don't do as I tell you? People get wounded."

Jax put direct pressure on Cole's inner thigh and glared at Henderson. "What do you want us to do now?"

"I'm leaving," Henderson said.

"So go."

"While I'm sure I've given you something to occupy yourselves in my absence, I can't risk leaving anyone behind who might feel inclined to come after me. So I'm taking some insurance."

Annja's stomach ached. Great, she thought. I know where this is going.

Henderson spoke again. "Annja will come with me, as will that fellow there." He pointed at Tom.

Jax shook her head. "We need Tom's help to take care of Cole."

"It wasn't a request," Henderson said. "He either comes with me or he dies here right now."

Tom looked at Jax. "Forget about me, just take care of Cole." He stepped forward and looked at Annja with a blank expression.

Annja frowned. "He's not necessary. You've got me, Henderson. Leave him behind."

"I need someone to drive the submarine while I keep you under guard," Henderson said. "Besides, two is better than just one for insurance, anyway, don't you think?"

"Depends," Annja said. "But it's your boat, so tell me what you want us to do."

"You're going on board first, followed by Tom. When I come down, I want you both back against the far side of the bridge. Any trouble and I'll shoot you."

"You're going to kill us, anyway," Annja said.

"If I get to my destination intact with the bomb, then you might just live. No guarantees, of course."

Annja frowned. "Fine." She climbed up the conning tower and down onto the bridge of the submarine. Tom followed a few seconds later and stood with her while Henderson clambered down.

He kept the gun on them the entire time. As he entered the bridge, he shifted position and then pointed at Tom. "Lock the hatch."

Tom went up the conning tower and secured the hatch. Then he dropped back down and Henderson nodded. "Get us out of here."

Annja frowned. Something was wrong. What was going on?

Tom took his seat at the controls and started punching buttons. Instantly, the motors kicked in. After a second, he looked at Henderson. "Ready."

Henderson smiled. "Excellent. Get us under way."

Annja felt the submarine shift and pull away from the dock. Tom guided it.

Henderson noticed the look on Annja's face. "I think Annja is a bit confused."

Tom glanced up. "She hasn't figured it out."

Henderson laughed. "May as well tell her."

Tom shrugged. "I work for Henderson."

Annja shook her head. "That's impossible. How would you even have known that we'd end up in Nova Scotia?"

Henderson laughed. "Haven't you learned that I'm a man who likes to cover my bets? We've had our spies looking after Hunter for a while now. And that meant we needed someone positioned with Cole, as well. Tom here was the perfect candidate for keeping an eye on him, in case Hunter fulfilled his potential."

Annja shook her head. "I'm still not getting this."

Henderson sighed. "Perhaps I gave you too much credit for being an intelligent woman."

"Go to hell."

Tom steered the submarine around and throttled up the motors. "Two minutes until we clear the tunnel and the cavern."

Henderson nodded. "Excellent." He looked back at Annja. "Hunter's treasure quest for the *Fantome* has been well known by us for several years."

"I didn't think he even knew about it until recently."

"Not true," Henderson said. "He's actually been quite vocal about his belief that the *Fantome* held a good supply of booty from the War of 1812."

"I thought you didn't care about the treasure," Annja said.

"Well, I don't really. The material goods mean little to me. However, when we discovered the vein of oil located here, we needed a convenient patsy to use as cover while we moved our teams of workers in."

"But I thought you wanted Hunter scared off the wreck— hence, the mechanical shark."

Henderson nodded. "We wanted him scared enough to stay out of the water but not so terrified that he left. That would mean someone else might wander into our area and we'd have to deal with them."

Annja frowned. "It's too sloppy. You're not telling me something."

Henderson smiled. "Well, there's one little thing we're leaving out."

"What?"

Henderson looked at Tom. "Did you get it?"

Tom nodded and reached around his neck, removing a chain.

Annja caught her breath. "The crucifix."

"Tom here's been diving each night while the rest of you slept. My mechanical sharks ensured that he was left unmolested while he searched the wreckage for this."

Annja shook her head. "Cole trusted you, Tom."

He shrugged. "So what?"

Annja looked at Henderson. "That's why you didn't care about the death and destruction. You've got the crucifix."

"And now I'm immortal," Henderson said.

"That's just a legend," Annja said.

"Like your sword?" Henderson asked. "We'll soon find out, anyway."

"How?"

Henderson pointed at Tom. "Put the crucifix back on."

Tom put it on and then looked at Henderson. "We'll clear the tunnel in one minute."

"Excellent. Once we clear that tunnel, Annja, you'll be glad we're in this submarine. The pressure would kill you otherwise."

Henderson turned and pointed the pistol at Tom's back. "Time now to see if this crucifix really works."

Then he fired the gun.

38

Tom's body spasmed in the chair as the round punched through his back and entered his heart, spraying blood out of the front of his chest and onto the instrument panel in front of him. Tom fell sideways out of his chair and abruptly jerked the steering wheel to the right and down.

The sub responded instantly and both Annja and Henderson pitched headlong toward the deck. Tom's body fell and his blood made the deck suddenly very slippery.

Henderson righted himself and yanked the steering column back and the sub leveled again.

Annja got up off the floor and saw that Henderson still aimed his pistol at her while he kept the other hand on the steering column. "Easy, Annja. Easy does it, girl."

"I don't like being called 'girl,'" Annja said.

He nodded. "I don't really care at this moment. I'm far more concerned that the crucifix doesn't seem to have worked."

"Well, you can't put your faith in these little sideshow artifacts, can you? Better to trust in yourself, I'd think." Annja cast a sideways glance at Tom's corpse and noted that he still wore the crucifix around his neck.

"I wonder if there's some sort of trick to it." Henderson frowned. "Take it from around Tom's neck."

Annja shook her head. "I prefer not to desecrate the dead. It's kind of sacrilegious and all."

"I could just shoot you and be done with it. I can steer this sub myself and do quite a good job of it."

Annja leaned down and scooped the crucifix from around Tom's neck. She didn't feel anything special when she slid it over her head and around her neck, but then again, what else was new?

"There. Happy now?"

Henderson frowned. "Feel anything…remarkable?"

"Not a damned thing."

Henderson leveled his pistol at her. "Perhaps I should shoot you and see if I get the same result as poor Tom there."

"I see you're all broken up about killing him. You must have a real problem with employee retention."

"Tom served his purpose and that purpose is now at an end. I'm a pragmatic man, Annja. I don't drag out goodbyes, but I do appreciate his service."

"I'll bet."

Henderson took a moment to set the autopilot on the submarine and then backed away from the instrument panel, giving himself a better drop on Annja. "So, what am I to do here? I was told that crucifix would grant the wearer immortality and now it appears I've been hoodwinked."

"It wouldn't be the first time," Annja said.

"What's that supposed to mean?"

Annja pointed at the bomb. "Your precious nuke there. Did you wonder why it didn't explode?"

"I assumed you'd somehow disarmed it, although I must confess I thought such a thing was well beyond your skill level."

"Thanks for the confidence." Annja shook her head. "I did disarm it. But that's not the whole story."

"What is?"

"That's not a nuclear device."

Henderson laughed. "You're lying. Of course it is."

"Nope. I think the scientist you murdered after he made this for you actually got the last laugh. He made you a dud. There's no nuclear material in there, at least none primed to explode. He might have sprinkled some dust around it so you got a nice read from your Geiger counters, but that's no nuclear bomb."

Henderson looked at the bomb and then back at Annja. "Open it up."

"What?"

"Do it."

"Sure." Annja walked to the bomb and unclasped the four locks on the lid. When she lifted it up, she saw something she didn't expect. There was a small packet at the bottom of the metal cylinder and a new timer. The timer was counting down and there were ten minutes left on it.

Annja looked up. "I've got a confession to make. I was lying to you."

Henderson gestured with his pistol. "I'm sure you were. Now step away so I can look at it."

Annja held up her hands. "Really, I was trying to get you to look inside there so I could jump you."

Henderson stopped and brought his pistol back up on Annja. "I warned you not to do that."

Annja nodded. "Can't blame a girl for trying to escape."

"Indeed," Henderson said. He brought the pistol up to Annja's chest. "And now you must pay the price."

The sub suddenly lurched as Tom struggled to get to his feet and reached for the steering wheel. Annja almost fell over. She grabbed at the nearest panel for support. How the hell was Tom on his feet? He was supposed to be dead.

Henderson fell back as the sub lolled to the right again. "Tom, for God's sake, boy, get the sub level."

Tom nodded dumbly, his chest still spouting blood as he jerked the steering column in the other direction. Henderson started to fall backward but managed to keep himself upright.

The bomb toppled over and fell, rolling part of the distance across the bridge before coming to a stop by the rail support.

Tom moved toward Henderson.

"Get away from me!" Henderson shouted. "I saw you die just a few moments ago."

Tom mumbled something and reached out for Henderson. Henderson's pistol exploded three times and Annja saw the impact of his bullets as they entered Tom's body and threw the young man back across the bridge.

This time he slumped to the floor and lay still.

Henderson rushed over and placed the barrel of his pistol at the base of Tom's neck and fired a final shot that penetrated Tom's brain.

"There. Now he's really dead."

Annja got to her feet slowly. Henderson was breathing hard and sweat poured down his face. He seemed short of breath and clutched the pistol to his chest.

"Maybe that crucifix you're wearing does indeed work," Henderson said. "Take it off."

"Make up your mind," Annja said.

"Take it off and give it to me," Henderson said. "I can just as easily remove it from your corpse if you'd prefer."

Annja wasn't sure what had happened to Tom but she lifted the crucifix over her head and handed it to Henderson. The old man looped it over his head and then tried to stand upright. "There. Now that's settled."

Annja looked at Tom's corpse. Had the crucifix really caused him to rise from the dead and try to attack Henderson? It wasn't possible. "It didn't look like Tom appreciated being used as your guinea pig, huh?"

"I suppose we'll never know," Henderson said.

"Seemed pretty evident to me."

"That's because you don't like me," Henderson said. "Now do me a favor and get the bomb upright again. No sense having an explosive rolling about the bridge. Rather dangerous, if I do say so myself."

Annja shrugged. "I don't see why you'd be worried, seeing as how you're supposedly immortal now."

"You don't believe it?"

"Maybe your bullet didn't kill Tom. Maybe he found a little life in him still and his only thought was to get to you, the man who tried to kill him. Guess I wouldn't blame the guy for trying."

"I don't know anyone who could withstand a point-blank shot through their heart, do you?" Henderson said.

"Well, not up until a few moments ago."

"Just do as I asked and get the bomb righted, would you?"

Annja set the bomb upright and then reached for the lid. As she did, she caught a glimpse of the timer, which now read two minutes. Annja had just two minutes to get out of the submarine or she was going to die in it with Henderson.

Worse, she had even less time since the submarine was headed out through the tunnel toward open water. If Annja didn't remain inside, she'd die from the pressure once they were out.

It was time to end this once and for all.

"You wanted to look at the bomb, remember?"

Henderson nodded. "I do indeed. Stand back and drop the lid, if you please."

Annja stepped away, still holding the lid. Henderson came forward, the crucifix dangling in front of him as he peered inside. He looked back up at Annja. "Why is the timer counting down?"

Annja shrugged. "Looks like someone managed to put a little treat in there for you."

She jerked the lid up and smacked him in the face with it.

The pistol went off and bounced a single round around the bridge. Annja heard the splang of the ricochet and winced as the bullet grazed her arm. She fought back the pain, though, and kicked Henderson in his chest.

Henderson flew into the nearby panel and then crumpled to the floor.

Annja looked at the display on the instrument panel near the steering column and saw that the sub was approaching the entrance to the cavern tunnel.

She dashed for the conning tower and climbed up the ladder. The upper hatch handle was right in front of her and she tried to jerk the wheel around to unlock it. It was stuck.

Annja grunted and tried to use her other arm, but the bullet wound must have been deeper than she thought because the wave of pain that washed over her was intense and she cried out in frustration.

"Dammit!"

She heard movement down below on the bridge. Henderson was coming after her.

She dropped back down to the bridge and saw Henderson approaching. Annja paused for a moment and summoned her sword.

Henderson lifted the pistol and fired as Annja dodged to the left.

Henderson tracked her and fired again.

Another bullet splanged nearby and Annja slashed at Henderson, who seemed to have remarkably fast reflexes for an old man.

Annja cut at him again and again, finding it hard to slash in the close confines of the submarine's bridge.

She figured she had maybe thirty seconds left before she passed the point of no return.

"I should have killed you earlier," Henderson said.

"Maybe you should have," Annja said. "But you missed your opportunity. Now it's my turn."

She ducked under the railing and thrust up, impaling Henderson as he came forward to shoot at her again. Annja's sword blade slid into his hollow chest with little difficulty.

Henderson gasped and fell forward onto the blade. As he did, his head came forward and Annja saw the crucifix dangling there.

"Give me that," she said, and scooped the necklace from around his collar. She jerked the sword free of his body and watched as he slumped to the floor. Then she slid the crucifix over her own neck and patted it once.

Annja turned back to the conning tower and grabbed at the ladder. Her arm still hurt like hell but the surge of adrenaline had dulled the pain. The energy coursing through her veins gave her the strength she needed.

She dashed up the ladder and jerked the hatch open. It flew off and Annja could see the tunnel entrance ahead of her. A wall of water awaited on the other side. Henderson must have developed some sort of almost force-field technology in order to preserve the cavern as he had.

But there was no time to delay. Annja swung out of the conning tower and onto the deck of the sub. With a final glance at the tunnel opening, she leaped off the sub and into the tunnel water.

Then she swam for all she was worth.

The submarine vanished through the wall of water and then exploded in a massive fireball just beyond. Annja saw the wall of water buckle and then suck outward with the force of the tremendous explosion. She heard a roar in her ears and felt a sudden immense pull.

The current sucked at her hard. Annja felt herself being tugged along toward the entrance of the cavern tunnel.

The force was too great.

And Annja felt herself losing the battle.

39

She couldn't give up. Not yet. Not after coming as far as she had. Annja took a deep breath and then tucked her head under the waves and started swimming as hard as she could. She felt that for every kick she took, she was being dragged back twice the distance.

But she refused to give in to the pull of the water. The explosion on the other side must have created some sort of massive suction force. It was sucking all the water out of the cavern toward the open ocean.

Annja swam harder, willing herself to keep battling the current until she could get back into the cavern itself where her friends waited for her.

Cole.

His wound needed medical attention. She wasn't sure if he would even survive.

The thought came to her almost at once. The crucifix. If there was ever a time to test the supposed legend of what it could do, that time was now.

Annja shifted direction and then started kicking harder than she had so far. She sensed a difference and she started making progress.

She swam back toward the cavern. The going still felt brutal and all of Annja's muscles burned. Her lungs heaved and the waves roared around her head as if she was in the midst of a massive storm surge. With every breath she took, she gulped down seawater. Her eyes stung and her leg muscles cramped.

But she pressed on.

Slowly, she felt as if part of the current was yielding to her indomitable spirit and the sheer willpower she demonstrated. Her legs kept kicking and her arms kept crawling forward, stroke after stroke.

Annja moved closer to the cavern tunnel wall and was using the walls of the tunnel itself to help her move back toward the cavern. The danger was that she might get crushed against the sides if a rogue wave picked her up and smashed her into it.

But she had to keep going.

Annja thrashed mightily against the swells and, ahead of her, she could see the light from the main cavern.

Cole.

She had to reach him. Had to get to him and place the crucifix around his neck so that it might save his life.

It felt as if she had already been gone for hours rather than minutes.

Too long.

The struggle to reach the cavern was exhausting her. She took another breath, dove deep underwater and then tried to pull herself along using handholds on the tunnel wall.

She gained a few yards and then surfaced again, sucking in oxygen.

How much longer can I do this? she wondered. I'm not getting anywhere fast enough.

She felt a sudden brush of movement past her leg.

Her heart pounded.

What the hell was that? Was there an animal in the water with her? Some kind of fish? She groaned. For the love of god, she thought, don't let it be a shark.

She felt something grab her around the ankles.

Annja ducked her head underwater again. A black mass with two eyes stared back up at her and then, abruptly, she was buoyed and almost lifted out of the water.

A spout of water hit her in the face. "Hiya, Annja."

Dave's body surfaced next to hers clad in a black wet suit. His beaming face smiled at Annja. "You look like you could use a little help getting back to the cavern."

"Dave! What the hell are you doing here?"

He shrugged. "I wasn't sure if my little going-away present would explode, so I took the liberty of tagging along with the sub and attaching one of my world-famous homemade limpet mines to its hull." He shrugged and, over the roar of water, Annja heard him say, "Glad you managed to get out of there in time."

"Yeah, me, too," Annja said. "But we have to get back to Cole, he's hurt really badly."

"How badly?"

"I think his femoral got nicked by a bullet."

"Shit." Dave took a breath. "Can you still swim for it? The current sucks pretty bad."

"I'm exhausted," Annja said. "But I'll keep going."

Dave grinned. "You make a swim like this with a spirit like that and you'll be as good as any SEAL I ever served with." Dave pointed to the wall. "Now, keep your head down and take a deep breath. I think we can make it back there if we follow a path through the water. I'll lead and you follow. Got it?"

Annja nodded. "I got it."

Dave ducked under the water and Annja followed. She watched as Dave's powerful legs scissored back and forth like a motor and Annja found herself inspired by the clean mechanical action of his body as he maneuvered his way toward the main cavern.

Annja fought for every inch she could and, gradually, they started making progress. Every time Annja surfaced for air, she could see they were farther along the tunnel.

But the current still refused to yield to their desire to get back. And Annja wondered just what was building within the cavern itself. If all the water was being sucked toward the entrance to the open ocean, then would that pressure also build up in the cavern itself?

And, if so, what would be the final result?

Dave pulled her along now, sensing that Annja was exhausted. Annja kicked as well as she could, but when they finally made it back to the water near the dock in the cavern, Annja was running an energy deficit and could barely crawl her way to the dock.

For his part, Dave seemed unstoppable. Annja knew that SEALs were conditioned like superhuman warriors and would never give up. Usually, Annja would be the same. But having just fought so hard for her life, her energy reserves were already tapped out.

The swim had basically finished her.

Dave appeared alongside of her. "Okay, Annja. I've got you. Just relax now and don't fight me."

Annja did as she was told as her heart hammered away inside her chest. She let Dave turn her onto her back and felt one of his arms come up under her armpits and position itself across her upper torso.

Then she felt him sidestroke them back toward the dock. Annja closed her eyes for a split second and then, from far off, it seemed as if Dave was calling to people on the dock for help.

Annja felt arms lifting her out of the water and laying her

on the dock. She wanted to do nothing but curl up and sleep forever.

But then she remembered Cole.

"Wait—Cole, how is he?"

She saw him immediately. His face was ashen gray and there seemed to be an immense amount of blood all over the dock. Jax knelt nearby and she looked at Annja.

Annja saw the briefest shake of her head and felt a renewed surge of energy, her last, flowing through her limbs as she struggled to reach Cole.

"No. Wait."

Dave saw her trying to get to Cole and helped her farther along. "I'll get you there, Annja. Just hang on."

Annja scrambled to move next to Cole. She could see Jax bending over to examine the wound. She looked up at Annja.

"I've done the best I can. I got the artery closed up, but he lost a fearsome amount of blood while I was working on him. I'm sorry."

Annja looked into Cole's eyes. He smiled up at her weakly. "Hey, you. Glad to see you made it back in time for me…to say goodbye."

"You're not going anywhere," Annja said. "You'll be fine."

He smiled. "If this is what fine feels like, then I'm pretty sure death is a lot worse."

"Don't talk like that, okay?"

Cole held up his hand. "Annja, it's okay. I know you tried. None of us could have seen what was coming." He frowned. "Where's Tom?"

Annja thought about telling him that Tom hadn't been who they thought he was, but decided against it. Knowing Cole, he might take the blame and that wasn't fair.

"I'm sorry, Cole. He didn't make it."

He nodded. "I wondered if he would. But thanks for trying to save him."

"I did everything I could," Annja said. "But it wasn't enough."

"Sometimes life is like that."

Annja slid the crucifix from around her neck and then eased it over Cole's head. "Here's a little souvenir from the *Fantome*. I thought you might like to have it for when we see Hunter again."

Cole nodded weakly. Annja could see the light going out in his eyes. "That will be nice. I'll miss my brother."

"You're going to see him again really, really soon. Just hang in there."

Cole grabbed Annja's hand. "Listen to me. I never wanted to put you in any danger. I hope you understand that."

Annja smiled at him through her tears. "Of course I do. I don't blame you for anything, Cole."

"Thanks."

"Now, just hang on. We're going to move you onto the shark and get you out of here. All right?"

Cole didn't respond.

"Cole?"

Dave moved in next to her and checked for a pulse in Cole's neck. Annja watched him prod Cole with his still-wet fingers. But then he dropped his hand away.

"I'm sorry, Annja. He's gone."

Annja looked at the crucifix hanging around Cole's neck. It seemed to sparkle brightly with the seawater still glistening on it. Or maybe it was the tears streaming down Annja's face that made it shine so brightly.

She looked up at Jax. "Thanks for trying."

Jax said nothing but looked away. Her face seemed wet, as well.

Dave got to his feet. "We need to get him the hell out of here. No one deserves to die in a place like this."

"I'll help," Jax said. She and Dave lifted Cole off the dock and carried him down toward the mechanical shark. They eased Cole's body through the hatch and disappeared from view.

Annja sat for a moment, willing the universe to give Cole back his life. He didn't deserve to die, she thought. He didn't deserve any of this.

Holly came up behind her. "Annja, it's time to go."

"All right."

Annja let herself be helped to her feet. The strain and struggle of everything she'd been through finally caught up with her and her legs buckled as she took a step.

Holly caught her. "Okay, okay, I got you. Just let me get you inside the shark. You can rest there."

"I'm fine," Annja said.

A sudden roar filled the air and Annja looked up.

The roof of the cavern started to fall apart. Massive boulders came down in chunks.

"We've got to get out of here now!"

40

Holly and Annja scrambled aboard the shark. Dave checked to make sure that everyone was in and then slammed the hatch. He pointed at Annja. "Are you okay?"

"I think so."

"Good, because I'm going to need your help to maneuver us out of here. We're going to be dodging boulders the entire way out."

Annja shook her head. "Why is the cavern collapsing like this, anyway? Was it unstable to begin with?"

Dave shrugged. "I may have used a little too much explosive on the mine I put on Henderson's sub. It's possible the explosion caused the water to draw out into the open ocean and the pressure became too great for the cavern."

Dave pointed. "Get up toward the front there and you'll see a small observation visor. It should give you a view of the water ahead of us. Try to see if anything is going to come crashing down on us from above. I'll steer us clear until we can get into the tunnel."

Dave powered the engines while Annja squatted by the viewfinder.

"Coming around," Dave said. "Give me a read, Annja."

"Clear as far as I can see," Annja said. But as she said that, a huge chunk of the cavern roof broke off and plummeted toward the water twenty feet from them. A wave from the splash washed over the mechanical shark and caused it to loll sideways.

Dave righted the shark and looked at Annja. "That's exactly what I'm talking about. Now try to make sure we don't get another one of those."

Annja nodded. "Go right. Ten degrees."

Dave made the course correction and kept his bearing. Annja could see the entrance to the tunnel but it seemed so far away through the tiny visor. More and more rocks came showering down from above.

"Go left now! Fifteen degrees!"

Dave jerked hard on the steering as another boulder crashed into the water on their right side. Another wave washed over their bow and Annja took a moment to catch her breath.

"You're doing fine, Annja," Dave said. "Now just keep us on our heading and we'll be okay."

More rocks tumbled out from the cavern ceiling, showering the water with stones of every shape and size. Annja could hear the smaller ones bouncing off the metal hull of the mechanical shark.

"We're almost there," Dave said.

Annja saw another section of the roof start to crumble. It was directly ahead of them, over the mouth of the cavern. "Twenty degrees to the right."

Dave corrected and then brought the shark around again as the rocks tumbled in alongside their left.

"Almost there," Annja said.

Dave throttled up the engines and the shark lurched forward.

Annja could see they were a scant twenty feet from the opening of the tunnel mouth.

A huge clang sounded on the exterior of their hull. Annja looked at Dave but he waved it off. "Can't be helped. If we took any serious damage, we'll just have to weather it for right now. We can't stop."

Annja peered out again through the viewfinder. The water in the tunnel was turning into a vortex of rushing waves that carried the shark along with it. She could hear them scraping against the sides of the tunnel.

"Can't we get out into the middle of the tunnel? We'll be smashed to bits if we stay here."

"I'm trying," Dave said. "The current's too strong now. I can't risk breaking the rudder by manhandling it too much. It might be better if we just let the current eject us as it wants to rather than fight it."

"There might not be anything left of us if we do that," Annja said.

Dave shook his head. "We'll be all right. Just hold on a little while longer."

Annja glanced over at Cole's body. Jax and Holly knelt close by, holding him so he wouldn't flop around. They held on to each other for support.

"Hell of a ride," Jax said. "Now I know why I hate submarines."

Dave grinned. "You ought to try getting shot out of a torpedo tube some time. It's a blast."

Jax groaned. "That was too horrible even for you."

"Probably."

Annja peered through the viewfinder again. Ahead of the shark, she could see the massive wall of water that seethed and boiled as if there were two converging storm fronts buried deep under the ocean.

"I can see the entrance to open water," she said.

"Better hang on," Dave said. "The ride's going to be brutal."

Annja looked at him. "Just how much explosive did you use on that mine?"

Dave smiled. "P for plenty."

"D for dead," Annja said. "You might have killed us."

"We aren't dead yet," Dave shouted over the building roar of water as they shot toward the wall ahead of them.

Annja risked another look outside. She could see the current actually twisting like spun steel cords, warping in on itself and torquing around as they got caught up in a jet-stream-like funnel of water.

The shark started to shake and rattle. Bits of metal came off the instrument panels. The bridge area shook and rumbled. Pings and clangs sounded everywhere. And, near the fused metal panels, small fountains of water started spraying everywhere.

"It's going to break apart," Annja shouted. "We're never going to make it out of here."

"She'll hold," Dave said. "She'll hold."

The rattling increased and the entire shark assembly started to rumble. Annja felt as if she was trapped in an aluminum can that someone was slowly starting to crush with their hand, twisting it as they did.

She grabbed the closest grip and held on for dear life.

"Here it comes," Dave said. "Hold on!"

The roar exploded in her ears and Annja thought that they were surely about to die. The shark seemed to accelerate forward and then slam right into a solid wall before again being ejected forward as if spit from the mouth of the cavern.

And then the roar died almost instantly.

The creaking stopped.

They were through.

The fused panels seemed to regain some of their structural integrity and the water leaks ceased for the time being.

Annja glanced at Dave, who seemed very pleased. "We made it."

She smiled. "Thanks to you."

He shook his head. "Thanks to us all. This was a hell of a ride."

"You're telling me."

Jax got to her feet and helped Holly. "We've got an injury here."

Annja looked at Holly and saw that she had a golf-ball-size lump on her head. "Anything serious?"

"Nothing that a little time on the ship won't cure." Jax laid Holly down and set about taking care of the swelling.

Annja looked at Dave. "How did you get down here, anyway?"

"I came down with Cole and the others, but I got off before they motored into the dock. I always prefer going in alone if I can. Anyway, I arranged with them to hold back until I got myself infiltrated and able to store that little improvised explosive in the bomb. Cole told me all about it, so I figured that Henderson might want to take it back. May as well give him his dearest wish."

"You did. A good one, too, by the looks of it."

"And then it was just a matter of slinking back into the water at the dock and waiting. I couldn't stop Henderson from shooting Cole—I would have been too exposed."

"So you rigged the mine?"

"Not until the sub was under way. I had to set the timer and hope that you knew you had to get out of there."

"I did, but not because of your mine. Although I did see the bomb. It toppled over and I saw your present."

"Yeah, I was hanging on when that happened. What the hell went down in there, anyway?"

"Just a little struggle for control," Annja said. "But as soon as I saw it I knew I had almost no time to waste. I got out of there as fast as I could."

"Good thing," Dave said. "If you'd have stayed any longer, you never would have made it out in time."

Annja frowned. "You were willing to take that chance?"

Dave smiled. "I had to. I didn't want to kill you, Annja. But sometimes the mission comes first."

"And, in this case, your mission was to neutralize Henderson."

Dave grinned. "I'll never testify to that if you drag me into court."

"Who said anything about court?"

Dave steered the shark on a course that slowly drew them farther and farther up. "Let's just say that we've known about Henderson for some time. And right now, if my internal clock is functioning, as I hope it is, the other station he built around here should be receiving a fairly large intake of visitors all too eager to make sure that his plans never see the light of day."

"Is that so?" Annja couldn't help the smile that was slowly spreading across her face. For some reason, she just felt good.

"Yep."

"But you'd never admit that under oath."

Dave shrugged. "I have no information regarding whatever supposed actions may or may not have been undertaken by my government in the interests of world peace and security."

Annja pointed at him. "That sounds like a speech you've delivered before."

"I may have had need of it once or twice in the past."

"Should I even ask how you came to be on the *Seeker* in the first place?"

Dave sighed. "I wasn't alone initially. Jock was a buddy of mine. Assigned to this operation from his SBS unit in the U.K.

We both went in because Henderson had been seen operating around here over the past several months. The *Seeker* was a good hunch for us."

"But if the shark wasn't real, then what happened to Jock?"

"Henderson had him shot and killed." Dave frowned. "We found his body floating farther down the coast. I don't know that Henderson had any idea of Jock's true identity, but he was a convenient way to drum up fear with the mechanical sharks."

"I thought they recovered body parts and presumed it was Jock."

Dave shook his head. "Henderson had a few stiffs on loan from a morgue that he chopped into bite-size pieces and scattered around. The evidence seemed to suggest a shark attack. And I even fell for it until I started to suss things out."

"Lucky for us there was no real shark."

Dave nodded. "I don't know how eager I would have been to tangle with a forty-foot man-eater."

"I don't think anyone would have been," Annja said.

Dave nodded and kept his hands on the wheel. "So, Cole tells me you've got this really cool sword."

Annja looked at him for a long moment and then grinned just a little. "I have no information relating to the supposed nature or existence of any such thing."

Dave smiled. "Sounds like you've rehearsed that speech before."

"I might have had need of it once or twice in the past."

"Yeah, well, if you ever get clearance to show it, I'd love to see it. I'm a big sword fan."

"I'll keep that in mind," Annja said. "For now, let's just get back to the *Seeker*. I'm sure Hunter is going out of his mind."

"Presumably," Dave said. "He was determined to come down with us but Cole told him no."

"He did?"

"Yeah, said he had a bad feeling about it and begged Hunter to stay with the ship."

Annja frowned. "I guess he had reason to fear the return trip."

"I guess."

"Anyone ever tell you two that you talk way too much?"

Annja whirled around. Cole was sitting up. Jax had one arm around him to keep him propped up.

"Cole!"

And then Annja was rushing, falling into his arms, crying and laughing all at the same time.

epilogue

The dark blue waters off Prospect, Nova Scotia, hummed with noise and activity. As the *Seeker* bobbed in the undulating swells, smaller boats zipped back and forth, ferrying divers and crews out to the dive site where the wreck of the HMS *Fantome* lay partially unburied.

From the deck of the *Seeker*, Annja stood with Cole and watched the recovery effort unfold. Cole was looking better than he had in the two weeks since he'd almost died in the underwater cavern. Spending time in a hospital ashore helped ensure that he'd be fine.

"I'm glad the surgery went well," Annja said.

"It was relatively minor," Cole replied. "They had to repair the arterial tear properly. Jax used duct tape to stop the bleeding, for crying out loud."

"A thousand and one uses," Annja said, laughing. "Where'd she go, anyway?"

"Hunter says she took off for a more sedate job piloting barges down the Amazon."

Annja nodded. She knew that if Jax really did work for Garin, there was no way she was going to stick around now. Not with the crucifix already recovered. The barge job was just a convenient exit for her.

"And Hunter?"

"Having the time of his life," Cole said. "Unearthing this ship means the world to him. And I've decided to stay here for a little while to help him get it all done."

"You're giving up the shark thing?"

"I don't know that I'm giving it up," Cole said. "It's unlikely I can purge my love of the study of them from my system. But I'm also a way from climbing back into the water."

"I'm relieved to hear you say that," Annja said. "No sense testing that fresh surgery by risking life and limb, huh?"

"Well, let's just say that I may have a newfound appreciation for life, having come so close to death."

"I understand."

Cole looked at her and smiled. "It's the strangest thing, Annja."

"What is?"

"Me. When I spoke to you on the dock, I genuinely thought I was dying. And I don't mean I was going out on this whole martyrdom thing. I mean, I really and truly thought that my life was ending. I was starting to hear things. See things, even. I didn't know what they were. But I knew that my time was almost over."

"Well, obviously that wasn't the case. Jax patched you up good and you just needed a little time to recover from your blood loss. That's all."

"That's not it and you know it."

Annja eyed him. "What are you driving at here, Cole?"

"Why did you put that crucifix around my neck, Annja?"

Annja started to tell him something else. She started to tell him that she wanted him to have peace of mind and that she thought perhaps seeing the cross would give him some of that. But she didn't think he would believe it. And she wasn't sure she would have in his place, either.

"I don't know what I thought," Annja said. "I just knew you needed to have it around your neck."

"Well, I'm glad you put it there. Because as soon as you did, the entire sensation that I was dying vanished."

"But you did die. Dave checked your pulse. You didn't have one."

"Yeah, I know. It felt like I went to sleep, but it was the most pleasant sleep I've ever experienced. But at the same time, I knew I wasn't dying anymore. I was just…going away for a little while."

"And what happened then?"

"I woke up and we were on board the shark. You and Dave were talking. And I felt really pretty good."

"Well, if it helps, you look pretty good, too."

"I'm being serious here, Annja. That crucifix saved my life. You know it and I know it."

Annja nodded. "Maybe so. But there are a lot of people who would kill to possess it."

"Yes."

"You've got to take care of it," Annja said.

"I shouldn't have it anymore," Cole said. "Someone else should take this thing and use it for others who might be in grave peril."

Annja shook her head. "It's yours now, Cole. And I can't think of a finer man to carry it with him."

"What about a finer woman? You could take it."

"No way. I'm already carrying around enough on my own. I don't need my life complicated any more with something new."

"But what about you? You're the first to admit that your life is pretty much always in danger."

"Yep. It sure seems to be. But that's because it's of my own design. I'm not sure, but I have the feeling that the crucifix isn't so much something that grants immortality as much as it is something that gives a better understanding of our own mortality. It grants us an appreciation for life. And it's what we do with that appreciation after we're given it that determines whether the crucifix works or not."

"That's pretty deep."

"I'm feeling very metaphysical today," Annja said. "And I'm very glad that one of my dearest friends is alive and kicking."

Cole looked at her. "Stay with me."

"What?"

"You heard me, Annja. Stay with me. I don't know what we have here, if anything at all. But maybe there's something. We shared that kiss and I've always liked you. Who knows what it might grow into?"

Annja smiled at him. "You're crazy, you know that?"

"I'm being serious."

Annja looked out at the ocean. Hunter's team was really progressing on the dive site. Each day they were bringing up more and more loot that would make them all wealthy beyond their wildest expectations.

But it wasn't what Annja wanted.

At least, not right now.

"I can't stay," she said sadly.

"Why not?"

Annja looked at Cole. "It's not that I don't care for you. You know that's not the case. But I'm not in a place yet where I can say for sure what my life is supposed to be. Maybe in that respect I'm jealous of you for having come so close to death—weird as that sounds."

"It does sound pretty weird."

"But you know what I mean. You have a clearer view of

what your life needs to be. My view, my perspective, they're still muddled. And until the time that I can figure it out, *if* I can figure it out, I won't be much good to anyone. And the last thing I want to do is hurt you, Cole."

He took a breath and nodded. "I guess I can understand that. I just hope that when you finally do decide, you'll come back."

"Maybe I will."

Cole nodded. "In that case, would it be too much if I asked you for one last kiss before you take off for wherever you're going next?"

It wasn't.

* * * * *